In
my

my (

Lila (1932-2014)

and Sister,

Heather (1956-2009)

Two courageous and inspiring women.

A light went out in my heart when you both left this world.

Part 1

Chapter 1

George

20th December 1980

I put my hands over my ears to drown out the girls screaming as they raced around me. Annalise might've only been five but she made an awful lot of noise. She and her sister, Lori, were fighting over the last Christmas bauble.

Vikki clapped her hands. 'Stop it. Both of you.' She turned to me shaking her head. 'You have to be firmer with them, Uncle George.'

I laughed at the little madam. Vikki, at ten, could be precocious at times, but she was right, I wasn't strict enough with the girls. They knew they could behave like little monkeys with me and get away with it.

Granville Hall's tradition was to have people in to decorate the Christmas tree but I'd insisted it was my job and foolishly had allowed my young sisters and niece to assist. I was fast regretting that decision. 'In that case' – I held the golden bauble up in the air – 'I think it's time Vikki had a turn.'

'No. It's not fair. Please, George, let me.' Annalise gave me her pleading smile.

'Not this time, young lady. You and Lori have done enough.'

Lori folded her arms. 'George is right. It's only fair Vikki has a turn.'

Vikki took the glass ball from my hand and hung it from an empty branch on the tree. 'There.' She twirled around. 'Doesn't

3

that look pretty? Can we carry on playing our game now, please? Hurry up, Annalise, it's your go.'

I picked up Tinkerbell. Although a bit tatty, and showing her age, she meant more to me than any of the shiny baubles. The lone survivor from my childhood Christmases at our two-up two-down terraced house in Wintermore. I was overwhelmed last year when Grace presented the wrapped fairy to me a week before Christmas Eve. It was like having a piece of Da with me. I could still see him placing Tinkerbell on the top of the tree. Afterwards, Mam, Alice and I would clap. Although I was only nine when he died, that memory was precious. My Da the coal miner. Now here I was, Lord of the Hall, not that I wanted the title. George Gilmore suited me fine.

Annalise jumped up off the floor. 'Tinkerbell. Hurray. Lift me up so I can put her on the top.'

'No, Annalise,' I said firmly. 'Go back to your game.'

She wiped her hand across her eyes. 'But I want to put Tinkerbell on the tree.'

Lori pushed her sister out of the way. 'Well, you can't. If anyone's doing it, then it's me. I'm the eldest and I'd like to put the fairy on the tree, please, George.'

'You're only two years older than me.' Annalise smacked Lori across the arm.

Lori screamed and slapped her sister back.

'Stop fighting.' I looked to Vikki who smiled her approval. 'Neither of you are doing it because I'm waiting for Grace.'

'How come you call Mummy, Grace?' Lori asked.

'I just do.'

'But why?'

'I'll tell you one day when you're older. Now go and play.'

Lori grabbed Vikki's hand. 'Let's finish our game.'

Snow was lighting on the window, a deep curtain forming, and it was covering the ground. I willed Grace and Adriéne to arrive soon. They were due back an hour ago.

'George, Lori's being mean.' Annalise was crying again. Grace would say it was excitement.

I sighed. 'Play nicely.' *Hurry up, Grace.* Whatever possessed me to offer to look after these three? And where was Alice? My sister was being a pain. She'd been gone ages. 'Let her play with you,' I said firmly to Lori and Vikki.

'We are but she's throwing a tantrum because she got knocked off. Look.' Vikki pointed towards the fireplace. 'She chucked her blue counter across the room.'

'Annalise.' I rolled my eyes.

Annalise screamed and threw herself on the floor, kicking her legs. As soon as Alice came back in, I'd get her to call Annie to watch them, I was worn out. Too bad Vikki's nanny had the day off when Elizabeth and Simon, Vikki's mother and father, had gone down to cousin Victoria's. With Grace and Adriéne joining them, Alice had volunteered us to watch over the girls but where was Alice?

Sniffling, Annalise stood up and tugged on my shirt. 'Please let me do Tinkerbell, George, then I'll be good. I promise.'

'No, I told you. I promised Grace we'd wait.'

Annalise's mouth dropped and she started crying again.

Alice charged into the room. 'George, quick.'

I rushed over to the doorway. Alice's face had paled. 'What is it?'

'It's Mum.' She sobbed.

Lori was up off the floor and standing next to me. 'What about Mum? And what's wrong with Alice?'

'Nothing for you to worry about,' I said. 'Vikki, be a big girl and watch Annalise and Lori for me, while I speak to Alice.'

She nodded and became a little mother. 'Come on, let's go and play house.' She took both Lori and Annalise's hands and they skipped across the room.

'Her and Adriéne…'

'Whatever it is, Alice, take your time. Tell me what's happened.'

She breathed quickly. '… a car crash.'

'Are they both okay?'

'I don't know. They've taken them to Golden Oak Hospital. Oh, George, what happens if she dies?'

'Let's not think like that.' I put my arms around my sister. 'Listen, can you find Annie or Joan and ask one of them to come and watch the girls so we can get to the hospital?'

'I'll try.' She sobbed, shaking.

In next to no time both Annie and Joan were in the room. 'You get off George,' Joan said, 'Annie and I can manage the children between us.'

'Thank you, Joan. I'll ring from the hospital as soon as we know what's going on.'

'Girls,' I called, 'we've got to pop out to buy some more presents to go under the tree. Joan and Annie are going to look after you.'

'Hurray.' Lori jumped up and down.

'Be good. All of you.' I kissed the girls on the cheek, one by one. Taking a deep breath to calm my banging chest, I left the room.

*

The chauffeur pulled up outside *Accident and Emergency*. Alice and I stepped out of the Rolls.

'Would you like me to wait, Sir?' he asked.

'Yes please, Eric. Why not park up and pop inside for a hot drink? It's too cold to sit out here.' The snow had stopped but it was still bitter.

'Thank you, Sir.'

Alice and I rushed through the entrance. A receptionist looked up as I approached the desk. 'Excuse me,' I said, 'our mother, Grace Gilmore and her husband have been brought in following a car crash. Where will we find them?'

'Let me check.' She ran her finger down a ledger. 'Grace Gilmore you say?'

'She may be down as Grace Ardant,' I added.

'Ah, yes. We have an Adriéne and Grace Ardant. I'll get someone to show you where to go.' She called to a porter, 'Matt, can you show Mr and Mrs Ardant's family to the relatives' room please?'

'Certainly.' He whipped across to where we were standing. 'Come this way.' We followed him along the corridor and through a set of swing doors. He pushed another door open. 'If you'd like to wait in here the doctor will come and tell you what's going on.'

'Thank you,' I said. Alice said nothing.

The hospital had tried to make the place homely. A red poinsettia brightened up the windowsill and a stack of magazines lay on the small coffee table.

'Would you like a cup of tea?' I asked Alice, signalling to the buzzing vending machine lighting up a small corner of the room.

She shook her head and paced up and down. 'I just want to know what's happened to Mum.'

I flicked through the magazines. 'Here, Alice, there's a *Look-in*. Something about Paul McCartney. Sit down and have a browse. I'm sure Grace and Adriéne will be fine.'

Alice snatched the magazine out of my hand sending it flying. 'I'm not interested in the bloody magazine. What's the matter with you? Aren't you worried?'

'Of course I'm worried.' I picked the pages off the floor. 'But one of us has to hold it together. Look at you, you're no good to anyone like that. Grace isn't going to want to see you in that state.'

The door creaked open.

'Why don't you both sit down?' The doctor led us to the couch and chairs, not meeting our eyes. With a serious expression he fiddled with the chart.

'Are they okay?' Alice asked.

'Sit down please, Miss…'

'Gilmore,' I said.

'I'll get a nurse to get you some tea. But first…'

'Please just tell us,' I said.

'I'm afraid…'

Alice gripped my hand. 'Please let them be okay.'

'I'm sorry to have to tell you that Mr Ardant died at the scene.'

'Oh my God.' I turned to Alice.

She screamed. 'No. Not Adriéne. George…'

Shaking, I looked up at the doctor. 'And Grace?'

'Your mother suffered a head injury but she's conscious. We've sent her to X-ray as a precaution and we'll know more once the results are back. From the police reports I'm surprised that she got out alive. Someone will come and let you know when she's back on the ward.' He patted Alice's arm. 'I'm sorry for your loss.' The doctor left us alone.

'Poor Adriéne,' I said, 'he was such a good man.' I thought back to that Christmas Eve when he'd asked my permission to marry Grace before proposing. A kind man who made her

8

happy and a great stepfather to me and Alice. How would Grace cope without him?

Alice blew her nose. 'Do you think Mum will be okay?'

I hugged my sister. 'I hope so.'

*

After what seemed an age a nurse came through the door. 'Mrs Ardant's relatives?'

'Yes, I'm her son.'

'Your mother's back on the ward. You can come and see her now.'

'Thank you.' Alice gripped my sleeve jacket.

We followed the nurse down the corridor and into a side room.

'Mum.' Alice rushed over to Grace.

'Grace.' I kissed her grazed, bruised cheek making her wince. 'Do you remember what happened?'

'The car skidded. Adriéne clung on to the wheel trying to keep control. A lorry. I remember a lorry. There was so much blood, on me, but worse for Adriéne. Blood was running down from his head.' Grace sobbed into her handkerchief.

I squeezed her hand. 'I'm so sorry, Grace.'

The doctor came into the room. 'Mrs Ardant, I'm pleased to say the x-ray shows no sign of a bleed on the brain but we'd like to keep you in overnight to check for concussion.' He turned to me. 'I think you and your sister should allow your mother to rest. If all is well she can be discharged tomorrow.'

'Thank you.' I let go of Grace's hand. 'We need to go now but we'll see you tomorrow.' I brushed my lips gently against her forehead.

'Bye, Mum,' Alice said. 'Don't worry about the girls. George and I can cope and Elizabeth will be back shortly.' She kissed Grace lightly on her cheek.

Grace was sitting up in bed staring into space when I arrived at the hospital the next day.

'Have they discharged you yet?' I asked.

'I'm still waiting for the doctor. Who's with the girls?'

'Annie and Alice. Alice wanted to come but I said it didn't take two of us.'

Grace pressed her temples.

'Are you in pain?'

'A bit.'

'Have they given you any painkillers?'

'They offered but I didn't want anything.'

'But if it helps… Oh look, here's the doctor now.'

It was a different doctor today. This one was older. He looked over his spectacles at Grace's chart. 'How are you feeling today, Mrs Ardant?'

'As well as can be expected.'

'I'm sorry to hear about your husband.'

'Thank you.'

'How do you feel about going home?'

'I'd rather be there than here.'

'Good because I'm about to discharge you.'

'Is there any follow up required?' I asked.

'Just watch out for any signs of vomiting, dizziness or memory loss.'

'She said she's in pain. Should she be taking anything?'

'Don't fuss, George.'

'I can see you're looking out for your mother. Paracetamol if she needs something.'

'Thank you,' I answered.

The doctor signed the paperwork. 'Once the nurse arrives, Mrs Ardant, you're free to go.' He shook Grace's hand.

A nurse pushed a wheelchair into the room.

'Ah, here she is now. Nurse will escort you to your car. Good day.' The doctor left.

'Did you bring some clothes for your mother?' the nurse asked.

I lifted a canvas backpack from the floor. 'Everything's in here.'

'If you'd like to wait outside while she gets dressed.'

'Certainly. I'll pop out and make sure the driver's ready.' I walked out of the room, along the corridor, downstairs, and towards the main entrance. Eric was standing outside by the Rolls, smoking. I gave him a thumbs up. He raised his hand to confirm he'd seen me and stubbed out his cigarette. Checking my watch, I rushed back to Grace just as the nurse was pushing her out of the ward in a wheelchair.

Grace protested. 'I said I can walk.'

'Hospital policy I'm afraid.'

'Don't give the nurse grief, Grace. Let her do her job and we'll be home in time for lunch.'

I walked alongside the nurse as she wheeled Grace along the corridor, into a lift and through the exit to where Eric was waiting by the car with the rear door open. He helped Grace into the back seat.

'Take care, Mrs Ardant.' The nurse looked at me pointedly.

'Don't worry,' I said. 'I'll take good care of her.' I climbed in next to Grace.

'Why do these awful things keep happening to me, George? As soon as I find happiness it's stolen away. What have I done to deserve it?' She cried on my shoulder as the driver pulled away and drove us home.

Chapter 2

Grace

Although still badly bruised, I couldn't stay in bed. I hobbled into the drawing room and stood at the window watching the snowfall. It was strange being back at Granville Hall after all these years. Elizabeth and Simon were coming back today. If only I hadn't insisted that we came home earlier. Maybe then we wouldn't have been caught up in that accident, I'd be in my own home, and Adriéne would still be alive.

Alice came into the room. 'How are you feeling, Mum?'

I shrugged my shoulders. 'It's snowing.'

She glared at me in silence.

'What's the matter?' I asked.

'Nothing.' She paced up and down.

'There's obviously something on your mind. What is it?'

She moved towards me. 'It's…'

'What is it, darling?'

She took my arms. 'You're a strong woman, Mum. You can do this.'

'I'm not sure, Alice.' I tried not to cry but I couldn't stop.

'You, can, Mum. I can't allow you to retreat into yourself again like you did after Dad and Beth died.'

George walked into the room. 'What's going on?'

'I've told her, she can do this,' Alice said. 'She needs to pull herself together.'

'Stop it. Leave Grace alone.' He scowled at Alice.

'You know what she was like after Dad died.'

'For God's sake, she's just lost her husband. What do you expect?'

'She…'

'Where's your compassion?'

'Please don't fight, children. Please don't.'

'Sorry, Grace.'

'I'm sorry too, Mum, but I'm just trying to stop what happened last time. I refuse to allow you to do that to Annalise and Lori. And you need to tell them what's happened to their daddy.'

'Grace has asked us to stop. So, stop now please, Alice.'

'But last time she went into herself and let you go off with Grandmother and then later when Beth died… She's not stealing those girls' childhoods like she stole ours.'

'I'm so sorry, Alice. I never meant to and I didn't realise that you felt that way.' I took a deep breath. 'I'll try, I promise.'

'You'd better. I know you've lost your husband and we're all devastated, but Mum, it could have been you dead in that car.' Alice sobbed.

'Shh, Alice. Grace needs a bit of time, that's all.' George held his sister.

'I'm frightened if we give her time then she'll… The best thing she can do is pick herself up right now.'

'Okay, Alice. I've got your message. I'll try, I promise.'

'You can start now by telling the girls. We'll be with you.'

'George, tell her. I can't do it,' I said.

'Alice, I suggest you wash your face before the girls see you like that.' George turned to me and rested his hand on my arm. 'Grace, they're asking questions so they do need to know but I'll help you, or if you prefer, I can tell them.'

'No, I can't ask you to do that. It should be me. But how on earth am I going to tell those little girls that their daddy's dead?'

'You'll find a way and I'll be right by your side.' George led me to the chaise longue keeping hold of my hand.

*

'Mummy, Mummy.' Annalise ran over to where I was sitting and hugged me tightly making me wince where I was bruised.

'Your pretty face is all scratched,' Lori said. 'What happened, Mummy? And where's Daddy? Is he coming back with Aunt Elizabeth and Uncle Simon?'

'Come and sit beside me.' I patted the space either side.

George stood behind me touching my shoulder. 'I'm here.'

'Listen, girls.' I took a deep breath and tried to hold back my tears. 'Listen, Annalise and Lori. I'm afraid Daddy and I were in a bad car accident.'

'Is that how you got your face bashed?' Lori asked.

'Yes, yes it was. But Daddy got hurt more than me. And Daddy...' I clung to their hands.

'What Mummy's trying to say,' George said.

'What George? What?' Lori asked.

Annalise scrambled on to my lap. I looked up at my son. 'It's okay, George. I can do this. Girls, I'm afraid that Daddy was hurt too badly and had to go to Heaven.' I squeezed their hands releasing my tears.

'You mean he's dead?' Lori screamed.

'I'm afraid so but he loved you very much and didn't want to leave you.' I was back in that little terraced house eighteen years ago when I was saying almost the same words to Alice and George. Alice was right. This time I must keep a grip on things. I wouldn't steal the girls' childhood. I'd never realised that Alice had felt that way. *Don't worry, Adriéne, I'll take care of our children.*

I hugged the girls tightly as we wept. George wrapped his arms around us all.

*

Elizabeth rushed into the room and came straight towards me. 'I'm so sorry, Grace. We came back as soon as we could. What with the snow…'

'Thank you.' I moved over and stood by the fire.

'Have you made the funeral arrangements?' Elizabeth joined me and rubbed her hands by the roaring flames.

'The vicar's coming later. I can't believe I've got to bury another husband. I'm cursed.'

'Don't think like that.' She put her arms around me.

Simon walked into the room holding Vikki's hand. 'Grace, what can I say? Except, I'm ready to help organise the arrangements.'

'Thank you, Simon.' I released myself from Elizabeth's hold. 'I think it's all in hand. George and Alice have been a great help. Especially George.'

'Did you fall over, Aunt Grace?' Vikki asked.

'I had an accident, Vikki.' I knelt down to my niece's level and stroked her face.

'Is that the one that killed Uncle Adriéne?'

'Yes, it is.'

'Annalise and Lori can share my daddy. Can't they Daddy?'

A tear pricked my eye.

*

How was I supposed to sort Christmas for the children while planning a funeral for their father? I sat on the floor wrapping up presents for their stockings. Dolls, felt pens, crayoning books, Lego. Adriéne had loved getting down on the floor with them playing Lego. The doorbell rang. I imagined that would be the vicar now. A little earlier than I'd expected.

15

Heavy footsteps echoed along the hallway. The door pushed open. Strong arms wrapped around me. 'Grace, my dear.'

'Max, thank you for coming. You too, Charlotte.'

Charlotte hugged me. 'You'll get through this. You're a strong woman and we'll help you.'

They were so suited these two, even though there was almost twenty years between them, Charlotte so elegant, and Max smart in his tailored clothing and looking nowhere near seventy-four. His white hair offered a distinguished look. What would I do without this pair? 'Thank you. The vicar will be here shortly so we can plan the service. Have you heard from Nancy?'

'Yes, she'll be here as soon as she can,' Charlotte said.

'But how are you, my dear?' Max said. 'I mean injury wise.'

'Just cuts and bruises. The doctor was surprised after reading the police reports that I got out alive. The car was crushed. If only I hadn't insisted we…'

Charlotte slipped off her faux fur coat. 'Now don't start blaming yourself. I believe it's fate. Remember I told you that after Jack?'

'You did. It doesn't make it any easier.' I packed up the wrapped gifts and put them inside carrier bags. 'For the girls' stockings.'

'I'll put them away until afterwards.' Charlotte took the bags and patted my shoulder. 'You'll get through this.'

*

Christmas Day at Granville Hall must have been the quietest it had ever been. The three girls, Lori, Annalise and Vikki sat down to open their presents from under the tree. We all gathered around: George, Alice, Charlotte, Max, Elizabeth and Simon. Nancy and Kevin hadn't managed to get here as they were stranded in Cornwall due to snow. Nancy was my oldest

16

friend, more like a sister, so I hoped she'd get back in time for the funeral. I needed her with me.

There were lots of *wows* and *yes just what I wanted*. I tried to smile as Lori unwrapped a box of Lego to build a castle. 'Will you help me do it, Uncle Simon?'

'Sure.' He got down on the floor next to her to fit the yellow bricks with red and blue doors and windows together. It even had a little car and figures.

'They're young,' whispered Charlotte. 'They'll be fine. We've been friends for a long time, Grace, and we've been through a lot together. How long has it been? Seventeen years?'

'It must be.'

'The girls will bounce back quickly. You'll see. But it's you I'm worried about. Once the funeral's over you need to start a new project.'

I knew she was right.

Annie came into the room. 'Dinner is served.'

Chapter 3

George

Seven of us sat around the huge table in the dining room. Christmas Day dinner at Granville Hall had never had so few people. We'd postponed other family members and friends because I didn't think Grace was up to it. The girls were shattered after an early start so Annie had taken them up to bed earlier.

Donna served out vegetables and Uncle Max carved a huge turkey that was far too big for seven of us.

'George,' Charlotte asked, 'who's the bubbly young maid?'

'Oh, that's Donna. She started last week, she's straight from school. Annie recommended her.'

'Is she living in?' Max passed a plate with sliced turkey to Charlotte.

'She is.' I took a sip of Pinot Noir and swilled the full-bodied red around my mouth. 'Mmm. That's good. Now, where were we? Oh yes, Donna. I was a little concerned she'd be homesick but seems fine.' I put my wine glass down on the table. 'I assume you know Martha's retiring?'

'Really? We had no idea,' Charlotte said as Annie served roast potatoes onto her plate.

'Too old to do chores now. Crippled with arthritis so she's going to live with her sister in Cumbria.' Personally, I couldn't wait to see the back of her. I thought back to my first day at Granville Hall when she forced me into the bath with disinfectant and later tugged a steel comb through my hair.

'You're hurting me,' I'd told her but she didn't stop. 'I don't have nits.'

'All your lot do.'

All your lot do. What right did she have to say that to me? And now because she was retiring, I was supposed to present her with a gift. Good riddance to her.

'So, have you sorted a retirement present?' Max asked.

'Well, Elizabeth has. To be honest I'm glad to see the back of the old cow.'

'George.' Charlotte was open mouthed in surprise.

'Well, after the treatment she gave me and Grace.'

Grace surprised me by sitting up and joining in the conversation. 'I'll be glad to see the back of her too. She caused nothing but trouble for me.'

'So, Elizabeth, are you going to tell us what you've bought for Martha then?' Max asked.

Elizabeth placed her knife and fork down. 'A Haller clock. It's gorgeous. It has a gold and crystal casing with a rotating pendulum. Have you seen them?'

'I can't say I have,' Charlotte answered.

'The plan had been to present it today but what with…' Elizabeth picked up her knife and fork.

Grace lifted her glass of wine to her lips, hiding her face.

*

Grace was downstairs pacing up and down. She wore a black dress that she'd designed herself with a matching jacket. Her small hat had a veil which reminded me of the one she'd worn to Da's funeral except this one had a flowered pattern on the net.

I walked over to her. 'Grace.' She jumped. 'Sorry I didn't mean to creep up on you.' I lifted her veil to kiss her moist cheek. 'How are you coping?'

19

'I'm all right.'

'What's the plan for Lori and Annalise?'

'Plan?'

'Is Joanie coming over to look after them?'

'No. Why would she?' Grace frowned. 'They're coming with me.'

'Are you sure? You do remember what happened after Da died?'

She looked at me, vacantly.

'You ended up on the grass and Alice and I thought you were going to get in the grave with Da. It was scary. That won't be fair on the girls.'

'Well, that can't happen this time, can it? Not when Adriéne's being cremated. It will be easier.'

'I hope so because I don't want those girls messed up.'

'Who do you think you are, George? They're Adriéne's children and shall attend their father's funeral,' Grace said as Elizabeth walked into the room.

'Is everything okay?' Elizabeth looked at me.

'I was just making sure Grace was going to be all right and advising it would be best to leave Lori and Annalise at home, so as not to frighten them.'

'Your Mum will be fine.' Elizabeth moved over to her sister and put her arms around her. 'I'll look after her, don't worry. And certainly, the girls must be there, as will Vikki.'

'Excuse me, Elizabeth, I don't mean to be disrespectful, but on this occasion, you don't know what you're talking about.'

'Your mother wants the children with her and there's nothing else to say.'

'But it might not be the best thing for the girls.'

'Did she stop you going to your father's funeral?'

'You know she didn't but you don't know what she was like.'

'Please can you stop talking about me as though I'm not here.' Grace adjusted her hat in the mirror.

I rested my hand on Grace's shoulder. 'I'm just concerned.'

'I know, darling but I promise you I will be fine.'

'Of course she will,' Elizabeth said. 'The children must go to their father's funeral and we shan't discuss this matter any further, George.'

I marched out of the room and forced myself not to slam the door behind me. What did Elizabeth know? She wasn't there when Da died.

Chapter 4

Grace

The hearse drove up outside the steps of Granville Hall. Clear to see, through its windows, were flowered wreaths of white carnations and red roses lying on top of the coffin. One *Daddy* and the other *Husband*. I slipped my hands into black silk gloves, walked down the steps and touched the glass of the vehicle, in line with the coffin.

'I'll never forget you my darling, Adriéne. If only I hadn't wasted so much time.' I held my palm in position until Alice was by my side.

'Come on, Mum. Let's get in the car.' Two stretched black limousines were behind the hearse.

I followed Alice. Elizabeth brought the girls to me. They looked beautiful. Their daddy would have been so proud. Although it had been hard, I'd forced myself to design their matching black corduroy pinafores and white silk blouses especially for today so they'd look their best. Joan was more than accommodating to run them up on the sewing machine. Joan had been more like a mother to me than a housekeeper and although now retired she was always ready to step in and lend a hand. Both the girls were so like Adriéne with their dark brown wavy hair and huge brown eyes and although there was two years between them, they could almost pass as twins. I kissed the girls and held them either side of me. No one was going to accuse me of stealing their childhood.

We took our seats in the car. George and Alice sat directly behind the driver, while I sat with the girls on the third row. It comforted me to know that my family and friends followed in the Rolls behind. Transport had been arranged for the servants and I would look out for Nancy and Kevin at the chapel.

'Why's that man walking in front?' Annalise asked. 'He'll get run over.'

'He's doing that out of respect for your daddy.' I patted her hand.

'And why's he got that funny hat and long coat?' Lori asked.

'That's his uniform. Like you wear a special uniform for school, this man has a special one for his job. That way everyone knows who the undertakers are.' I kissed the girls' cheeks in turn.

'What's an undertaker?' Annalise sat upright to get a better view.

I took a deep breath. Thankfully, George stepped in.

'He makes sure your daddy's final journey goes well.'

'What journey?' Annalise bounced on the seat.

'Stop it now.' I tried to hold my tears back. Perhaps George had been right, maybe I should have left the children at home. Annalise at least. She was so young and didn't have a clue what was going on. At least Lori had recognised that her father wasn't coming back.

'Is Mum okay?' Alice whispered to George.

'I can hear you,' I said. 'And yes, thank you, I'm all right.' I took another deep breath.

'We're here for you.' George turned around from his seat and smiled. 'Now girls why not see who can stay quiet for the longest?' He took out two one-pound notes from his wallet. 'A pound each if you can stay silent for the rest of the way.'

Lori and Annalise giggled and snuggled up either side of me. I hugged them both. When we reached Granville's gates the car stopped.

'Why have we stopped?' Lori asked.

'Because the undertaker's going to get inside the hearse. Watch.' George held up the green notes. 'But remember no more questions if you want this money.'

As the hearse pulled away, we followed at a snail's pace turning right on to the main road, past barren trees. Thankfully the snow had gone but the roads were still icy from frost. We turned left off the road and pulled into St Michael's Chapel.

George guided me out of the car. 'You can do this.' He gripped my hand before turning to Alice. 'You take the girls and I'll look after Grace.' I let him lead me into the small church and along the aisle to a row by the altar. Alice and the girls sat behind us along with Charlotte and Uncle Max.

I turned around wondering where Nancy was just as she, Kevin and Rebecca walked down the aisle. Nancy came up to me and kissed my cheek. 'I'm so sorry, Grace.'

'Thank...' I broke down.

'Oh darling.' Nancy hugged me. 'It must be so hard for you.'

'I'm so relieved that you made it.'

'There was no way I wasn't going to get here when my best friend needed me.'

Nancy knew more than most what I was going through as we'd buried our first husbands together. Despite her losing John, she'd been a tower of strength to me at Jack's funeral. We were more like sisters than friends. Our tears mingled. I moved from her hold. 'Thank you. I'm so glad you're here. Will you sit with me?'

'I wouldn't have it any other way.' She smiled and even through grief her happiness with Kevin shone through. She deserved that happiness after not only losing John but having several miscarriages and stillborn babies too.

I moved along to make room and she eased herself down next to me. Here I was again, sitting between Nancy and George, just like eighteen years ago when we'd buried Jack.

The pews filled up. Doors had to be left open because of the overflow crowds. Adriéne was well loved. He'd been a great employer as well as a loving husband and father. He didn't deserve to die when he was only forty-seven, leaving me a widow at forty-six. A widow again, for the second time in my life. It wasn't fair. What had I done to deserve this? I wanted to scream but I'd promised Alice that I'd keep my emotions in check. What did she know? She hadn't lost two husbands.

George passed me his handkerchief to wipe my eyes. 'You're doing really well.'

I gave a half smile. Everyone stood up as the pallbearers carried my husband down the aisle in his beech casket. They set it down. The flower spray was exquisite. I chose red and white because Adriéne was a Manchester United supporter, despite being a Frenchman.

The vicar began to speak. I thought of how the quality of Adriéne's coffin was so much better than the one poor Jack was buried in. Jack, my first love, whom I'd been hesitant to let go for Adriéne and now they'd both gone.

I gripped George's hand, just like I'd gripped it when we buried his father.

'And now we will sing, *Morning has Broken.*' The vicar broke my thoughts.

Everyone stood up. The choir boys in their red and white smocks sang the first verse and then the rest of the congregation joined in.

'And now Simon Anson will say something about Adriéne.' The vicar moved to the side to let Simon speak.

'Adriéne and I became good friends. In fact, he was more like a brother to me and nothing delighted me more than when Grace and he came home and announced that they'd married in secret. He was a wonderful husband and father…'

How would my girls cope without their daddy? Alice's words echoed in my ears. *You're not stealing their childhood like you stole ours.* I hadn't known she felt like that. I thought I'd always been a good mum but if she was right then I needed to make sure I didn't make the same mistake again.

Alice stood up and read Psalm 23. 'The Lord is my Shepherd…'

George was next. He touched my shoulder. 'Will you be okay?'

Nancy took hold of my hand. 'I'll look after her.'

George moved to the front and read out John Keats' *Endymion.* He returned to his seat as the vicar stood up and said, 'Will you please stand for the committal?'

Everyone stood up.

'And now the family will come up and say goodbye to their loved one, Adriéne.'

I waited at the end of the pew for Elizabeth to bring out Lori and Annalise. I took their hands and showed them their white roses to pick up from the basket in front. I chose a red one. We took our single flowers and placed them on the top of the casket. 'Goodbye my love,' I said.

'Where's my daddy?' Annalise asked.

'He's in there.' Lori pointed to the coffin.

Annalise started screaming. 'I don't want my daddy in there. I want him here with me.'

I picked up my youngest daughter and rocked her in my arms.

Chapter 5

George

Grace positioned herself at the top of the twelve-seater boardroom table in her home. The family waited in anticipation.

'What's all this about?' Charlotte asked.

'Are you going to put us out of our misery, Gracie?' Uncle Max laughed.

'If you let me speak.' Grace took a deep breath. 'I've decided to build a memorial for Adriéne and wanted to run it past you all to see what you thought.'

'Sounds lovely,' Charlotte said. 'Any idea what and where? It's good to see you moving forward.'

'I've an idea, and I'm hoping it will be at Gerrard's Cross.'

'Do you have a plot in mind?' I asked.

'That's partly where you, Simon and Elizabeth come in. I'm hoping you'll sell me a small piece of Granville. The outskirts would be perfect. What do you think?'

Simon chewed on his pen. 'I think we need to know a little more about the project before a decision can be made.'

'Absolutely. I was thinking a palm house.'

'What, like the one at Sefton Park?' Alice asked.

'Yes.'

'May I ask why you've chosen that?' Elizabeth asked.

'Adriéne fell in love with the one there when we visited Liverpool last year. It was his dream to have one of his own and fill it with banana plants. What do you think?'

'In theory I don't have a problem.' I turned to my aunt and uncle. 'How about you, Simon? Elizabeth?'

'The palm house at Sefton brings back memories for us all.' Uncle Max clasped Grace's hand. 'Are you sure you're not confusing Adriéne's love with Jack's? You know it was Jack's favourite place, although he favoured the Peter Pan statue.'

'Positive, Max.' Grace smiled. 'You've no need to worry. This is about Adriéne not Jack.'

'Tell us a bit more.' Simon scribbled on the notepaper. 'Size, etc, and then if you don't mind, I think George, Elizabeth and myself need to discuss your suggestion in private before getting back to you.'

'That sounds perfectly reasonable to me. As for size, I was thinking a similar size to the one at Sefton Park with a memorial plaque outside.'

'Do you mind me asking why you haven't considered building it here?' Simon looked left and right towards the double aspect windows. 'It's not like you don't have enough room.'

'I had considered it but the plot at the side of Granville's far lake would be perfect. Also, Granville's a family estate so it will always be passed down to a family member, whereas this place… It could be sold anytime. And obviously the palm house may be used by all at Granville Hall and I wouldn't expect your gardener to do the work, I'd employ someone.' Grace lifted her cup to her mouth. 'But there is something else.'

'What's that?' I asked.

'I'd like you to design it. I know it's a much smaller venture than you're used to. But would you think about it?'

'I don't need to. There's nothing I'd like better than to be part of Adriéne's memorial. Let's fix a meeting for the two of us to draw up plans.' I took a gulp of my tea. 'I'm presuming you'll want to go ahead even if it isn't on Granville land?'

'That would be the plan. Charlotte said I should have a new enterprise and this is it.'

'In that case I think we should make a toast,' Charlotte said.

'I agree, we must.' Simon got up from the table and stretched his legs. 'But it's a bit early for champagne. You're right though, we should celebrate but why not wait until a decision has been made as to where it will be built?'

'George, are you going to have time to do this with your architect business?' Nancy asked.

'It's only a small job and I'll do it in my own time.'

'But you own the business.' Alice picked up a cheese scone from the plate in the centre. 'I don't see why this shouldn't take priority.'

She'd no idea. 'Just because I own "Stylistic Symmetry", Alice, doesn't mean I can do what I like. I'm still answerable to my board of directors.'

'Mum could pay and then you move her to the front of the queue.'

Everyone in the room stared at my sister.

Grace coughed. 'Alice, it's fine. George and I will make the arrangements.'

'How's the business going, young man?' Uncle Max asked me.

'Building up nicely. We now have a payroll of twenty employees. Did Grace make you aware of my grandfather's wishes?'

'Yes, vaguely. Don't you have to manage the estate? How's that working out along with running your own business.'

'I'm fortunate enough that Simon agreed to continue running the estate, despite Grandfather's terms in the will which stipulated I must be involved. Simon only calls on me when my signature is required.'

'That's very decent of you, Simon,' Uncle Max said.

'I knew how much George wanted to be an architect, and if he took over Granville, then I'd be redundant, so it worked out fine. I'm happy and so is George.'

I was happy. I'd got my family around me and although I hadn't been able to convince Grace to move into the Hall permanently, we were a family again.

Charlotte topped up everyone's cups with tea and coffee. 'To Adriéne.'

'To Adriéne.' We raised our cups to my stepfather.

'And to new beginnings.' Uncle Max raised his cup again. 'Next time it will be the real thing.'

'If we're finished here, Elizabeth and I have an estate meeting shortly, so if you don't mind…' Simon pushed his chair back and stood up. 'Are you ready, darling?'

'I'll see you both out.' Grace stood up and left the room with Simon and Elizabeth.

Nancy moved over to the window seat and beckoned me over. I followed her. 'Sit down,' she said, patting the seat next to her. 'While your mam's not here and there's just you and me…' She looked across to where Uncle Max, Charlotte and Alice were chatting at the table. 'How's she really doing?'

'Better than any of us expected, considering it's not even two months since the accident. She's coping extremely well with Lori and Annalise and those girls can be a bit of a handful, I can tell you.'

'A handful? Surely not. How are those lovely girls?'

'They're okay. Well at least they seem okay, you can never really tell. Can you?'

'That's true. I remember after your mam lost your dad, Alice seemed fine at first but then…'

'What?'

'Well, I'm not sure whether her problems were due to losing her daddy, and her brother, or because of how your mam was. Anyway, tell me about the girls. I'm so excited to see them.'

'Lori's settled back in school and Annalise started reception last month. She loves it. Lori keeps an eye out at break for her sister. I'd hoped Grace would move in permanently at Granville but she insisted on getting back to her own home.'

'You can't blame her for that. Your mam's an independent woman.'

'I know. I was being overprotective. You know, after everything.'

'I'm pleased she's doing well.'

'How long are you staying for?'

'Just a few days. Grace and I need to go through some textiles for the huge order that's come in. Actually, my suitcase and bags are still in the car. Would you mind helping me?'

'Sure thing. Let's do that now.'

Grace came back into the room as we were leaving. 'Where are you two off to?'

'To get Nancy's stuff from the car.'

Grace patted Nancy's arm. 'Would you like to get settled into your room before our meeting?'

'I think I would. Are Max and Charlotte joining us?'

I checked my watch. 'If you let me have your car keys, Nancy, I'll get your bags in, only I've an appointment myself shortly.'

'Thanks George.' Nancy rummaged through her handbag. 'Here they are.'

I left Nancy and Grace chatting and headed outside to the maroon Clubman Estate parked outside.

Chapter 6

George

'Vikki not joining us this evening?' I asked while sitting at the table with my aunt and uncle.

'No, she's been at a friend's house all day. An early night was called for.' Elizabeth pushed a bit of cabbage and mashed potato onto her fork.

'Shall we discuss Grace's proposal then?' I asked.

Simon poured red wine into our goblets. 'I had the same thought.'

'Cabernet Sauvignon, my favourite.' I swirled the glass, smelling the blackcurrant aroma.

'Elizabeth's too,' Simon said.

'What do you think of the memorial being built where Grace suggested?' I asked.

'I have no objection and neither does Elizabeth, do you darling?'

'None at all. As I told you on our way home from Grace's, I'm all for it.'

'And anything that's going to help her move past losing Adriéne has got to be a good thing.' I took the last bite of chicken breast from my plate. 'Annie's turning into a great little cook.' I put my cutlery down in the finished position. 'We're in agreement then? Grace should have the land?'

'Yes, definitely.' Simon topped up his wine.

'How do you feel about us gifting the plot rather than making it a sale?' I asked.

'I actually think that's a good idea. You know how much Adriéne meant to me too. Elizabeth?' Simon turned to his wife.

'I think it's an excellent idea. After all, if Father hadn't disowned Grace, all of this would have been hers.'

I raised my glass. 'To Adriéne.'

Elizabeth and Simon raised theirs too.

'I'll telephone Grace first thing as I'm not seeing her until Sunday morning,' I said.

After a tap on the door, Annie and Donna entered. 'Is it okay to clear the table now?' Donna asked.

'Certainly.' I moved my arms away from the table.

Annie stacked the last of the plates. 'Can I get you anything else? Dessert or cheese and biscuits?'

'Not for me, thank you.' I patted my stomach. 'I'm sufficiently full.'

'Me neither,' Elizabeth said, 'I'm trying to watch my waistline.'

'Mr Anson?'

'No thank you, Annie.' Simon took a cigarette from his Embassy packet and flicked his lighter on as the girls left the room. He puffed on the cigarette. 'I miss him so much.' He sighed.

'I know you do, darling. We all do,' Elizabeth said.

'I'd like to be hands on with this project.' Simon blew out smoke. 'I know Grace will insist on paying for stock herself but I'll have a chat with her and maybe she'll let me help order the plants.'

'And I can help with the furniture.' Elizabeth smiled. 'I'll speak to Nancy about designing special cushions for wicker seats.'

'Did I mention that I'm expecting Alice tomorrow afternoon? She's bringing a guest. You and Simon are welcome to join us.'

'Thank you,' Elizabeth said. 'What time?'

'Three-ish apparently. I've no idea who this mystery guest is.'

'I'll check our diary. We'll certainly try and be there, won't we, Simon?'

'Absolutely. If you'll excuse me.' Simon stood up. 'I think I need to retire for the night. Are you coming, darling?'

'I think I should. It's been a long day. Good night, George.' Elizabeth tapped my shoulder.

'Sleep well,' I said as they both left the room. Poor Simon, he'd taken Adriéne's death harder than I'd first thought. They were like brothers. Always fooling around doing something together. More recently they'd taken up golf. I should've realised how much Simon must miss my stepfather. I tipped back my glass and drank the remainder of my wine.

*

Tea and cakes were laid out ready on the coffee table. Alice peeped her head around the door.

'Hello, you.' I waved. 'Is Grace coming too?'

'Not today. She's quite fired up about the new project after your phone call giving it the go ahead, and Charlotte, Max and Nancy are still with her.'

'I thought you were bringing a guest. Did you change your mind?'

She pushed the door open wide and walked in. 'No.'

I was staring at the doorway waiting for the mystery guest when Robert Sanders wandered in. 'George, my old pal.' He patted me on the back. 'How are you doing?'

'I'm fine, thank you.' Curious to know why my old roommate was with my sister, I opened my mouth to ask when Alice cut in.

'Robert and I are together.' She moved closer to him and took his hand.

'What do you mean you're together?'

'We've been seeing each other. For a while now, actually.' She grinned.

'Him?'

'Excuse me, pal. You may be Lord of the Manor but that's hardly any way to speak about me. I've got a lot to offer Alice.'

I shook my head. 'What's that supposed to mean?'

'Ta da' – Alice wiggled her fingers – 'we're engaged.'

I cleared my throat. 'Does Grace know?'

'Yes, and she's happy for us. It would be nice if you were too.'

'Sorry. You surprised, me, that's all. Congratulations.' I kissed Alice on her cheek and shook Robert's hand. I was going through the motions but my head was spinning. This couldn't be happening. This bully, this bastard, I'd hoped I'd never meet him again in my life and now...

I rang the bell. Donna came into the drawing room. 'Yes, Sir.'

'Please can you bring in a bottle of champagne from the wine cellar. And also ask my aunt and uncle to come through.'

'Certainly, Sir.' Donna left the room.

I poured tea into the cups and cut the cake, passing a slice in turn to my sister and Robert. 'I had carrot cake made especially for you, Alice.'

'Oh yes, it's my favourite. How's the new cook working out?'

'She only lasted five minutes so Annie stepped in. Cook's still coming in once a week to help train her but alas, she's moving to Cornwall with Jimmy, her nephew, at the end of the month.'

'What a shame? Steph's doing a good job as new housekeeper for Mum but Joan is always around to help out if there are any problems. She and Ted are getting on a bit but Mum's told them the cottage is theirs for as long as they want.'

'Yes, she told me that too. One of the reasons she didn't want to move into Granville Hall, I think.'

'Madness.' Robert brushed his mousey coloured hair away from his gold-rimmed glasses. 'She should be getting rent for that property, not letting ex-employees live there for nothing.'

Alice frowned at him.

'You don't know what you're talking about, mate. Joan and Ted are like family,' I said as Simon and Elizabeth came into the room.

'What's all the fuss?' Simon asked.

Alice and Robert stood up. Alice held out her ringed hand. 'Aunt Elizabeth, Uncle Simon, we're engaged.'

'Congratulations.' Simon kissed Alice and shook hands with Robert.

'Congratulations both of you.' Aunt Elizabeth inspected the diamond ring. 'Wow, this must have cost you a pretty penny, Mr Sanders.'

'Nothing's too good for my Alice.'

'You don't seem very surprised, Aunt Elizabeth.' I glared.

'Well, to be honest, I'm not but I was sworn to secrecy. I think it's a great match and makes sense. It's a good allegiance between our two families.'

'For pity's sake, Aunt Elizabeth. It's nineteen eighty-one not Victorian times. It was bad enough that Grandfather spoke like that in the sixties but...' I shook my head.

'George, don't speak to your aunt like that.' Simon scowled.

'I'm sorry, Aunt Elizabeth, I hadn't meant to be rude. If you'll excuse me, I need some fresh air.' I stomped out of the room, took my wool overcoat off the peg and made my way out into the garden where the sun was melting the last of the snow. I paced up and down the gravel path. How could Alice have chosen Robert Sanders? Didn't she know what a bully he was? I thought back to my first day at the village school. I felt sick as I remembered what he'd done to me. Then it made me remember the kidnapping. I thought I'd come to terms with that part in my life, so much so that the therapist discharged me a couple of years back.

The back door slammed and the sound of high heels click-clacked up the path.

'Are you all right, George?'

'Aunt Elizabeth. You shouldn't have come out here. I'm fine.'

'Are you sure?' She shivered.

I took my coat off and wrapped it around her shoulders. 'It was just a bit of a shock.'

'It must have been. I should have warned you, I'm sorry. I thought you knew that she was seeing him though.'

'No. I'd no idea at all.'

'She should have mentioned it. Is there anything else though? You look pale and you're shaking.'

'It was seeing him. It brought a lot of bad memories back to the surface.'

'Like what?'

I shrugged my shoulders.

'Come on, George. Talk to me.'

'About the kidnap.'

'I don't see the connection.'

'Robert Sanders is a bully. My first day at school he shoved my head down the toilet and if that wasn't bad enough, it was the same day as the kidnap.'

'You poor thing.' She put her arms around me. 'You're freezing by the way. We should go inside. And George, do you need to start seeing the therapist again?'

'I don't think so.'

'Might be worth considering. It's been a tough time, what with the accident, your mother and then this. You're vulnerable at the moment.'

'I'll think about it. You're right, we should go inside, it's far too cold out here.'

We wandered back inside and upstairs towards the drawing room. I took a deep breath before pushing open the door. 'Sorry about that.'

'I'm sorry too. I didn't mean to give you such a shock. I wanted to surprise you.'

'You did that. Well, I'm very pleased for you both.' I kissed my sister and shook hands with Robert.

Donna brought in a chilled bottle of champagne and poured the sparkling liquid into fluted goblets and passed them around.

I raised my glass. 'To Robert and Alice.'

'To Robert and Alice.' Elizabeth and Simon said.

'To us.' Robert and Alice clinked glasses.

*

Elizabeth and Simon were already in the conference room when I joined them.

'What's all the secrecy?' I asked.

'No secret,' Simon said. 'I know you're not involved in the day to day running of Granville business and although presently we're not short on funds, I wondered what you thought about some ideas I've had to help move us forward.' He laid down the plans on the table. 'If we're going to survive as an estate in the future then I believe we need to change with the times.'

'Are you sure you want me involved?' I looked at the drawing.

'Yes, definitely. I'm hoping you can help me come up with some ideas. From a younger man's perspective.'

'What are you proposing?' Elizabeth asked.

'I'm suggesting we use this plot of land, here' – he pointed – 'and set it up for daily shoots as deer thrive in this part of the estate.'

'That's not a bad idea' – I pulled back a chair and sat down at the table – 'but I'd rather a clay pigeon shoot, as you know my feelings on game.'

'I've obviously missed something, somewhere, because I'd no idea you thought that way. But okay, a clay pigeon shoot will work, I'm sure.'

'What else?' I scribbled on the piece of paper in front of me.

'I wondered if you two had any ideas?'

'We could grow a maze and open up to the public,' Elizabeth said. 'That should bring in some money during the summer.'

'I like that.' I added it to my list.

'I was thinking we could do up one of the barns.' Simon pointed to the diagram. 'We could hire it out for parties and even wedding receptions.'

'And we could include the catering,' I said.

'I don't think we should mention any of this to Grace at this stage.' Simon folded up the plan. 'Otherwise, you know what she's like, she'll refuse to accept the plot of land for Adriéne's memorial as a gift.'

'True. Fancy a drink?' I stood up and poured three glasses of Scotch on the rocks.

Chapter 7

Grace

I stood staring out into the garden. The spring flowers were starting to push through and the nights would soon draw out. Three months since Adriéne had been killed. I longed to retreat into my sadness but Alice wouldn't allow that, so instead I kept going for Annalise, Lori, Alice and George, despite my heartbreak.

Adriéne's memorial should be ready by the end of the year. George had worked fast on the drawings and submitted them to the planning department. Hopefully we'd get the go ahead shortly to start building. I moved away from the window, over to the table, and looked at his portrayal of the palm house again.

Alice entered the room. 'Are those the plans?'

'Yes, come and see. George dropped them off earlier today.' It looked just like Sefton Park Palm House and would be a great tribute to my late husband. It brought a tear to my eye as I remembered him taking my hand as we toured around looking at all the plants. He knew all their names. I told him he must've been a botanist in a past life.

'It looks fantastic. I can't wait. Lori and Annalise are going to love it too.'

'I think they will, and as they get older, they'll have that special place to go and think about their father. Have you and Robert set a date yet?'

'No, but I promise it's on our list. I think I'd like to get married in August. What do you think, Mum?'

'August sounds lovely. It will be nice and warm which means you can have a nice off the shoulders gown. I'm going to be so proud when you walk down the aisle. Have you thought about who'll give you away?'

'George of course. And Lori, Annalise and Vikki will be bridesmaids. I'm not sure about an off the shoulder dress though. I'd like one of those big frocks with a long train. I want a fairy tale wedding.'

'And you shall have it my dear.' I hugged my gorgeous girl. Twenty-five, where had the years gone?

'Is George coming over later?'

'Yes, he's coming for dinner. Max and Charlotte left early this morning for the States and George didn't want me to be on my own.'

'You wouldn't be on your own. I'm still here.'

'I know you are, darling. You're a good girl.' I kissed my daughter on the cheek. 'I think George was worried that I'd find it a little quiet in the house with Max and Charlotte gone and you out and about with Robert.'

'I suppose so. What about Nancy? Isn't she coming to see you?'

'She's busy. She and Kevin are sorting out Rebecca's wedding.'

'It's a shame Nancy was never able to have children of her own.'

'Yes, but Rebecca's like a daughter to her.'

'What's Rebecca's wedding dress like?'

'Now you know I can't tell you that. I'm sworn to secrecy. You'll see on the day. I imagine you're looking forward to being bridesmaid.'

Out of the blue I was taken back to planning my first wedding with Jack, when I was living with Max and his first wife and my best friend Katy.

We'd all been chatting in their drawing room when I stood up and announced I was going upstairs to finish the last touches on my gown.

'What's it like?' Katy had pleaded.

'You'll have to wait and see.'

Then there'd been the time that she threw a tantrum because she didn't like the colour of her bridesmaid dress. What was it? Pink? Lemon. I really couldn't remember.

'Mum.' Alice was waving her hands in front of my eyes. 'Are you listening? In answer to your question, yes, I am looking forward to being Rebecca's bridesmaid. It's funny how we're both getting married the same year. Were you thinking about your wedding with Adriéne?' Alice put her arms around me.

'Strangely, no. I was thinking about my wedding to your dad. You know your father was a wonderful man. He'd have been so proud of you and George. George looks just like him.'

'Can we look through the photos again, Mum?'

'By all means. I'll dig them out.' At least, I'd dig out the few we had. Jack and I never had many photographs and what we did have I'd put away when I married Adriéne. It wasn't fair to expect him to live up to a dead man. I never loved him like I loved Jack but I did love him. It was just different. And he'd given me two wonderful girls. I missed him so much but I wasn't going to make the same mistake this time around. I wouldn't put my life on hold. Life was too short. Losing two husbands had taught me that.

'Is it okay if Robert comes for dinner this evening?' Alice kissed me on the cheek. 'Oh, Mum.' She soaked up my tears with her clean handkerchief.

'I'm sorry. I don't know what's the matter with me.'

Lori and Annalise came running in ahead of Joan. Joan and Ted had taken them out to the park. I was so lucky to have met Ted that first day in London, he'd been such a friendly taxi driver. It wasn't long before I invited him to join my employment as our chauffeur and Joan became a machinist, and later, housekeeper. Joan was the grandmother my children never had. Now in her late sixties, despite her permed hair turning completely white, she still looked well for her age with soft, blemish free skin. The other day Alice was teasing her about shrinking, but she was round and loveable, just the way we loved her. The girls adored her and she was like a mum to me. I wasn't sure how she managed to keep up with the children though.

'Hello my gorgeous girls.' I hugged them either side of me. 'You know, Joan, I worry about you looking after them. Are you sure they're not too much for you and Ted?'

'We're fine, Grace. It's not like we do a lot else these days now that you've got Steph in doing the housekeeping.'

'You must tell me if it becomes too much. Why don't you and Ted join us for dinner this evening? George is coming over.'

'Do you mind if we don't? I think we'd just like to put up our feet and turn on the telly. Dallas is on this evening with that gorgeous Bobby Ewing.' Joan giggled like a schoolgirl.

'What are you like?' Alice nudged Joan. 'You'd best not let Ted hear you.'

'Don't worry, dear, he knows.' Joan laughed, before turning to the girls. 'Right my little lovelies, come and give your Aunty Joan a big kiss and cuddle.'

Annalise and Lori rushed into her arms.

'I want you to do our bath.' Annalise tugged at Joan's blouse.

'No, Aunty Joan can't.' I said. 'Now let go of her blouse before you rip it.'

Joan lifted Annalise's hand away from her top. 'Another day, Annalise. You've worn old Joanie out.'

Annalise started whining. 'It's not fair. It's not fair.'

'Stop that now.' I took hold of my youngest daughter. 'Carry on like that and Joan won't take you out again.'

'Don't be too hard on her, Grace. I think she's just tired.' She leaned over to me and whispered. 'And she's been asking when Daddy's coming home. I don't think she's quite got to grips with it yet.'

'Thank you for letting me know. I'll talk to her later. I'll see you in the morning.'

'Bye girls, bye Alice.' Joan left the room.

'I know,' I said, 'who'd like a story?'

'Yes, please, yes please.' Annalise ran to the bookcase and brought back *The Very Hungry Caterpillar*.

'I like that one too. Can I read it?' Lori asked.

'Yes, you can. Come along, girls.' We curled up on the settee together.

Lori turned over the page.

*

Lori and Annalise were settled in bed when George arrived.

'I hope you don't mind me coming early,' he said, 'but I thought you and I could have a little chat before everyone arrives?'

'That sounds ominous.' I carried on tidying the girls' books and toys away.

'Not at all. Shall we sit down?'

'Certainly. Just let me get rid of these few bits.' I picked up the remainder of the girls' things and popped them into a toybox in a cupboard.

'Now if I were my sister, I'd be saying, I'm surprised you don't have a maid doing that for you.'

'Quite. I may have been a Granville, but that was a long time ago. I certainly don't think I'm too good to clear up after my

44

own children.' I sat down next to him. 'Now what's this all about?'

'I was just wondering what you make of this engagement?'

'Alice and Robert's?'

'Yes.'

'He seems a nice young man. Why? Is there something I should know?'

'Not especially but...'

'What?'

'Probably nothing but you know his father bullies his wife, and well let's face it, Robert's never been backwards in the intimidation department. He tried it on me at school, but once he saw that wasn't working, he turned to poor Neil.'

'Do you still hear from Neil?'

'No, I haven't heard from him in years. The last I knew he was studying at Sussex University in Brighton. I don't even remember what he was reading.'

'Brighton. I have some very special memories of that place. Why don't we take a trip down there once the weather gets warmer?'

'Yes, if you like. But never mind that now. What about Alice? I'm concerned how Robert will behave once they're married.'

'George.' I took hold of his hand. 'Darling, I think you're being overprotective. Anyone can see that he adores her. I know you've had your problems with him in the past but he's grown into a fine young gentleman. Alice is lucky to have him.'

George grunted under his breath.

'You need to be happy for your sister. Now come on, let's go and find the betrothed couple. They're probably in the dining room already.' The doorbell rang. 'That will be Elizabeth and Simon.'

George smiled. 'Oh, I didn't realise they were coming too?'

45

'Well yes, Alice invited them to help celebrate.' I took George's arm and we entered the dining room together. Simon was patting Robert on the back.

'Grace.' Elizabeth hugged me.

Simon kissed my cheek. 'How's my favourite sister-in-law doing?'

'I'm fine,' I lied. It wouldn't do any of them any good to know how churned up I was still feeling. After all what did they expect? It was only three months since Adriéne had been killed. Did they think I was made of wood?

'Robert' – I looked around the room – 'are your parents coming?'

Robert glanced at his watch. 'Yes, they are. I did tell them eight o'clock. That sounds like a car now.' He moved towards the window. 'It's them.'

'Good.' George frowned. 'Grace doesn't want the meal ruined.'

'Shh, George,' I said, 'there's plenty of time, we're still waiting for Nancy and Kevin to arrive. Charlotte and Max are really upset that they can't be here too. But don't worry, they said they'll be here for the wedding. Whenever that is.'

Steph entered the room. 'Lord and Lady Sanders.'

'Thank you, Steph.' I smiled. 'I'm still waiting for Nancy but she'll use her key.' I missed having Nancy around but understood she needed to move on. I couldn't believe it had been five years but she still had her key, and Charlotte kept a key too. I'd insisted they must always consider this as their home.

'How do you do?' I greeted Robert's parents. 'I'm Grace. Alice and George's mother.' This was the first time I'd met the future in-laws. Elizabeth and George had met them on lots of occasions when Father was still alive. Lord Sanders was a big man, broad and tall. His whitened beard made his face appear

46

longer and slimmer than it probably was. Lady Sanders looked petite next to him.

'Donald, please.' He held out his hand. 'And this is my wife, Frances.'

I shook hands with Frances. 'Please help yourself to a glass of sherry.' Steph had poured sherry into crystal glasses before everyone arrived.

Frances picked up a glass showing off her wrinkled hands. I reckoned she must be in her fifties, he closer to sixty. She must've been quite old when she had Robert.

'Isn't your daughter coming this evening?' I asked.

'Unfortunately, not.' Donald fiddled with his ear. 'She's away in the States. Didn't Robert mention it?'

The phone rang in the hallway. 'Excuse me.' I walked out of the room to see what was happening. 'Was that Nancy?' I asked Steph. 'Is she on her way?'

'I'm afraid she's unable to come. It was Kevin. Nancy was on her way out and slipped on black ice.'

'Oh dear, is she okay?'

'They're at the hospital now. Kevin said she's had an x-ray and luckily no bones broken but needs to go home and rest.'

'Thank you, Steph. I think we'll start dinner. Has the girl from the agency arrived to help you?'

'Yes, she's in the kitchen now.'

I was so relieved that I'd hired someone from the catering agency to help Steph with the guests. Normally Alice or myself would muck in and help but I wanted this evening perfect for my daughter. As I made my way back into the dining room, I heard raised voices.

'There's not really been the opportunity, Father. But yes, Emma has gone to Chicago on business.'

'Hmm, time that girl got herself a husband,' grunted Donald. 'How about you, young sir?' He turned to George.

47

'What about me?'

'Isn't it time you started looking for a wife? Emma will make a delightful catch.'

'When I'm ready for a wife, I'll choose my own, thank you.'

'Shall we sit down.' I interrupted to prevent a row. 'Donald, you're here next to Elizabeth, and Frances, you're sitting next to Simon.'

The talking stopped while everyone placed their empty sherry glasses on the sideboard and sat down at the table.

'You could do worse than my daughter.' Donald picked up where he'd left off but George wasn't the least bit interested.

'Leave the lad, alone, Lord Sanders. He'll find a wife when he's ready,' Simon said, butting in.

'I'm just saying. How old are you now? My daughter's a fine match. Your Grandfather…'

George jumped up from his chair. 'Can you please stop?'

'I agree.' I stood up. 'George, sit back down please.'

'My brother and Mum are right.' Alice frowned as George and I returned to our seats. 'We're here to celebrate our engagement.'

'Well said, Alice.' Robert put his arm around my daughter. 'Can everyone please remember that this is our engagement party?'

'Exactly.' I turned to Simon, George and Lord Sanders.

'Sorry, Alice, Robert.' George looked them in the eye.

'As am I. Forgive me, please.' Simon smiled.

I turned to Lord Sanders. 'Donald?'

After a long pause he finally opened his mouth. 'My dear Alice, please accept my apologies. I got a bit carried away there thinking how our two families could join together further and heighten both our empires.'

Empires. We weren't interested in empires. He was just like Father. I glared at Lord Sanders and shook my head.

The agency girl was circling the table pouring wine. 'Red or white,' she asked as she reached everyone. She seemed a polite young girl. I'd find out more about her later. Steph could do with a permanent hand to help her.

Steph pushed the food trolley into the room. She took the dishes from the under shelf and began serving chicken soup into the bowls.

I raised my glass. 'To Alice and Robert.'

Everyone joined in. I hoped George was wrong and Robert was nothing like his father.

Chapter 8

George

Laughing, I walked into the drawing room to find Simon and Elizabeth reading.

'Can you believe that Lord Sanders last night? Who the hell did he think he was?'

Simon looked at me with a serious expression on his face. 'You are coming up to twenty-eight after all.'

I glared at him.

'I'm joking.' Simon laughed.

'You got me there. Coffee anyone?' I poured myself a cup from the percolator on the sideboard.

'No thank you. Simon and I had coffee earlier. But listen, I agree it wasn't the right time last night to talk about you finding a bride but maybe it's something we should talk about?'

I shook my head. 'No thanks, Aunt Elizabeth, there's no rush for me to marry. When am I supposed to find this wife? I never go anywhere.'

'Why don't we throw a party? Grace is designing me a new dress which will need an entrance.'

Simon folded his newspaper, got up and moved over to the cabinet. 'I've changed my mind; I will have that coffee. Elizabeth, are you sure you won't have one?'

'No, thank you. Too much caffeine. What do you say, George?' Elizabeth closed her book and put it down on the lamp table.

'About what?'

'Me organising a party and I'll invite lots of young ladies.'

Simon poured two coffees and carried the cups over. 'Leave the man alone, Elizabeth. He said *no*. I'm sure he'll meet someone in his own time.' He put my drink down on the table.

'Thanks, Simon.' I folded my arms.

'Let's still have a party. It's been ages since we had dancing at the Hall.'

'No, Elizabeth'– Simon sat back down– 'it's too soon after Adriéne. There'll be plenty of time for a new frock and dancing at Alice's wedding.'

'Yes, of course you're right. I wasn't thinking properly. I got carried away by the idea of music and dancing filling the Hall's ballroom. Now, George, Grace mentioned that you're not happy about Robert and Alice's engagement. Why is that?'

'I don't trust him.'

Simon sipped his coffee. 'It's a good match and Alice is happy.'

'Good match, bloody hell, Simon, that's Donald Sanders talking. These days we marry for love, like you and Elizabeth did.'

'But Alice does love Robert,' Elizabeth said. 'She's very happy.'

'But does Robert love her?' I shook my head. It was pointless. Everyone thought he was such a nice man.

*

There was nothing I could do. I knew Alice was making a big mistake but no one would listen. Not Elizabeth, not Grace and certainly not Alice. They were all blinded by Robert's charm but I knew what he was really like and didn't believe he'd changed. The most I could hope for was a long engagement. Maybe during that time he'd show his true colours.

Throwing my coat on, I wandered down the steps from the house and towards my brand-new Ferrari. I patted her long red

51

bonnet. I'd nicknamed her *Jessica*. Everyone thought I was mad but who cared?

I climbed into the car and sank myself into the deep seat, turned the ignition and spun the wheels as I drove off. 'Yay, you can certainly move, girl.' The roads were quiet for Saturday lunchtime so it didn't take me long to arrive at the local Con club where I'd agreed to meet Robert. How the hell did Alice meet him in the first place? I thought I'd seen the back of that bastard when we finished school. He knew how to put on the charm. Like he did with me, pretending to be my friend and then as soon as my back was turned, hit on my girl. What was her name? Ah, yes, Patsy. She was my first proper girlfriend. What did I mean first? I hadn't had any proper female company since. No wonder Elizabeth was worried about me. I'd been so busy with study and then work. If it hadn't been for Sanders, who knows where our relationship may have led. No, I didn't trust him. Fooled everyone all the time. Pretending to be your friend when he was out to get you. And now he just wanted Alice because his father thought he'd have links to Granville. By the time I pulled up into the almost empty carpark, I was seething. At least if there weren't many people inside we should get a chance to speak without being disturbed. I took a deep breath as I reached the entrance. There was no need to confirm membership as the door manager recognised me instantly.

'Good afternoon, Lord Granville. Mr Sanders is waiting for you.'

'Thank you.' I walked through the double doors, searched the large room and found Robert sitting at a small table in the corner. I wandered over. 'Robert.' I shook his hand.

'What's with the formality, old pal?' Robert patted me on my back. I wanted to keep it formal though.

'Let me get you a drink?' I said.

'Pint of bitter. Cheers.'

I walked over to the bar and ordered our drinks, returning to the table with two pints of bitter.

'I was pleased that you called. It's about time we had a catch up. Unfortunately, I had to put Alice off.'

'What, you'd arranged to meet her and cancelled because of me?'

'Yes, but don't worry, she was fine about it.'

So already he was putting others before my sister. 'When did you and Alice first meet?'

'Ooh, let me think. One of the dinner parties at your place, I believe. While you were away.'

He didn't know? Surely when marrying someone you should remember the first meeting. 'Do you mind me asking, what is it you see in her?'

'Blimey. What a question. Well, she looks like dynamite for starters. I suppose as her brother you can't see her that way.'

'I suppose not. But do you love her?'

'Ah I see. This is one of those conversations is it? You want to make sure that I have good intentions?'

'I suppose I do.'

He patted my hand. 'Rest assured, big brother, my intentions are good. And just think, we'll soon be family.'

I lifted my glass and swigged a slurp of beer. *Not if I can help it, mate.* I licked my lips. 'Do you love her?'

'What's love? It's a good match. It's what Father wants and it's what your family want too.'

'Maybe I don't.'

'What's this all about?'

'I'm not sure what you mean. I just want to check your intentions towards my sister.'

'I know what this is all about.' He sniggered. 'You're still cut up about me and that girl at school, aren't you?'

'I don't know what you're talking about.'

53

'You are. I can see it in your face. That's the reason you don't want me to be with your sister. For fuck's sake, Granville, that was, how many years ago?'

'It's nothing to do with that. I want to make sure my sister is going to be happy and with a man who'll treat her right.'

'And why can't that be me?'

'Because you're a slime goat. You always have been and I don't trust you.'

Robert got to his feet, leant over and grabbed my tie, forcing me to seize his arm and twist it until he squealed and let go.

The club manager was at our side. 'Gentlemen, please. This is a respectable establishment. Please don't give me cause to ask you to leave.'

'Please accept my apologies.' I straightened my tie.

'Mine too.' Sanders smoothed down his jacket.

'Well, keep it civil. I won't stand for aggression in my club.' He walked away as we sat back down in our seats.

Robert adjusted his gold-rimmed specs. 'That was your fault for calling me a slime goat.'

'Just don't start. You heard what he said.'

'Well, just get this into your head. I'm marrying your sister and there's not a bloody thing you can do about it.' Robert took a swig from his pint of beer.

'I'm telling you now, Sanders. If you hurt my little sister, I'll…'

'You'll what? Do you think just because you've inherited a swanky title that you're better than me now?'

'It's nothing like that. I'm just concerned about my sister ending up with a bully like you.'

Robert tossed his head back and laughed. 'If it makes you feel any better, I love her to bits. I promise I won't hurt her.' Using the back of his hand he wiped the froth from his upper lip.

'You'd better not. That's all I'm saying.'

'Or you'll do what?'

I pushed the table back, ready to throw a punch to wipe off that slimy grin, when the club manager headed over. 'Just don't try me, Sanders.' I turned to the club manager. 'Sorry, Miles.' Adjusting my suit, I strode out of the place.

Chapter 9

Grace

Some of my guests, in particular Robert and his father, were getting impatient as we waited in the drawing room for George to arrive. This evening's dinner party was to be a small gathering, giving us all a chance to get to know each other better. Elizabeth and Simon had arrived early while Lord and Lady Sanders – Donald and Frances – were prompt.

Elizabeth joined me by the fireplace and rubbed her hands by the glowing flame. 'I can't believe it's the end of June and so chilly.'

Alice paced backwards and forwards, searching the hallway through the open door. 'Hurry up, George. Where is he?' Her black spotted rah-rah skirt, teamed with a plum gypsy blouse accentuated her gorgeous figure and the blonde ponytail hanging to one side highlighted her porcelain skin. It was hard to comprehend that she was twenty-five and soon to become a wife, although I was only eighteen when I'd first married.

'Alice, relax. Come and drink your snowball.' I looked at my watch. 'I'm sure he'll be along shortly.' He was ten minutes late, no wonder she was getting anxious. I hoped this wasn't a protest from him, against the groom. Why couldn't he be happy for his sister instead of looking for problems?

Alice slumped down on the couch and picked up her glass, stirring the advocaat cocktail. Robert banged his Scotch down on the coffee table. 'Where the hell is he?'

'Calm down,' Simon said. 'He's on his way.'

I hoped he was. Alice looked like she might cry and as for Robert's father, I hadn't taken to him at all.

The front door banged shut and heavy footsteps ambled along the hallway. George strolled into the room, smiling. 'Sorry I'm late. I got caught up with a phone call.'

'You're here now,' I said, 'and that's all that matters.'

'About time too,' Robert said. Simon glared at him.

Robert's father stood up to shake George's hand. 'Good to see you again, young man. Perhaps I can call on you sometime with a matter that I think would be of mutual interest?'

'Sure.' George didn't seem interested in the slightest.

'Well now that everyone's here,' I said, 'shall we make our way into the dining room?'

Name settings with alternate male and female positionings were placed around the dinner table to avoid confusion when everyone came in. I was at the head of the rectangular table with George and Robert either side of me facing each other, while Elizabeth sat opposite me. Simon was on one side of her facing Donald Sanders on the other. Alice was in the middle between Robert and Donald, and Frances Sanders was opposite Alice between George and Simon.

Steph pushed the food trolley into the room while Paula, the young girl I'd hired following the agency trial, circled the table serving wine. She was a big help for Steph. Paula was pouring the cabernet into Robert's glass when he knocked her arm causing her to spill the wine.

'Stupid girl,' he shouted, 'look what you've done.'

'I'll get a cloth.' She ran out of the room.

'It wasn't her fault,' George said, 'you nudged her.'

'I did not.'

'Actually, Robert, you did,' Simon agreed.

'Well not on purpose.'

'Fair enough,' I said, 'but maybe you should apologise to the girl when she comes back in.'

'What, you've got to be kidding me?'

I smiled. 'No, Robert. If you could have the grace to apologise, I'd appreciate it.' I stood up from the table. 'If you'll excuse me, I'll just check that she's all right.'

I needed an opportunity to leave the room to calm down. Was George right about Robert being a bully, or was it that too much alcohol had made him aggressive? He'd been hitting the Scotch rather hard before dinner. Poor little Paula looked like she was going to burst into tears. She was only just sixteen. At this rate she'd be handing in her notice. I found her in the kitchen crying. 'It's all right,' I said, 'he didn't mean to shout. We know it wasn't your fault.'

'You're not going to sack me then, Mrs Gilmore?'

'No, dear. I'm not. Now pop to the bathroom and wash your face and we'll see you in a few minutes.' I returned to the dining room where everyone was chatting nicely except Frances Sanders who appeared subdued. She'd been quiet since they'd arrived, maybe I could help her open up. I sat down. 'How are you, Frances?'

'I'm fine, thank you.' She unfolded the white cotton napkin and laid it across her lap.

'Frances hasn't been too well of late, have you, dear?' Donald looked across to his wife.

'I've been getting dreadful migraines, but I'm fine. Red wine doesn't help, hence why I'm not drinking.'

'No, I'm sure.' I was outraged how Donald had embarrassed her. And as for her son, he was certainly making up for her lack of intake of alcohol.

Paula rushed back in and over to Robert with a cloth. 'Here you are, Sir. I am so sorry.'

'Thank you.' He took the cloth and dabbed his jacket. I glared at him. 'And I'm sorry too.' He forced a smile.

We chatted small talk over prawn cocktail followed by the main course. 'The steak is cooked beautifully.' Simon speared another piece on to his fork.

'A bit overdone for me.' Robert screwed up his nose. 'I prefer mine rare.'

I took a deep breath. 'I'm sorry it's not to your liking.'

'Behave yourself, Robert.' Donald Sanders' face looked like thunder 'Where are your manners?'

'Sorry, Father.'

'Have you young people set the date?' Simon asked, trying to keep the peace.

Alice put her knife and fork in the finished position. 'Yes, we have. Shall I tell them Robert, or will you?'

'No, you can.' He clattered his cutlery down on the plate and picked up his wine.

'Well don't keep us waiting.' Elizabeth glared bright-eyed.

'Oh, all right then. Twenty-second of August.' Alice beamed.

'Will Emma be able to come, Frances?' I asked.

'She certainly better had,' interrupted Donald.

'That's if she's not jaunting around the world.' Robert gulped the last of his wine and poured a refill from the bottle on the table.

'She's obviously a successful entrepreneur,' I said. 'What is it that she does?'

'A photographer,' Frances muttered under her breath.

'Sorry, I don't think we quite got that,' George said.

'She's a photographer.' Robert slammed his empty glass down. 'Is there any more wine?'

'Twenty-second of August. That's not even two months away, Alice,' Elizabeth said trying to change the subject. 'Not much time to order a new hat or frock for that matter.'

'Never mind hats, Mum needs to design my gown and the bridesmaid dresses. Sorry, Mum, for not giving you more time.'

'I'm sure I'll manage,' I said unable to miss the tension between Robert and his father. Was that why Robert was behaving this way? 'It will keep me focused.' I smiled at my daughter. I did wonder how I was going to fit everything in but it wouldn't be the first time I'd sat up all night finishing off a gown.

'And don't forget my dress, too.' Elizabeth picked up her glass. 'We should have a toast.'

Steph was by my side. 'Would you like me to bring champagne, Mrs Gilmore?'

'I don't think so, thank you. I think everyone's had enough alcohol for one evening. Some more than others.' I looked directly at Robert.

'Very well. I'll get Paula to bring in dessert. I've baked Alice's favourite, black forest gateau.'

*

'We should get started on your wedding dress.' I held up some samples.

'But I want to see what Princess Diana's wearing first,' Alice pleaded.

'That will give me less than a month to sort out your gown.'

'You can be getting on with the bridesmaids' dresses, can't you? And it's not like you have to make the dresses yourself, is it?'

'I know, darling, but I'd like to complete the final embroidered touches myself. And let's be honest, it's your gown that's going to be the challenge. Why don't we try and

60

work out a plan at least? This is the sort of thing I was thinking.' I drew a sketch. 'A silk V-necked bodice with off the shoulder three-quarter lace sleeves and a full skirt trimmed with matching lace and a long train.' I lifted the drawing. 'What do you think?'

'It looks lovely, Mum, but can we make the skirt much fuller and I'd like a six-foot train.'

'Yes, I can add lots of net underskirts and how about matching lace for the train?'

'Yes, that sounds gorgeous and then if it doesn't look as good as Princess Diana's, you can adjust it so it looks better, can't you?'

'I can do that but you shouldn't be in competition with the royal bride. You should be choosing what you want because you like it. You're going to make a stunning bride.'

'Do you think so, Mum?'

'Absolutely, darling. How could you not be? You're beautiful.'

'I just don't want to let Robert down.'

I shook my head. 'How could you?'

'If I don't look as good as he's expecting me to look.'

'In that case, he won't deserve you as his bride. Now let's not hear any more nonsense like that. What about your bridesmaids? Have you thought what colour you'd like them to wear?'

'Yes, peach.'

I scribbled a design on the notepad. 'How about this?'

'Oh yes, Mum. I love the ruffled tiers and puffed sleeves.'

'And I can embroider little rosebuds on the tiers. Now how about your matron of honour? Has Rebecca given you any inclination of what she'd like?'

'She's happy to wear what I say.'

61

I laughed, thinking back to when I'd married Jack, and Katy had made a big fuss about the colour I'd chosen for her to wear. That seemed such a long time ago yet at the same time every moment of my first wedding and the planning was still fresh in my mind. I wiped away a tear.

'What's the matter, Mum?'

'Nothing. I'm just happy for you.'

'I wish my brother was. Honestly, what's got into him lately?'

I slipped the tape measure around her bust and wrote the measurement down. 'He's just worried about you. Just be thankful you have a big brother looking out for you.'

'I suppose so.'

'You're so tiny, Alice.' I wrapped the measure around her waist.

'How much am I?'

'Not even twenty-two inches. That's smaller than I was when I got married.'

'What was Dad like?'

'Just take a look at your brother and you'll see your dad. It's uncanny the way they are so alike.'

'I wish he was here to give me away. I always thought at least I'd have Adriéne but we don't even have him anymore.'

Another tear escaped my eye.

'I'm sorry, Mum. I didn't mean to upset you. You haven't had it easy, have you?'

'No, I haven't, darling, but look at it another way. How lucky was I to have found two men to love and for them to love me?'

'And you might find love again?'

I shook my head. 'I don't think so.'

'But, Mum, you're still young. Never say never.'

Chapter 10

George

I was looking forward to seeing Betty and John. Even after ten years it felt odd to call my old primary teacher by her first name. I still thought of her as Miss Jones. After finding her ten years ago we'd kept in touch. In fact, they'd asked me to be godfather to their six-month-old son, Nathan. Ben and Susie had been invited to the christening too so this was a great opportunity to hook up with them again.

I'd sought out Betty on my eighteenth birthday after having left her class when I was nine. Now I was twenty-eight. Where had those years gone? And me, still a single man. And although I was cross when the subject of getting married was brought up, deep down, I knew it was right. I'd been so busy studying for my dream job as an architect that I hadn't time to go out with a girl, never mind see one on a serious basis.

I slowed down the Ferrari, pulled up outside Betty and John's house and switched off the ignition. It was half past eleven but there was a light on, so thankfully I hadn't kept them up. I grabbed my backpack and wandered up the path to the front door.

Betty opened the door before I got to the bell. 'I thought I heard a car.' She kissed me on the cheek. Tassles, the red setter, pushed her way towards me, sniffing. In no time at all she was on her hind legs with her front paws against my chest.

'Hello, old girl.' I patted her greying coat.

'Come in, come in.' Betty ushered me through into the lounge. 'You're looking well, George.'

'John not in?' I slipped off my shoes.

'He's on a late shift but he should be home by midnight.'

'I was worried about waking you up so the light on in the sitting room was a welcome sign. The journey hasn't been the best.'

'Poor you. Sit down and I'll make you a cuppa. Have you eaten? Would you like a sarnie?'

'Thanks, that would be nice.' I held my hand over my stomach as it rumbled. I laughed. 'I should have stopped at the motorway services but I was concerned about getting here even later. Is Nathan in bed?'

'Yes, he is, although he's due another feed. But don't worry, you'll get plenty of time with him tomorrow. He's a right pickle. Crawling now.'

'No way.' I laughed. 'Are you planning on going back to work?'

'Not for a while. I don't want to miss a moment with Nathan but I'll have to return sometime to help pay the mortgage. I'll go back part-time and with John's shifts we should be able to cover childcare between us. Anyway, enough about me. Sit down.' She gently pushed me into the dark brown armchair. 'I'll stick the kettle on and get you a towel.'

'Thanks. I'll just use the little boy's room if that's okay?'

'I'm sure you remember where it is. Straight up the stairs and on the left.'

'Cheers.' I crept upstairs to use the bathroom. By the time I returned Betty had a mug of steaming black coffee on the coffee table.

'Cheese and cucumber sarnie okay?' She threw me a striped towel.

'Thanks on both counts.' I rubbed my hair dry. Who'd have thought I could have got soaked in just the few minutes running from the car to the door. 'More like April showers,' I called into the kitchen, 'than the beginning of July.'

'I know what you mean.' Betty came back into the sitting room with a plate of triangular sandwiches and a lettuce salad on the side. 'Here get that down you.'

'Thanks.' I bit into the brown bread.

'Now tell me what's been going on in the world of George.'

'Well, I wrote and told you that Alice is marrying that plonker Sanders, didn't I?'

'You did indeed. But I thought he was your friend?'

'He was never my friend, I just put up with him. To be honest, Betty, he's a bully and I don't reckon he's marrying Alice for the right reasons.'

'You don't think he loves her then?'

'No, I don't. He said he did, but I don't believe him. I reckon it's more about keeping his father happy by marrying into the Granville clan. Would you believe his father suggested I marry his daughter?'

Betty laughed. 'By the sound of things, I think I might.'

'Bloody cheek. I'll marry when I'm ready and who I want.'

'Without a doubt. Calm down though, otherwise you'll do yourself a mischief.'

'Sorry.' I took a swig of coffee. 'Ah, this is nice. Just what I needed.'

The front door slammed and Tassles ran out into the hallway. 'Hello, girl,' I heard John say. 'Hello, George,' he said coming into the lounge.

I stood up to shake his hand. 'How are you?'

'I'm fine. You sit down and eat your supper. Anything there for me, Bett? I'm starving.'

'Sure. Sit yourself down.' Betty went into the kitchen and in no time at all returned with a sandwich just like the one she'd made for me, and a steaming hot drink. 'Here you are, darling. How was work?'

'Okay but tiring. How's Nathan been? I missed giving him his bath and story.'

'You can feed him when he wakes up.' She turned to me. 'He's dropped the ten o'clock feed but still wakes for one in the middle of the night. Still, it works well because then he sleeps through until seven. We need him to be bright-eyed and bushy tailed for his big day tomorrow.'

I stacked my mug onto the empty plate. 'That was lovely, thank you. A bit rude of me, I know, but would you mind if I turned in? I'm absolutely shattered and struggling to keep my eyes open.'

'No problem,' Betty said. 'You're in the usual room.'

'Night, John. Night Bett.' I kissed Betty on her cheek. 'And good night to you too, Tassles.' I ruffled her ears.

I grabbed my rucksack from the hall then tiptoed upstairs and made my way across the landing. I peeped into Nathan's room but he was fast asleep. I was looking forward to seeing him tomorrow. This would be the first time I'd been a godfather. I went into the familiar spare room where I'd slept on numerous occasions. After undressing I climbed into the clean cotton sheets, put my head down on the pillow and closed my eyes.

*

Betty placed Nathan in the baby stroller.

'Hang on.' John attached a matching green parasol. 'I'll push.' He steered the pram down the front step and opened up the flowered sunshade.

'This is your big day, Nathan,' I said making him gurgle.

It took us about twenty minutes to walk to St Andrew's and the sun shone the whole time. I followed Betty and John into the church. The pews were filling up and there were two more couples with babies to be christened. We were allowed to sit in the front rows. Just as we were sitting down I heard a voice I recognised.

'George, how you doing, mate?'

I turned around to see my old friend, Ben. 'Where's the kids?' I asked him.

'With Mam. We didn't want them messing about with us being busy as godparents.

I was so pleased that Ben and Susie had become good friends with Betty and John over the last few years as it meant we could all meet at The Woodcroft when I came up for a visit.

'Shh,' said an old woman sitting in the pew behind us.

It took me all my time to keep my mouth closed. It wasn't like the service had started yet. The vicar hadn't even come in.

Ben rolled his eyes. 'There's always one.'

I smiled and whispered, 'Isn't there just?'

The vicar walked in and made a greeting. 'Welcome everyone, particularly to our newest members of the church, Nathan, George and Samantha. There will be a bible reading and we'll talk about what baptism means. Will the godparents and parents please come forward?'

Ben, Susie and I followed John and Betty. The other couples and their godparents went to the front too. A curator handed us cards to read from. The vicar went through the promises one by one and only the parents and godparents answered until he said, 'People of God will you welcome this child and uphold them in their new life in Christ?'

The congregation joined in and said, 'With the help of God, we will.'

The vicar took hold of Nathan, made the sign of the cross on his forehead and poured water over his head. He didn't make a sound. The vicar took the other babies in turn, one was good like Nathan but the other one screamed. I think the vicar was glad to give that one back to his mother.

The parents or godparents were given an ignited tapered candle to hold on behalf of the child. I was given that honour. Afterwards photographs were taken and Nathan smiled when he was in my arms. He really was a dear little baby.

'Right,' said John, 'let's get this little boy home to bed. Are you coming back to ours?' he asked Ben and Susie.

'Just for half an hour and then we'd best rescue Mam from the kids,' Susie said. 'They'll be driving her up the wall by now.'

Ben and Susie now had four children, yet looking at Susie you'd never have guessed it because she was still as trim as ever. Her youngest, five-year-old twin boys, were quite a handful. Ben's mam must've had some energy.

When we got back to Betty's house, I was allowed a little cuddle with Nathan before John said he needed to get him ready for bed. Betty had bathed him before the christening so it was just to be a top and tail. 'You can feed him if you like?' he offered.

'I'd like that.'

Betty carried a tray of tea and chocolate fingers into the sitting room.

'Shall I be Mam?' Susie poured tea into the cups.

Ben helped himself to a chocolate finger from the plate and took a bite. 'Do you remember when we used to have these at school?'

'I do.' I laughed.

'Less talk of that.' Betty giggled. 'You'll make me feel old thinking back to my three former pupils when they were only eight and nine-years old.'

John came back in with Nathan. 'Are you ready for him?' he asked me.

'Yes, I'll just get rid of this.' I finished off my tea and put the cup down.

John passed the six-month-old to me. 'I'll just get his bottle.' He disappeared into the kitchen.

Nathan started crying. I rocked him up and down. 'Shh, it's okay. Your bottle's coming.' He started to scream.

John rushed in with the bottle. 'Here, give him this.'

I popped the teat into Nathan's mouth. He snatched it, gulped and started sucking and guzzling.

'Look at you. You'll make someone a great wife.' Ben winked.

'Oi, leave him alone. He'll make a fabulous dad one day.'

'I'm only ribbing him, Betty. George knows that. Don't you, mate?'

'Aye, I do.' I looked down into Nathan's little face. It made me feel warm inside. I couldn't wait to be a dad. With still about an ounce of milk left at the bottom of the bottle, Nathan was out for the count. 'What about winding him?' I asked.

'He'll be fine.' Betty took Nathan from me and carried him upstairs.

'So how long are you down here for?' Susie asked.

'Going back tomorrow evening.'

'So, time to come out for a drink this evening then?' Ben asked.

'Err...'

'You go,' John said, 'don't worry about us. We can let you have a key.'

'That sounds great but what will you do about the kids?'

'Our Sandie will babysit, so long as I pay her.' Ben laughed.

'Right. Where shall I meet you?'

'Woodcroft at eight.' Ben stood up. 'On that note, once Betty comes down we should get going.'

As if on cue Betty walked back in. 'He's fast asleep. Hopefully that will be him for a few hours. I'm exhausted.' She flopped into an armchair.

'We'll leave you be as we need to get off.' Ben kissed the side of Betty's face and shook John's hand. 'Thank you for allowing us to be part of Nathan's big day.'

'Thank you for coming.' John kissed Susie on the cheek.

I kissed Susie and patted Ben on the back. 'See you both later then.'

I turned to Betty and John. 'Do you mind if I have a quick nap if I'm going out later?'

'No, of course not. Treat this like your home.'

*

It was just after eight when I arrived at The Woodcroft. Every time I came to this place it stirred up memories of Alice and I sitting outside on the wall waiting for Da. Somehow the cheese and onion crisps used to taste nicer then, as did the Coca Cola we drank from a bottle through a straw. I pushed the door open.

Ben waved at me. They were sitting by the window and had someone with them. I made my way over.

'I got you a pint in. This is Mandy.' Ben turned his head towards a woman with long dark hair. 'I hope you don't mind us bringing her along.'

'Not at all.' I winked at this stunning woman. 'It's a pleasure.'

'You don't remember me, do you?'

I put my hand to my mouth. 'Hmm, should I?'

'She used to sit next to me at school,' Ben said, 'Mandy Brown.'

'Never.'

'I could say the same about you.' Her eyes sparkled. 'Who'd have thought you were that lanky lad.'

'I wasn't. Was I?'

She laughed. 'Well, yes.'

By the end of the evening I felt like I'd known Mandy forever, which in a way, I suppose I had. 'Can I walk you home?' I asked.

'That will be lovely.'

'Are you coming up for Alice's wedding?' I asked Ben and Susie.

'Yes, we'll be there.'

'Great, I'll see you then.'

I took Mandy's hand as we left. 'Which way then?'

'Down Shepherd's Street. Do you remember it?'

'Ah, yes, the posh area.'

She blushed. 'Not as posh as I understand you are now. Susie said you're a lord.'

'I am but I don't really use the title. I'm still the same George.'

Mandy told me how she was a teacher and in fact worked in the reception class at our old school. The boys most likely looked into her big green eyes and fell in love with her, just like I'd fallen in love with Miss Jones, Betty, when I used to stare into her blue eyes.

'It's here.' She stopped outside a semi-detached house that looked like it was built fairly recently.

'Do you live here with anyone?' I asked. My way of finding out whether there was a Mr Mandy.

'No, I live alone. I got divorced last year. Found out he was cheating on me. You can come in for coffee if you like?'

'Well, only if you're sure.'

'I wouldn't have asked otherwise, would I?' Her eyes glinted.

My heart pounded like I was a schoolboy. I hadn't felt this excited for years. I walked into the house and slipped off my shoes.

'No need for that,' she said.

'It's fine.' I followed her into the kitchen and watched her draw water from the tap to fill up the kettle. She flicked the switch. 'He was mad,' I said.

'Who?'

'Your ex. If you were my wife, I'd never have cheated on you.'

She blushed and I could feel myself aroused. I pulled a pine chair out from under the table and sat down crossing my legs.

'How do you like it?'

'Sorry, what?'

'Your coffee.'

'Oh.' I laughed. 'Black with two sugars.'

'Fancy a biccie?'

'What's on offer?'

'I've got chocolate fingers or you can try out my homemade cookies.'

'No contest. Your cookies.'

After pouring water into the mugs, she lifted a Quality Street tin off the shelf and pulled out a handful of biscuits, placing them on a plate. 'Why don't we sit down in the lounge where it's comfy?'

'Shall I take the coffees?'

'If you don't mind, thanks.' She picked up the plate of cookies and I followed her into the sitting room with the steaming cups of coffee.

She made her way to the modern armchair while I sat down on the matching settee. 'I can't believe I'm sitting opposite you after all these years,' I said.

'No, me neither. I really missed you when you upped and left. No one knew where you'd gone, not even Ben. What happened?'

'Well, you know me da was killed in the big accident at the mine?'

'Yes, I remember that. It must have been an awful time for you.'

'It was.'

'So, what happened after your dad…?'

'Mam didn't cope very well.' I thought it was strange how I'd slipped into the old dialect, but being with Mandy was like travelling back in time. Here I was in Wintermore and it was like I'd never left.

'How so?'

'Well apart from crying a lot you mean?'

'Understandable.'

'Yes, but it was more than that. Then one day Mam's mother turned up out of the blue. Her parents had disowned her when she married Da.'

'Why did they disown her?'

'They were titled, and Mam marrying a coal miner wasn't in their plan.'

'I see, so that's how you became a lord.'

'Sort of.' I bit into the ginger cookie. It was nearly as good as Cook used to make. 'These are lovely.'

'Thank you. Go on with your story.'

'No. I don't want to bore you.'

'I'm not bored at all.' She smiled at me making my heart beat fast.

I looked across the room to the record player. 'Shall I put something on?'

'If you like. You choose.'

I stood up and stepped to the music centre. Kneeling on the floor, I browsed through the albums on the rack underneath. I took an LP from its sleeve and placed it on the turntable, carefully positioning the stylus.

'What have you chosen?'

'Wait and see.'

The turntable spun around and *I don't want to know* burst through the speakers.

'*Rumours*,' she said, 'my favourite,' and began joining in with the song.

'Mine too. I love Fleetwood Mac. Has anyone told you that you've got a lovely voice?'

'Well actually… yes, but thanks. I used to be the soloist in the school choir.'

'I'm not surprised.' *Dreams* was up next. 'Dance with me.' I held out my hand to take hers. We smooched on the shag pile carpet and Mandy sang sweetly in my ear. I hadn't been this relaxed for years. People talk about love at first sight and I'd always laughed it off but here with Mandy's breath on my skin, I was quickly being converted.

As we danced a slow beat to the next track, I twisted her under my arm making her twirl and when her dress rose up, she giggled. 'We should sit down,' she said, 'our coffee will be getting cold.'

I aimed for the settee. 'Only if you sit with me.' I gently pulled her to the couch. As we continued to listen to the tracks, I moved closer and kissed her softly on her lips, wrapping my arms around her. We kissed and cuddled only coming up for air when the needle reached the end of the record and clicked itself off. I looked at my watch. 'That must be my cue to leave. It's gone midnight. Can I phone you?'

'How do you know I'm on the phone?'

'The green one on the hallway wall was a bit of a giveaway.'

74

'No catching you out, is there Mr Gilmore? Oh sorry, I forgot, you're Granville now.'

'I'd prefer to be Gilmore. But never mind that. Let me have your number.' I smothered the back of her neck with kisses.

'Oi, behave.' She got up and took a small notepad and biro out of the sideboard drawer and wrote on a sheet of paper. 'Here.' She tore the sheet off the pad and passed it to me.

'Wigan 3921. It's etched on my brain.'

She laughed. 'So, are you going to give me yours or do I just have to hang around waiting for you to call?'

'Sure. Pass the pad and pen.' I took the notepaper and pen from her and wrote down my number, adding five x's underneath before handing it back and making my way to the front entrance. Before she opened the door, I leant forward to kiss her. 'I'll call you.' I couldn't wait to see her again.

Chapter 11

Grace

Slowly I was coming to terms with life without Adriéne. I didn't think that meant I loved him less than Jack but this time I had my family around me. Riding helped and I was able to do a lot of that at Granville Hall.

I was leading the stunning chestnut mare, Lady, out of the stables when George came trotting towards me. 'Hi, Grace, how are you?' He climbed off his horse and kissed my cheek.

'Fine, thank you. Riding this beautiful girl helps.' She'd been a gift from George last Christmas but it was only over the last few months that I'd managed to become acquainted with her.

'It's hot out there so don't stay out too long. Not just for you but for Lady too.'

'I won't. Just a quick trot over the meadow. Fancy joining me?'

'No, I won't if you don't mind. I think this poor fellow needs a good brush down and rest. Don't you, Murphy?' He stroked the exquisite black stallion. 'Come in for tea once you've finished.'

'Will do. Joan has taken the girls out so I'm free until quite late.'

'See you later then.' George walked into the stables and chatted to the groom.

I trotted off. The slight breeze lifted my hair and it felt good to be alive. Everything was coming together; Alice would be settled in a month and she was going to be the most beautiful bride. Her wedding would be so different to both of mine. I thought back to my wedding with Jack when I was young and innocent. If it hadn't been for Uncle Max and his wife, I didn't know what I'd have done. I made my own dress and when we spent our wedding night at Halliwell Lodge, Jack was so gentle as he took me into womanhood. When I married Adriéne it was a quiet occasion with two strangers for witnesses in a little registry office. Alice was inviting the whole world. For a coal miner's daughter, nothing phased her. The more expensive the better.

'Phew. George was right, wasn't he, Lady? It's very hot.' I pulled over by a huge oak tree to give us some shade. Taking out a plastic bowl that I'd packed in my saddle bag, I poured water from a flask for my horse and tipped some in the cup for me. She sucked it up while I sipped mine. I lay down and closed my eyes knowing that Lady would be fine under the tree's canopy.

I was dreaming of Jack on our wedding night when a horse whinnied. 'Shh, Lady,' I said, rolling back to sleep to continue my dream. Jack's hands were caressing my arms, moving upwards to my neckline when I was woken with a jerk, sensing someone leaning over me. I sat up. 'You. What are you doing?' I pushed Richard Anson off me. I looked around for help but all I could see was his horse tied up next to Lady.

'Don't be like that,' he said with a wide grin. 'Lie back down.'

'I don't think so. It's time I was going. Go home to your wife.' I stood up and went to reach for Lady but Richard was up on his feet too and backed me towards the tree, his face reddening. My shoulders tightened. 'What the hell do you think you're doing?'

'Come on, Grace. Don't be such a tease.' He scowled. 'Do you know how long I've waited for this?'

I pushed him away, looking about me again but no one was around. 'Waited for what?'

'For you? I've been waiting for over thirty years.'

'Well, you can wait all you like, Richard Anson. I wasn't interested in you then and I'm certainly not interested in you now.'

'Don't give me that. You must be longing for a man. A proper man.' He put his hand across my breast.

'Get your dirty hands off me.' I jerked backwards and reached for the riding crop to thrash it across his body but he was too quick for me, grabbing it out of my hand and throwing it to the ground.

'I see.' He smirked. 'So, you want to play rough.' He pinned me against the tree so I couldn't move and ripped my blouse open.

'Get the hell off me.' I kicked his shin.

He leant down to clutch his leg, inching away, giving me enough space to push him from me. My nails hit flesh and I dug deep, but he caught me by the arm, and wiped his cheek with the other hand. 'You bitch. What have you done?'

I wriggled under his grasp and finding enough space I raised my knee and thrust it into his groin. He let me go and keeled over screaming. 'Bitch.'

'You picked the wrong woman to mess with, Richard Anson.' I untied Lady and climbed up onto the saddle. 'Good luck explaining the mess of your face to Mrs Anson. Oh, and one last thing, if you ever come near me, or any of my family again, in that way, I'll kill you. And that's not a threat but a promise.' He was still lying on the ground holding himself, his face contorted. I galloped off and didn't look back. I was shaking. I looked down at my torn blouse. Thank God I'd found the strength to fight him off.

*

78

After parking the car, I jumped out and hurried to the house. I longed to get in the shower and wash away his filth. Steph rushed to the hallway. 'Mrs Gilmore, Charlotte and Max are here.'

'They're early. I wasn't expecting them until tomorrow.'

Charlotte came out of the drawing room. 'I thought I heard your voice.' She hugged me. 'How are you, darling?'

I burst into tears.

'What is it? What's happened to you?' She ushered me into the drawing room.

Max stood up away from the chair. 'Grace, dear, it's so lovely to see you, but what's wrong?'

'I don't know yet,' Charlotte answered. 'I hugged her and she just burst out crying. Sit down, Grace, and tell us what's happened.'

'Where's Alice?' I sobbed.

'She's out with her fiancé, apparently. What's this chap like? Sorry, never mind that, let's sort you out. What is it? Have you had an accident?'

'It's nothing.'

'It doesn't look like nothing.' She tugged at my torn clothes.

'Would you mind if I slipped upstairs and had a shower first? I've been out riding and feeling a bit worse for wear.'

'Have your shower, darling, and then come down and tell us all about it.' Charlotte gently squeezed the top of my arm.

The events ran through my head and I thought how different it could have been if I hadn't had the strength to battle him off. 'I can't tell you.'

'It's me. Charlotte. I'm the one that's seen you through all your tragedies. You can tell me anything, you know that. And Max isn't going to judge you either.'

I looked her in the eye. 'There's nothing to judge me for. I haven't done anything, it was…'

79

'Who?' Max pressed.

'If I tell you, you must promise not to go storming off, no taking the law into your own hands.'

'We promise, don't we, Max?'

Max nodded.

Charlotte led me to the sofa and sat down next to me. Max sat the other side.

I knew I had to tell someone. 'It was…' I took a deep breath, wiped my eyes and pulled a handkerchief from my pocket. 'It was Richard Anson, Simon's twin brother.'

'What's he done?' Max jumped up. 'What's the bastard done? I'll bloody kill him.'

I tugged on Max's arm to get him to sit back down. 'You can't because then you'll be locked up. Please. It's okay, I'm fine. Just shook up. Nothing happened.'

'It doesn't look like nothing has happened, Grace.' Charlotte put her arm around me. 'Your clothes are ripped.'

'You're right. I think he was going to rape me. He was drunk and going on about waiting for me for so many years and how he'd show me what a real man was like. Thank goodness I had the strength to get him off me. I scratched his face so I imagine that will prove difficult explaining to his wife.'

'But you're going to the police? I'll phone now.' Max was back up on his feet.

'No, Max. Don't. Sit down,' I said.

Charlotte took my hand. 'You must tell Simon or George then.'

I shook my head. 'I hadn't planned to.'

'You must.' She gripped my hand tighter. 'Then they can sort him out and make sure that he doesn't step on Granville property again.'

I released my hand from Charlotte's hold. 'I'll arrange refreshments before getting cleaned up and then you can tell me all about what you two have been up to. And how long you're here for.'

'Don't worry, Grace. I'll sort out the tea. You go and get that shower.' Charlotte hugged me.

Max stood up next to me. 'I can't promise that I won't say something. You're like a daughter to me and the thought of any man touching you against your will, well it makes my skin crawl.' He kissed me on the cheek.

'Thank you, Max. You've been like a father to me too. I won't be long.' I left the room and walked upstairs in a trance like state.

Chapter 12

Grace

22nd August 1981

The day was here. My daughter's wedding. I slid the matching long burgundy jacket over my linen pencil dress. It was one of my latest designs. Standing at the hallway mirror I pinned the white orchid corsage onto the right-hand side of my jacket before turning towards the stairway as Alice was coming down.

'You look beautiful, darling.'

She came downstairs carefully holding the wide span of skirt and the six-foot train trailed behind her. The gown was a perfect fit.

'Thank you, Mum.' Alice kissed my cheek as she reached the bottom. 'You've done wonders sorting it in time. I like it better than Princess Diana's.'

George appeared at our side. 'Wow, is that really my kid sister? The little monster that used to get on my nerves. You look gorgeous.'

'Thank you, George. That means a lot. Now you're not going to start today, are you?'

'Definitely not, Sis. I'll be on my best behaviour. And look at these three little darlings too,' he said, turning to the children who had followed Alice down, all dressed in peach satin dresses. 'The cars are here.'

I was to take the first car with Vikki, Lori and Annalise. George and Alice would follow in the next, arriving last at the church. Just like I did when I married Jack although hopefully

Alice wouldn't be asking George to stop the car like I did when panic set in on my way to the church. Not that I didn't want to marry Jack but everything had got on top of me, not having my father give me away and not being able to have my sister, Elizabeth, as a bridesmaid. Max told the driver to pull over and advised me that the best thing to do when things got on top of you was to find an open space and scream. The driver stopped by a field and I climbed out and did as Max instructed. And yes, I felt heaps better for it. Thankfully we didn't arrive at the church too late.

'Grace, did you hear what I said?' George was tapping my arm. 'The cars are here. You need to go now with the girls.'

'Sorry.' I walked over to the sideboard and picked up Alice's bridal bouquet of white roses and freesia. 'These are beautiful, darling.' Although nothing had been said I knew she'd chosen roses for her father as they were his favourite.

Annalise grabbed my hand while Vikki and Lori skipped on in front.

*

The limousine pulled up outside Guildpool Cathedral.

'That's a big church, Mummy,' Lori said.

'It's not a church, it's a cathedral,' Vikki said. 'I've been here before with Mum and Dad.'

Annalise tugged at my arm. 'What's a cathedral, Mummy?'

'It's a big church,' Vikki answered, 'wait until you see inside.'

'It looks scary.' Annalise started to cry.

The chauffeur opened the door of the car and helped us out one at a time starting with Vikki.

'Don't worry.' I hugged my youngest daughter. 'Rebecca's coming and she'll look after you.'

'I'll look after her too.' Vikki took Annalise's hand.

Where was Rebecca? She'd told Alice that she'd meet us here because she wanted to travel with her husband.

'Aunt Grace, look, she's here,' Vikki announced as a white Triumph 2000 pulled up across the road. Rebecca climbed out looking elegant in a long lilac dress, her blonde hair pinned up loosely with soft curls at her cheeks.

'Aunty Grace.' She kissed me. Although she wasn't my real niece, she'd grown up knowing me as her aunt.

'You look gorgeous, Rebecca. I knew that colour was right for you when Alice chose it from the swatches.' I'd seen it on her before for fittings but not all dressed up as she was now with make-up and hair done. Unlike my daughters, Lori and Annalise, and my niece, Vikki, Rebecca's bridesmaid dress wasn't tiered but draped loosely brushing her lilac satin high heeled shoes.

We walked up to the vestibule while chatting.

'Thank you,' Rebecca answered. 'You remember my husband, Michael, from our wedding?'

'Yes of course. How are you, Michael?' I shook his hand.

'Enjoying married life. Look ladies, the bride has just arrived so I think I'd better get inside.'

'I shall be there myself in a moment.' I glanced at my daughter and son stepping out of the white Rolls. Alice certainly did look like a princess but I was also filled with pride watching George take her arm and lead her up the footpath to the cathedral. My heart leapt as he walked towards us. It was like going back all those years when I married Jack. 'Jack,' I whispered, 'look at your children.'

'What are you saying, Mummy?' Annalise tugged at my dress.

'I was saying, now be good girls and enjoy your special time being bridesmaids. You all look beautiful.' I turned to Rebecca. 'Are you sure you can manage with the three of them?'

'Yes, I'll be fine and I'm sure Vikki will be helping me.'

'I will be.' Vikki clutched my girls' hands.

Before going inside, I took one last glimpse as my son and daughter walked closer. I blew a kiss to them both and headed inside to the pews on the left-hand side. Max, Charlotte, Nancy and Kevin were already seated. I sat on the front row next to Nancy while the others were on the pew behind.

'You look lovely, Grace.' Nancy kissed my cheek. 'I love your hat. The cream sets off the colour in your dress and you always did look great with a wide brim.'

'Thank you,' I whispered, as the organist began playing '*Here comes the Bride.*'

George and Alice started the procession. They walked slowly towards the altar. It was a long walk, much longer than if they'd married in a regular church. This was the type of wedding I'd have had if Mother and Father hadn't disowned me but I was thankful for a smaller ceremony in the little village church. Alice must have got all these fancy ideas from her grandparents, despite never knowing them. Her V-neck off the shoulder gown accentuated her slender figure while the three-quarter lace sleeves showed off her slim hands. The full skirt brushed along the floor with Vikki holding the long train. Lori was next, dropping rose petals from her wicker basket and Rebecca and Annalise followed hand in hand. The dresses looked divine. I'd spent hours embroidering little rosebuds on the ruffled tiers. It had paid off.

As they reached the altar, Robert turned towards Alice and smiled. George had to be wrong. This looked like a man in love. I didn't recognise his best man. I beckoned the little bridesmaids over to sit with me and Rebecca lifted the net veil from Alice's face and took hold of her bridal bouquet before joining us on the front pew.

The bishop stood on the steps in front of the altar and welcomed the guests before we sang the first hymn, 'Give me joy in my heart.' Vikki sang above us all. When we got to the 'sing hosanna', her soprano voice rang out. Then the bishop began with his talk about marriage. 'Love is the gift, and Love is the giver…'

'Mummy, I need the toilet.' Annalise was dancing on her feet.

'I'll take her,' whispered Nancy and shuffled down the pew holding Annalise's hand.

'Is there anyone here who sees any reason why this couple should not marry?' The bishop looked up at the congregation.

Everyone turned to look at each other but no one answered. My heart started pounding. I hoped that George wouldn't say anything but the church stayed silent.

The bishop turned to the bride and groom to ask them the same question. Alice gave a nervous giggle as she answered *No*.

Next came a bible reading. The best man walked over to the pulpit. He looked about the same age as George and Robert. I wondered who he was as he started reading from Corinthians. A cousin of Robert's maybe. When he got to the end he stepped away from the podium and swaggered back to his seat. The bishop began the vows.

'Alice, say after me. I, Alice Rose Gilmore, take you, Robert Edward Sanders to be my wedded husband.'

'I, Alice Rose Gilmore, take you, Robert Edward Sanders to be my wedded husband.'

'To have and to hold…'

Suddenly little footsteps ran down the side of the church. 'Alice is getting married.'

'Shh, Annalise,' Nancy was whispering but not before those close enough to hear smiled and offered quiet laughter.

I was taken back to my wedding with Jack. He was such a wonderful man. So gentle and he spruced up well on our wedding day. No one would ever have guessed he was a coal miner. Uncle Max had made sure Jack was suitably attired and Eliza had helped me plan my wedding. I smiled thinking of Eliza, she was such a lovely lady. So sad what had happened to her after Katy, my best friend, committed suicide. It was too much for Eliza and she'd ended up in a mental institution and died there.

'I now pronounce you man and wife. You may kiss the bride.'

The congregation clapped as Robert kissed my daughter.

*

We threw confetti over the bridal couple. I was so proud of my daughter. She looked enchanting. Alice had always wanted a princess wedding and that's exactly what this was. The photographer sorted everyone in position to snap group shots, one of George and Alice, lots of the bride and groom, some with the bridesmaids and she took one of just George, Alice and me. My mind wandered back to the day I'd married Jack. It was a small do but Max had hired a photographer to take a few snaps so that we always had that to look back on, unlike today when the photographs seemed to be never-ending.

Alice's gown looked wonderful on her. It was worth sitting up most of last night to finish off the final touches. I'd covered the bodice with diamond sequins and pearls. She wanted a dress more unique than Princess Diana's and she had one. The silk hung beautifully showing no signs of creases.

Max held his hand up in the air. 'Everyone, the bridal couple are now ready to leave.'

Ted opened the back doors of the Rolls for them to step in. We could have hired a chauffeur but Ted insisted that he wanted the honour. And Joan, Ted's wife, was happy to travel with Nancy and Kevin.

George gripped my hand as we travelled in the car behind Alice and Robert.

'Didn't she look gorgeous?' I didn't usually get over emotional but today, I couldn't contain it.

'Here.' George passed me a handkerchief. 'It's clean.'

Touching the cloth took me back to the times I'd been passed a handkerchief by Jack and he'd say exactly the same. Our driver started the car and pulled away following the bridal Rolls. The flowers and ribbons were exquisite. Nancy and Joan must have sat for ages creating such beauties. I was so lucky to have such a fine family. Annalise and Lori were well behaved bridesmaids, along with Elizabeth's daughter, Vikki. They followed in a car behind us with Rebecca, the chief bridesmaid. She'd been Alice's roommate at Greenemere. More tears as I thought about my Greenemere roommate, Katy, the girl who changed my future by introducing me to her cousin Jack so avoiding a future with one of the Anson twins. So yes, I had a rough deal in losing George for a time in my life, losing my lovely man Jack, and then later losing Adriéne, but I'd known love, real love, not once but twice. My life would have been so different with an arranged marriage. I wiped my eyes again.

George placed his arm around me. 'Look at you, all emotional today. We've arrived and you cried the whole way here.'

'Sorry, George.' I sniffled. 'I'm not sure what's the matter with me. It was just seeing Alice like that, all grown up and beautiful. Your father would have been so proud of her.'

'Yes, he would have.'

Chapter 13

George

A huge marquee erected in Grace's garden was filled with tables and chairs for the guests. I sat at the top table next to Grace, with Robert's sister, Emma, on my other side. Grace was unfortunate enough to be seated next to Robert while Donald Sanders was next to Alice. Uniformed agency staff rushed around serving the meal. First up was a tasty vegetable soup with croutons, followed by tender sea trout in a tomato and tarragon cream sauce, and a boozy sherry trifle to finish.

'I see we've been suitably partnered,' Emma said, during a lull between courses.

'Yes, I imagine that was your father's doing.'

'For certain. But don't worry, I'm not interested either.'

'Oh good. Nothing against you, I'm sure you're a lovely girl but…'

She squeezed my hand. 'It's okay. I'm taken.'

The Master of Ceremonies stood up and announced it was time for the speeches. 'Lord Granville, you're first as stand-in for father of the bride.'

'Excuse me,' I said to Emma, before standing up. 'Well, what can I say except that it has been an honour to stand in for our father. Unfortunately, due to no fault of our own, Alice and I were parted for a few years during our childhood but going back to my early memories of her I can tell you she was a gorgeous little girl. If you remember what Shirley Temple looked like, that was my sister. And look at her now, she's grown into this stunning young woman that any man would be proud to have as his wife. And if our father were standing here today, I don't think he could be prouder than I feel right now.' I finished off by smiling and saying, 'So Robert, I'm expecting you to take care of my little sister or you'll have me to answer to.' Everyone laughed thinking I was joking. She looked radiant. I hoped with all my heart that he would make her happy so she never lost that glow. 'And without further ado, will you be upstanding and raise your glasses, to the bride and groom.'

Everyone stood up and raised their glasses. 'To the bride and groom.'

It was Robert's turn next. He shuffled up to his feet. He was already looking like he'd had too much to drink. 'What can I say to follow that great speech from my old roommate.' He went on about how he'd been at school with me and if we hadn't become friends then he might never have met Alice. We were never friends. He ended his speech saying, 'So there's nothing else for me to say except thank you, George, for allowing me the honour of marrying your sister. Will everyone be upstanding and raise your glasses to my bride, Alice.'

Everyone stood up and raised their glasses. 'To Alice.'

He then turned to Lord Sanders. 'I've done you proud, haven't I, Father?'

Donald frowned as Robert sat back down leaving the floor for his best man.

It turned out that the best man was a cousin of Robert's on his father's side which could explain why he seemed just as full of himself. He waffled on about times as kids when they'd climbed trees, played footie and rugby. I shut myself off from listening to the drivel until he asked us all to stand to toast the bride and groom when glasses were raised again.

'You're nothing like your brother,' I said to Emma.

'Thank the Lord for that. I'd hate to be as arrogant as him or dear Daddy for that matter.'

'Hmm. Not nice men. How does your mother put up with him?'

'She loves him and to be honest he loves her. He does look after her. Intimidates her sometimes but I don't think he realises he's doing it. Oh look, the bridal couple are getting up for their first dance.'

Alice and Robert took the floor as the music played Smokey Robinson's *Being with You*. As they danced, she leaned on Robert's shoulder until he lifted her face towards his and kissed her lips. Everyone applauded. I felt sick.

The Master of Ceremonies announced it was time to join the bride and groom on the dance floor.

'Shall we,' I asked Emma.

While we glided around the room, I said, thinking out loud, 'I've recently met someone who I think will become my wife.'

Chapter 14

George

I set off early on the Monday morning after the wedding and arrived at Wintermore around nine-thirty. After parking the Ferrari, I dropped into the florist and picked up a bunch of white roses to take across to the cemetery. I had no problem finding where Da was these days as the enormous yew was a great guide. I strolled along the gravelled pathway and reached his gravestone. Stooping on the ground, I placed the flowers in the vase, adding water from a bottle I'd brought with me. 'Da,' I said, 'I wanted to tell you that I'm going to propose to a lovely working-class girl, you may even remember her. Mandy Brown. Simon and Elizabeth are going to kick off, particularly Simon, but I don't care. Mandy will become Lady Granville because Grandfather had my name legally changed when I was a child and there would be too many repercussions to change it back, but I'll always be a Gilmore, Da, you know that, don't you? I'm not interested in all these fancy things and ideas like our Alice, I'm still a coal miner's son. So, what do you think?' I knew he couldn't answer but felt better saying it aloud. 'I'll bring her here once we're wed.'

When I left the cemetery, I called into the little café Grace had brought me to that first time I'd visited Da's grave. Somehow, I hadn't been able to call her Mam again, she'd always be Grace now. Even though I loved her, the word mam wouldn't form in my mouth.

A bell pinged when I opened the glass door and a middle-aged woman waddled out from behind the counter. The café was empty. It was a wonder they didn't go bankrupt. I sat down by the window.

'Hello, dear.' She looked me up and down. 'Are you new around here as I don't think I've seen you before?'

'Actually, I was born here. Just been to visit me da's grave.' I made a point of saying *me* to emphasise I was local. 'What happened to the man that used to run the café? Has he retired?'

'Ah that would be me dad. Unfortunately, he died earlier this year. Stroke. Very sudden.'

'I'm sorry.'

'Not your fault, sunshine. Now what can I get you? A full English?'

'Sounds good. And I'll have a mug of black coffee to go with it please. Need something to wake me up after driving up from London.'

'I'll get you a coffee straight away and a top up once your brekkie arrives.'

'Thanks.'

As she disappeared into the kitchen, I dug into my jacket pocket and pulled out a small red box. I opened it up and stared at the platinum diamond solitaire ring. I hoped Mandy would say yes.

*

After leaving the café I drove around to Betty's. It was six o'clock, hopefully I was in time to have a play with my godson before bedtime.

I parked outside their house. John answered the door with Tassles sticking her head out of the open doorway.

'Hello, girl.' I ruffled her fur.

'How are you doing, George?' John shook my hand.

'Fine, John, and you? How's fatherhood?'

'Exhausting. But come in, let's not stand on the doorstep.'

93

I walked into the hallway and slipped off my shoes. 'Am I in time for Nathan?' I said walking into the lounge.

'Hello my favourite pupil. You certainly are.' Betty kissed me on the cheek. 'He's just had his tea and there's time for a play before his bath.' She pointed to the blue blanket which was a gift from me. 'I don't know why I bother putting that down, he never stays still long enough. He's speedy at crawling now.'

'Oh wow, aren't you a clever little boy.' I got down on the floor to play with him but he just glanced at me, giggled and darted across the room on all fours.

'See what I mean?' Betty said. 'He's so funny.' She laughed.

'Is it okay if I pick him up?'

'If you can catch him, go for it. He's missed his Uncle George.'

I chased him around on the carpet before sweeping him up for a hug. Betty and John said it was better for me to be known as Uncle out of respect. It wasn't good practice for a child to call adults by their first name. I sat down and bounced Nathan on my knee making him giggle. 'He weighs a bit more than last time.'

'That's what happens when you feed them,' John said, 'you should see what he eats. None of that strained stuff. Although, Bett still mashes the food up but even so. She makes little portions and freezes them. These freezer things are a godsend. I suppose you've had one for a while at Granville Hall?'

'I haven't forgotten what it's like to be poor, John. And I can tell you, we were a lot poorer than you.'

'Of course, sorry I didn't mean to offend you.'

'No, you didn't. I just wanted you to know that I haven't forgotten my roots. Even if I do have a title.'

Betty padded in from the kitchen wearing a pair of plaid slippers with a pompom on them.

I stared down at them and laughed. 'Aren't they a bit grandma for you?'

'Yes, but they were a gift from John's mum. Don't mock them, they're really comfy. Shepherd's Pie for dinner, all right with you?'

'Lovely, thank you.'

'I thought we'd get Nathan bathed and in bed first.'

'Sounds good. I had something to eat in the little café.'

'Have you seen Ben yet?' Betty asked.

Nathan started to cry.

'Let me take him.' She took the wriggling baby from my arms. John had gone upstairs to run the bath.

'No, I hope to meet up later. Those twins of his keep him busy though.'

'They are a bit of a handful, aren't they? Hope Nathan's not going to be like that.'

'I'm sure with your teaching skills you'll be able to handle whatever he gives you.'

'Hope so. Some say it's different when it's your own. By the way, how did the wedding go?'

'A success but too many people for my liking.'

'How about Alice? I bet she looked gorgeous. What was her frock like?'

'She looked stunning. Hard to imagine she was my kid sister. Her dress was very pretty but huge.' I demonstrated with my hands a yard wide. 'And she had a really long train.' I pulled out a Polaroid snap from my wallet. 'Here.'

Betty placed Nathan down on the carpet before taking the photo from me. 'Oh George. She looks like a princess. I see what you mean about the dress being big.'

'Bath's ready,' John called from upstairs.

'Come on little man, let's go.' Betty picked Nathan up as John came downstairs.

'I'll bath him to give you two time to catch up.' John took Nathan from Betty.

'Thanks, John.' She turned to me. 'Come in the kitchen and we can chat while I finish off dinner?'

'Sure. Anything I can do?'

'Yep. Can you set the table?' I went straight to the correct drawers for the mats and cutlery as I'd done so many times before. Betty mashed the potato, spread it across the mince and added sliced tomato and grated cheese before placing it under the grill. 'Let's sit down while that's cooking.'

I pulled out one of the pine kitchen chairs and sat next to her.

'You've been itching to tell me something since you got here, haven't you?'

'Err yes. You know me too well, Miss Jones.' I laughed.

'Come on then. Out with it.'

'I'm planning on asking Mandy to marry me.'

'Really? I didn't think you'd been together that long.'

'We haven't. Only since June when I came down for the christening but she came up to London once and I managed a quick trip down here a couple of weeks ago. You just know when it's right, don't you?'

'I suppose you do. I'm really pleased for you, George.'

'Thanks.' I took the box from my pocket and flipped it open. 'What do you think?'

'Wow. Diamonds are a girl's best friend as Marilyn Monroe said.'

'Yes, I hope so.'

'She'll love it, George. I'm surprised you're not seeing Mandy later rather than Ben.'

'I would've done but she had to go into work to get things ready for the new term next week. It's a shame she's moved schools, otherwise you'd have been working together.'

'Where's she gone?'

'St Agatha's as Deputy Head.'

'Would you guys like to come up and say goodnight to Nathan?' John called down.

'You go first,' Betty said, 'I'll check on dinner and then you can make sure it doesn't burn when I go up.'

I took the stairs two at a time reaching Nathan's bedroom as John lifted him off the changing mat. 'All nice and clean.' He handed me Nathan in his blue Babygro. I lifted him up to my shoulder level. 'He's wearing the one I bought.'

'Yes, he is. Bett saved it especially for your visit.'

'Don't you smell delicious,' I said. The smell of baby talc made me think about Beth, the baby sister who I never really got to know. She was a hazy memory now, as I'd missed her last months of life. She'd only been a few weeks old when I'd been sent to Granville Hall. I was lucky to have the chance to see two other little sisters, Lori and Annalise, grow up. 'Shall I read him a story?' I asked John.

*

Nathan's screaming woke me. I turned to the clock. The time glowed nearly seven forty-five. I'd overslept. Betty was supposed to wake me so I could spend some time with Nathan before I left. Climbing out of bed, I threw on a robe and hurried into the bathroom. Once I'd finished, I met Betty on the landing with Nathan in her arms.

'Morning sleepyhead,' she said, 'I'm just going to change him so I'll see you downstairs when you're ready. John's gone to work.'

'Why didn't you wake me?'

'Because you needed the sleep. Get dressed and we'll chat over breakfast.'

Betty disappeared into the nursery and I went into my room. It was chilly so I threw on a jumper over my shirt and made my way downstairs to the kitchen. I plugged in the kettle and stuck two slices of Hovis into the toaster.

Steam evaporated from the kettle. I added the water to the pot and got two mugs ready. I knew Betty would have already eaten but she never said *no* to a cup of cha. She walked in just as I carried the mugs over to the table.

'You've made me a cuppa? That's so kind of you, George.'

'Where's Nathan?'

'I'm sorry, love, but he dropped off to sleep. I left him in his cot for a few minutes while I washed my hands after sorting him out and when I went back, he was fast asleep.'

'Not to worry. I need to get off handy.'

'Your toast has popped up. Stay sat down, I'll get it for you.'

'No way, Betty. You sit down and have a break while the young man's sleeping.' I jumped up, laid the toast onto a plate and spread butter thickly over it.

'You do know they reckon that's bad for your heart, don't you?'

'So they say. But I like it.'

Betty laughed. 'Are you ready to pop the question?'

I finished chewing a mouthful of toast. 'Mmm. I am. She will say yes, won't she?'

'I'm sure she will. She'd be mad not to. I can't believe that you're marrying someone you sat with in primary school.'

'No, me neither. I always thought I'd marry you. Oops.'

'What? Was that your daydream?'

'Yes. But don't tell John.'

She tapped my shoulder. 'Bless you. I'm glad that your eyes are now wide open and you've found yourself a beautiful girl. How do you think your family will take to her?'

'Grace will be fine, I'm sure. How can she not be? Bit hypocritical if she isn't, but, hmm not so sure about Simon and Elizabeth.' I took my mug and plate to the sink and washed up quickly. 'Right, I must be off. Give Nathan a kiss from me and I'll see you all shortly. Thanks for having me.' I picked up my bag and made my way towards the front door. Tassles bounded towards me.

'Sorry, girl, did you think I'd forgotten about you?' I felt bad because indeed I had. 'I'll come back soon and maybe Mandy and I can take you to the park.' I stroked her head.

Betty kissed me on the cheek. 'See you soon favourite pupil.'

*

The sun glared through the rear-view mirror as I pulled up outside Mandy's house. She was at the open front door as I got out of the car.

'I've missed you.' She hugged me on the doorstep.

'I've missed you too. Shall we go inside though as it's turned rather chilly.'

She closed the door behind us and I slipped off my coat and hung it over the bannister.

'Am I too early?' I checked my watch noting Mandy in her dressing gown.

'No, you're bang on time. It's me who's running late. Fancy a cuppa?'

'I've just had one.' I moved closer to her and stroked her face. 'You're gorgeous, you know? I've missed you so much.' I kissed her slowly on the mouth and she moved with me, her tongue in tune with mine. My hand moved down across her shoulders until I was caressing her breasts.

'Would you like to come upstairs?'

'Are you sure?'

99

She took my hand and led me to her bedroom. I slipped off her robe and pink negligee revealing her naked body. My beautiful Mandy. 'You're so lovely.' I kissed her from her neck down guiding her onto the bed. 'Are you sure,' I asked again.

'I'm sure.'

Afterwards we lay in each other's arms and slept. On waking, I discovered it was close to two o'clock. No wonder my stomach was moaning. 'Mandy.' I shook her arm gently.

She stirred, put her arms around me and started to kiss me.

'No, listen, Mandy. I've something to ask you.'

'Later.' She kissed me.

'Aren't you hungry?'

'Yes, for you.'

'Much as I'd love to my darling, there's something I need to do. And I'm not leaving here today without completing the purpose of my visit.'

She sat upright. 'So you didn't come for me?'

'Absolutely I did, but I don't just want sex. I want you.' I climbed out of bed, pulled on my jeans, and rushed downstairs. I grabbed the ring box out of my coat pocket and ran back upstairs again. I knelt down by the bed. 'Mandy Brown.' I held out the opened ring box. 'Will you do me the honour of becoming my wife?'

She slipped her arms into the lace negligee and sat on the bed with her mouth open.

'Well? Put a man out of his misery.'

'Yes, George. Yes, I will. Are you sure though? What about your family? And won't they think it's too soon?'

'I don't give a damn what my family think. I love you, and life for me is nothing without you. I'm tired of spending nights alone. I want you by my side, day and night.'

'But what about my job?'

'They have teaching jobs in Gerrard's Cross. But there's more. I've checked with the registry office and they have a free slot on twenty-first of September.'

'What, next year?'

'No, this year.'

'So soon? But what about my notice?'

'I'm sure your school will understand and I have contacts to get you a placement somewhere near home. Say, yes, and I'll organise a special licence.'

'Yes. Yes, let's do it. I love you, George Gilmore, Granville.'

'And I love you too.' I wriggled out of my jeans, climbed back into bed with Mandy and put my arms around her. 'Now what was it about being hungry for me?'

Chapter 16

George

Grace would be here shortly to mark the occasion to the foundations for Adriéne's memorial on the outskirts of Granville land.

The building foreman swaggered over to me. His toolbelt around his drooping belly was loaded with drills and hammers. 'Morning, Lord Granville. As you can see, we've finished the footings and are ready to start building. Can I just confirm something on the plans?' He unrolled the drawings across a portable table.

'What's the problem?'

'No problem, I just want to check something.'

'Sure?'

'It says here that you want two foot high of red bricks and the rest glass?'

'That's right.'

'Hmm.' He frowned, tilting his head to one side.

'Look.' I pointed. 'See the arch shaped windows here, they'll take it up to the ornamental balustrade and these square windows will sit towards the roof. This layer of arch windows will be added before reaching the final dome.'

'Ah, I think I get it.'

'Have you been to Sefton Park Palm House?'

'Where's that, Guvnor?'

'Liverpool. You obviously haven't.' I took a photograph out of my inside pocket. 'See, it's to be a version of this.'

'I got ya. We're off to dinner now but we'll start bricklaying at two.' The foreman blew his whistle and the men put down their tools and wandered off over the hill. As they disappeared, Grace and Alice arrived.

'Sorry I'm late,' Grace said, 'but your sister wanted to come too, and then we had to wait for Simon to drop us off.'

'Fab,' I said to Alice, trying not to sound disappointed. 'I wasn't expecting to see you today.'

'I didn't want to miss the moment so thought I'd tag on with Mum. That's okay, isn't it?'

'Sure,' I said. Alice looked positively blooming. Maybe I'd been wrong about Robert. I hoped so.

'I wanted to see how far they'd got.' Alice looked ahead towards the site. 'But there's not much to see, is there?'

'The builders have gone for their break but will start building this afternoon, and the windows are due to arrive on Friday. It'll be erected before we know it. What do you think, Grace?'

'The positioning is perfect, darling. It's going to be wonderful. Thank you for helping me make this happen.'

'Can we go up to the hall for tea now?' Alice folded her arms. 'I'm freezing.'

'Not yet.' Grace sighed. 'I did warn you there wouldn't be much to see. Well except…'

'She hasn't seen the best bit yet, has she? Follow me.' Grace and my sister trudged up the bank behind me. I stopped a few feet in front of the site.

Grace looked down towards the lake. 'Alice, imagine you're sitting here on a bench. Take in that view.'

Alice stood with her mouth open before finally saying, 'It's amazing.'

'A piece of Heaven,' Grace said. 'Worth being cold for?'

'I suppose so.' Alice rubbed her hands.

Grace moved further forward. 'Adriéne would've loved this spot.'

'Yes, he would have.' I linked my arm in hers as she continued to stare ahead towards the lake with the sun hanging over it. 'He'd be so proud of you, Grace, as I am.'

'Me too.' Alice linked Grace's other arm.

'This moment needs to be kept for posterity.' I lifted the Polaroid from around my neck. 'Turn around and I'll take a piccie with the view behind you both.'

Grace and Alice huddled together. I opened the shutter on the camera and brought them into focus. 'Say cheese.'

'Cheese,' they said in unison.

I clicked the switch and captured the moment. 'We're so lucky to have this cracking sky and sunshine. You'd never believe how misty and frosty it was earlier.'

'I think Adriéne must be looking down on us,' Grace said.

'Here.' I passed Grace the developed picture. 'One for the scrap book.'

She held the snap up. 'Thank you. I'll treasure it.'

'Let me see.' Alice peered over Grace's shoulder to take a peep. 'Don't we look happy?'

'Yes.' I laughed. 'No one would believe you were moaning. Grace, I've taken snaps of the foundations too and I'll get more at each of the building stages.'

Alice nudged me playfully, reminding me what a great sister she was, making me feel guilty for resenting her earlier presence. 'If you've seen enough,' I said, 'we'll go up to the house and have coffee or something a little stronger?'

'Coffee will be fine,' Grace said.

'The Land Rover's just the other side of the hill by the barn.'

We traipsed across the crunching grass where frost hadn't quite cleared. After piling into the truck, I drove us up to the Hall.

*

I poured coffee from the percolator into the mugs. 'Shall we sit by the fire?'

Alice was warming her hands by the high flames. 'I think that's a good idea. I can't believe how cold it is?'

'What do you expect when you've been in Tenerife for the last couple of weeks?' They'd delayed their honeymoon as Robert, apparently, had some things to tie up. God knows what, as he never seemed to do anything. I thought he was a lacky for his father.

Grace sat on the winged armchair adjacent to the fireplace. It was a right monstrosity and had seen better days. Every time one of us brought it up Elizabeth would say it was staying because it had been Cousin Victoria's. I sat opposite on the modern settee. 'Have you given any more thought to the plants you want in the palm house?'

'You mean apart from the obvious, palm plants, cheese plants etc. Yes. I've been looking at bougainvillea.'

'That's a bit of a mouthful, Mum,' Alice said, 'what on earth are they?'

'They're evergreen climbers and bloom with lovely pinkie/lilac petals in summer and autumn. I imagine with the glasshouse heated they may flower out of those times too. I haven't investigated that yet. I'm also thinking of something tropical like red and orange cannas. I've ordered a few plants already.'

'And the furniture?' I asked.

'Bamboo lounge chairs, dining table, coffee table, that sort of thing and an arch bookcase unit, also in bamboo. I want to

105

commission a carpenter to make a couple of special benches. One to go outside the glasshouse and another further down by the lake. I think they will be idyllic places to sit and think. Not just about Adriéne, but for anyone with a problem where they can enjoy space and solitude.' Grace turned away but not before I noticed a tear fall to her cheek. A lump formed in my throat.

'Ah, that's why you asked me to imagine I was sitting on a bench,' Alice said.

'Yes.'

'I know what.' I stood up. 'Why don't I see if Annie's got any of her special cookies? They're not quite up to Cook's, well not yet, but pretty close.'

'Don't you ring a bell and get the maids to do that?' Alice took a sip from her coffee.

'No. I don't like them waiting on me all the time.'

Alice shrugged. 'That's their job. You know you could be upsetting Donna and Annie by not letting them do it.'

I shook my head. Where the hell did she get those bloody airs from? I felt sorry for the staff in the Sanders' household. As I walked out of the room Simon and Elizabeth came in. 'I'm just going to get some cookies. Can I get you two anything?'

'Coffee would be nice.' Elizabeth kissed her sister and Alice in turn.

*

Donna and Annie were busy in the kitchen preparing tonight's dinner. Donna was peeling root vegetables and a pan bubbled away on the stove.

'Lord Granville,' Annie said, 'what can we do for you?'

'George will do, please.' I hated lording over them. 'I've come for some of those scrummy cinnamon cookies if you have any?'

'I do indeed, Master George.' Annie lifted a square tin down from a shelf. Her figure was looking rounded like Cook's. She was so tiny when I'd arrived at Granville Hall in nineteen sixty-two. I felt myself blushing remembering her seeing me as a nine-year-old in the bathtub on that first day.

'You know, Annie, I think it's time we promoted you and offered you a pay rise.' I sat down at the pine kitchen table. 'After all, now that Martha has gone your workload has increased.'

'That's very kind, Sir,' Annie said. 'Thank you.'

'You too, Donna. You're taking on a lot more now than when you first came here.'

'You're such a good employer, Master George.' Annie spread the biscuits on to a plate. 'Your grandfather always looked out for us too but you, Sir, you go that extra mile. We really appreciate it. Don't we, Donna?'

Donna lifted her face from chopping carrots. 'Yes, Sir. We do. Thank you.' Her eyes glinted.

I wondered why Annie had never married and whether she'd even had a boyfriend. Were we giving the staff enough time off for recreation? I'd speak to Elizabeth and Simon. I stood up away from the chair and walked over to the window to fill a percolator with coffee.

'Sir, let me do that for you,' Annie said.

'No, Annie. I can manage. You're busy making dinner. What are we having this evening?'

'Roast lamb, Sir, with dauphinoise potatoes and vegetables. Will Mrs Gilmore and Mrs Sanders be staying?' Annie opened the oven door and pulled out the sizzling lamb. She prodded it with a fork before sliding it back onto the shelf.

'I'm not sure. Do we have sufficient if they decide to?'

'Yes, Master George, we always make extra for unexpected guests.' Annie placed the oven glove on the back of the chair.

107

'Right, ladies. I must be off. Upstairs will think I've been making these.' I signalled to the plate of cookies in my hand.

As I climbed the kitchen stairs towards the drawing room, my thoughts wandered to my soon to be wedding day and how I hadn't told any of my family. I had hoped to speak to Grace today while we were alone but then she turned up with Alice. It was probably better to surprise them all when I brought Mandy to her new home. My wedding would be nothing like Alice's, I didn't want a big affair like that. Mine would be a complete contrast, small and quiet.

Chapter 17

George

Ben pulled up outside Betty's house. I opened the front door as he walked up the path. I looked at my watch. 'Bang on time. I was a little worried as you didn't have Susie to sort out the twins.'

'I know. I don't know how she manages to get off to work every day when coping with those two.'

'You did well then?'

Ben laughed. 'Err actually me mam came around to help. Mind you, she nearly made me late going on about Susie being Matron of Honour and how it wasn't fair that she couldn't come to the wedding too.'

'I hope she wasn't too upset. I feel a little bad now especially as she's offered to look after Nathan while we're at the reception.'

'Don't worry about it, mate. Are you ready?'

'As I'll ever be.'

'You boys look very handsome,' Betty said. 'Burgundy goes well with that off-white. 'If only I were ten years younger…'

'Oi you can stop that now.' John nudged her.

Grace would be so disappointed that she didn't get the chance to design something for me. I'd considered inviting her when we were looking at the memorial foundations but Alice was there too. Still, it was probably the right thing not to have asked her. It would have meant inviting Alice, Elizabeth and Simon too. And then before long it would have turned into some monstrous affair like Alice's wedding. I tapped my finger on Betty's arm. 'You look nice too. Bottle green suits you.'

'Thank you, George. It's velvet so should be nice and warm.' She held up a white corsage. 'Have you got time to pin this on for me? If not, I'll get John to do it.'

'No. I've got a minute to do that.' I pinned the flower spray on the right-hand side of her jacket. 'There. All done. Are you ready now?'

'Not quite. You go on and we'll follow shortly. I've got to finish getting this one sorted but it won't take long.' Betty scooped Nathan up and rested him on her hip.

'Don't be late,' I said.

'Stop panicking, George,' Ben said. 'All is in hand. We'll see you three later,' he said to Betty before dragging me out of the house to his Ford Anglia. 'Look I gave her a good polish and prettied her up with ribbon. What do you think?'

'Perfect.' The black bodywork shone in the sun.

'Silk ribbon that, you know. Susie got it from the department store. None of that cheap market stuff.'

'Thank you. I appreciate it.' I patted my friend on the shoulder before moving around to the passenger door and sinking into the customised sports seat.

Ben started up the engine and drove us into Wintermore village centre, pulling up outside the registry office. As I stepped out of the car my legs shook.

'Bit nervous, mate?'

'I am.' I laughed. 'No idea why.'

'It's normal. You should have seen me before I married my Susie.' As we reached the entrance at the top of the steps he looked at his watch. 'Ten to two. Should we wait here for the girls?'

'Sure thing. Hang on, looks like that's them now.' A white Ford Zodiac pulled up outside and a driver got out of the front to open the rear door. Susie stepped out first and Mandy followed, both of them looking hot.

I headed towards my fiancé, soon to be wife, and took her hand to lead her into our marriage venue. 'You look gorgeous. I'm the luckiest man on earth.' Her dark hair was piled on her head with curls teasing either side, framing her face.

'Do you like the headdress, George?' Susie asked.

Mandy looked dynamite. I imagined peeling off that tight cream dress and making love to her.

'George, I said, do you like the headdress?'

'Sorry, Susie, what did you say?'

'I said, do you like her headdress?'

I looked up towards Mandy and smiled. 'Yeah sure. Very pretty.'

'We made the roses ourselves. Didn't we, Mand?'

'Yes. Took us ages.'

'You'll get on with my mother,' I said, following the signs to the wedding room where the registrar opened a door. 'Mr Granville?'

'Yes,' I said holding Mandy's hand.

'Come on in. Ah, and these are your witnesses?' He glanced at Ben and Susie.

'No, not quite. My friend' – I indicated to Ben – 'is to be one witness but the other witness hasn't arrived yet but she shouldn't be long.'

The sound of high heels running along the shiny floor echoed in the hallway and Betty and John came through the door with Nathan sleeping in John's arms.

'Here she is now,' I said.

Betty caught her breath. 'Sorry we're late. We had trouble parking.' Nathan opened his eyes and started screaming. 'Give him here,' Betty said. John passed the baby to her who immediately stopped crying.

111

'Not a problem,' the registrar said. 'You're here now. Come along in. If the bridal couple can come to the front while we sort out some preliminaries and the rest of you take a seat.' The registrar had a look of Phil Collins particularly with his hair receding from his forehead. 'Do sit down,' he said in a deep voice and followed with the formalities of checking our names, occupations, dates of birth, etc. 'Do you have your birth certificates?'

'Yes, certainly.' I passed him mine.

'Excuse me, Sir, but this says Gilmore, I thought your name was Granville?'

'Oh yes, sorry.' I handed over the deed poll document.

'Ah, yes. That all seems to be in order. And Miss Brown?'

Mandy handed her birth certificate. 'As my fiancé mentioned on the phone, I've been married before so I've brought in my decree absolute as instructed.'

The registrar inspected the paperwork. 'What about you Mr Granville, have you been married before?'

'No.'

'Then everything seems to be in order so we may begin the ceremony.'

*

We stood on the steps of the registry office and our friends poured coloured confetti over us. After a few snaps of Mandy and me, a passer-by offered to take a photograph of us all.

'Right, now that's done with,' Ben said, 'time for the boozer.'

We got in our cars and drove around to the Woodcroft. As we parked outside the pub, Ben's mam turned up. 'Congratulations, George and Mandy. Is your mam not here?' she said to me.

112

'They got married in secret, Mam. Remember, I told you?' Ben said.

'Ah yes. So you did. Is the babby ready?'

'I really don't like leaving him.' Betty strapped Nathan into the stroller.

'Don't worry, love, he'll be fine with me. Look he's fast asleep and you'll have him back before you know it. Do you the world of good to have a couple of hours without him. Have you got his bag?'

Betty passed over the baby backpack. 'There's a spare set of clothing, bibs and a bottle with my milk.'

'Ta, dearie.' She put her hand on Betty's shoulder. 'Don't worry, I'll look after him. Me house is only down the road. I'll send our Sandie to get you if I've any problems. I best get back now because she's looking after the twins. Have a good time and don't worry.' She took the pushchair from Betty and waddled down the street.

'He'll be fine.' John took Betty's hand. As we walked in the pub door more confetti was sprinkled over us by some of the regulars and glasses of sparkling wine were poured out ready.

'George and I will go to the bar,' Ben said. 'We'll push those couple of tables over there together.' Betty, John, Mandy and Susie made their way to the far corner.

The landlady set a tray of sandwiches onto the counter. 'You've got cheese and pickle on brown, and salmon and cucumber on white. Ah and here comes the sausage rolls, Scotch eggs and cocktail sausages.' The barmaid put the trays down next to the sandwiches and then the chef came out carrying a two-tier cake with a bride and groom decoration on white icing.

'Wow, quite a spread.' I turned to Ben. 'You organised all this?'

He patted me on the back. 'What are mates for? Well, actually Susie did most of it. Got us mates' rates too.'

'You should let me settle up. You can't afford all this. I can.'

'We won't hear of it. It's our wedding present. Now accept graciously. And mine's a pint.'

I laughed. 'Coming up.'

*

We strolled through the revolving glass door of Northern Lodge Hotel and up to the entrance desk.

'Mr and Mrs Granville.' I turned to smile at Mandy.

The receptionist ran her finger down the ledger. 'Ah yes. Here you are. Congratulations. You're booked into the honeymoon suite.' She smiled and passed us a key on a numbered tag. 'Room 306. The lift's straight ahead.'

We stepped into the elevator and pressed the button for floor 3. In no time at all the doors shot open and we made our way along the green carpeted hallway, stopping outside our room. After unlocking the door, I lifted Mandy into my arms and carried her across the threshold.

'The room's beautiful.' Mandy bounced on the mahogany four-poster bed that almost filled the room. 'I love this pink, satin bedspread. And look.' She jumped off the bed and darted over to the long window. 'The curtains match the bedspread but velvet. I love how they go down to the floor.' She ran her fingers across the soft pile. 'Can we have some like these for our bedroom at Granville Hall?'

'You can choose anything you like. After all you'll be the lady of the house.'

'I don't think I'll ever get used to being Lady Granville.'

'Tell me about it, I still haven't got used to being a lord which is why I don't use the title if I can get away with it. You can do the same if you prefer.'

'Suppose your family think I only married you because you're a lord?'

'Then I'll put them in their place.'

'I love you, George Granville.'

'And I love you too, Mrs Granville.'

'Catch.' She threw an orange from the wooden fruit bowl. 'You've thought of everything.' She touched the petals in the crystal vase on the sideboard. 'Chrysanthemums and asters are my favourites. How did you know?'

'A lucky guess, I expect. I'm glad you like them.'

'The burnished-gold are the chrysanthemums...'

'Now I've had my nature lesson, come here. Have you any idea how many hours I've waited to get you out of this dress?' I held her in my arms, kissed her lips and lowered her down onto the bed.

'Oh look, George.' She picked up a small package from the pillow. 'Chocolate hearts. And wrapped in gold-metallic paper. Everything's so posh.'

I sighed. 'You can eat them later. Right now I want my wife.' I lightly threw the chocolates on the bedside cabinet and began smothering her in kisses, gently removing her clothes.

Chapter 18

George

It was wonderful to wake up with Mandy by my side as my wife. I rolled over towards her and kissed her lightly on the lips.

'Good morning, Mrs Granville, how are you feeling?'

She yawned and stretched her arms out. 'Sleepy.'

'Sleepy? Sleepy when you're lying next to your new husband.' I laughed.

'I'm afraid so. Can I have ten more minutes please?'

'Go on, then.' I kissed her forehead. 'You sleep while I shower. We need to be on the road by ten at the latest though.'

'Thanks.' She turned over on to her side and went back to sleep.

*

John was standing outside the hotel next to his Cortina. He'd come to collect us so I could pick up the Ferrari from theirs.

'Hello, Mrs Granville or should I say, Lady Granville?' he said to Mandy before turning to me. 'Get in the back with your missus. I'm fine as a chauffeur so long as you don't forget my tip.'

'I'll give you a tip. You and Betty must come and stay a night in this hotel. Our treat. And what's more, Mandy and I will babysit. When's your anniversary?'

'Not until March 4th.' John started the car and pulled away.

'Right, it's a date, I'll sort it out and it can be a surprise for Betty.'

'Thanks, George. That's really kind.'

'It's the least I can do after everything you and Betty have done for me.'

John drove down the High Street and turned right into Rainham Gardens. He stopped outside their house and turned off the engine. 'You two coming in for a quick cuppa?' he asked plunging the car keys into his coat pocket.

'Try and stop us. It'll have to be quick though as we've a long drive ahead and I don't want to be late home.'

The front door opened before we got to it. Betty was on the doorstep holding Nathan in her arms. Tassles rushed out to greet us.

'Hello, girl.' I stroked her coat.

Mandy stepped away.

'She won't hurt you, darling. She's just a bit excitable. Aren't you, girl?' I ruffled the red setter's ears. 'Go on. Stroke her.'

Mandy was apprehensive but she put out her hand and patted Tassles gently.

'She likes you,' I said.

'Can you all come in, please?' Betty said. 'You're letting the cold air in.'

We followed her into the house and slipped off our shoes, our feet sinking into the brown shag pile. 'It's not a bad day out there, Bett,' I said, 'there's even a bit of sunshine.'

'Even so. I was getting a little chilly and I don't want Nathan to catch cold.'

I held out my arms to take the baby. 'And how's my favourite godson?'

'You only have the one, don't you?' Betty laughed.

'I'll go and put the kettle on,' John said. 'They can't stay long as they need to hit the road.'

'We knew that would be the case.' Betty patted the settee. 'Come and sit down. Have you had breakfast?'

'No, but don't worry, we can get something at the service station, can't we Mand?'

'A piece of toast would be nice if it isn't any trouble.' she answered.

'No trouble at all, Mandy. John,' Betty called through, 'can you pop a couple of slices of bread in the toaster?'

'Sure thing,' he shouted back.

I got down on the floor to crawl with Nathan, pretending to chase him. He loved it and giggled as he sped around the carpet.

'Here we go?' John carried a tray through and placed a tray of mugs on the coffee table? 'Tea for four. The toast is almost ready. Who's it for?'

'Just me,' Mandy said, 'unless George has changed his mind.'

'No, I'm fine thanks. I'll get something later. I ate far too much yesterday.'

'It was a lovely wedding. Thank you for letting us be part of it.' Betty stooped down beside me and squeezed my arm.

After a quick cuppa, we kissed Betty, John, and Nathan goodbye, and ruffled Tassles, before climbing in the car, waving as I pulled away.

Chapter 19

Grace

'That's wonderful news, Alice. Has the doctor confirmed it?' I asked.

'No, not yet. But I just know. You can tell, can't you? And I've been sick.'

'Well how far do you think you are?'

'Six-seven weeks? Something like that. I reckon it probably happened on our wedding night. So the first possible chance.'

'I'm really pleased for you but I wouldn't go announcing it yet. Wait until you're at least twelve weeks, especially as you haven't had it confirmed.'

'Had what confirmed?' George walked into the drawing room.

'Oh nothing,' I said, 'just girl talk between mum and daughter. I didn't hear the door?'

'Steph saw me pull up. Anyway, never mind that. I have some news for you both.' He left the room for a second, re-entering with a young woman. They were holding hands. 'Meet the new Lady Granville.'

I shot up from the chair in shock, trying not to stare at my new daughter-in-law. It was like looking at my younger self. Dark hair fell in waves caressing her shoulders and her small frame was akin to mine before I had the children. It could have been Jack and me standing there, not George and his new wife.

'Grace, Amanda. Mandy, Grace, my mother, and my sister, Alice.'

'I'm really pleased to meet you, Mrs Granville.' Assured, she came towards me beaming, and held out her hand.

Catching my breath, I shook her hand. 'You too, Amanda. It's Gilmore though, not Granville.'

'And please call me Mandy.'

George winked at his new wife. 'We were married two days ago in Wintermore.'

She seemed a nice enough girl, spoke well, and good mannered. 'I'm afraid,' I said, 'you've caught me off-guard as George hasn't mentioned you. In fact, I'd no idea he was seeing someone.'

'I think George wanted to surprise you.' She smiled at her new husband accentuating the magnetism between them.

He'd certainly done that.

'What? You got married without us.' Alice frowned. 'You should have had a big do like mine.'

'That's exactly why I kept quiet. It wasn't what we wanted.' George turned to Mandy. 'We didn't want any fuss. Did we darling?'

'No.' Mandy's eyes twinkled. 'It was quite a surprise to me too. He only asked me a month ago and then everything was sorted so quickly.'

'Do sit down.' I ushered them towards the settee. 'I'll stoke up the fire so you can get warm.' I picked up a couple of pieces of coal from the scuttle with the tongs and poked the fire, before sitting down opposite Mandy. 'Why don't you tell me how you two came to meet?'

'You're never going to believe this,' George said, 'but Mandy and I used to sit together in junior school.'

'We met again this year on a blind date organised by mutual friends,' Mandy said.

'Ben and Susie,' George said. 'They've been up here a few times so Grace knows who they are.'

'Was your father a coal miner too?' I asked.

'No, he wasn't. I'm so sorry about George's dad. It must have been awful for you.'

'It wasn't the best time but life goes on as they say. We never forget those that go before us.'

'No,' she answered softly.

'So, let me get this straight,' Alice said, 'you were in the same class at school as George?'

'Yes, and at the same table.' Mandy smiled. 'Who'd have thought I'd end up marrying him?'

'Quite.' Alice leaned forward. 'So, did you live in Bamber Street too? I don't remember you but then I was only young when we left.'

'No, I lived around the corner in Union Street.'

'Wasn't that up by the local shop?'

'It was. My mam used to work there.'

'I hate to tell you this but I fear you have a few obstacles ahead. Don't you think so, Mum?'

George glared at Alice. 'My sister means my Aunt Elizabeth and her husband Simon. But don't worry, it'll be fine.'

Mandy ignored me and turned to Alice. 'Obstacles. Why?'

'Because George, as Lord Granville, is expected to marry a woman of his own class. I don't mean that disrespectfully because you seem like a lovely woman but they may not understand.'

George put his arm around Mandy who'd gone very pale. 'Well, considering we're from the same class, Alice, I don't think they can argue and it's too bad if they do.' He brushed his lips against his wife's hand. 'Don't worry, darling, you're the new Lady Granville and there's nothing they can do about it. Everything will be fine. Trust me.'

George was a good man and it was clear from the way they looked at each other that they were very much in love. I stood up from the chair and moved to the couch next to my daughter-in-law. 'George is right. Don't worry. You have my blessings. Welcome to the family.' I kissed her on the cheek. 'I recognise that fragrance. Chanel N° 5?'

'Yes, it was a birthday present from George.'

'It's one of my favourites.' I clasped my hands. 'Where are my manners? I'll organise some refreshment. Do you like tea, Mandy?'

'Yes, tea would be lovely. Thank you, Mrs Gilmore.'

'Nothing for me, Mum. I need to get going.' Alice stood up and went over to her brother and his wife. 'It's good to meet you, Mandy. I've always wanted a big sister. And you.' She nudged George. 'No more surprises, please.'

'Will you excuse me?' I said. 'I'll just see Alice off home and then pop down to the kitchen.' I headed out of the door with my daughter and once we were out of earshot, I asked her what she thought.

'This may sound a bit silly but she looks a bit like you in your wedding photo with Dad.'

'I thought the same. She seems a nice girl though, wouldn't you say?'

'She does. I don't envy her though. She's going to have a right fight on her hands.'

'You're probably right but George will look after her and she'll have you and me in her corner too.' I helped Alice on with her coat before opening the front door. 'Take care, sweetheart, and I'm sorry your news got drowned out a bit.'

'That's all right, Mum. It wasn't your fault.'

'See you tomorrow, darling.' I hugged my daughter.

'Bye, Mum.'

I waved as she got into her orange Audi and drove off.

*

George was consoling his wife when I returned to the drawing room.

'Is everything okay?' I asked.

'Not really,' George replied.

'I'm afraid your sister has never been gifted with tact.'

Mandy looked like she was about to pass out just as Paula walked in with a tray of tea and biscuits. 'Is she all right?' the maid asked. 'I'll get her some water.' She rushed out of the room and was back within a couple of minutes. 'Here, Miss.' Paula handed Mandy a glass.

Mandy sipped the water. 'Thank you.'

'This is George's wife,' I said. 'They were married a couple of days ago.'

'Awesome. Congratulations.' Paula turned to me. 'Is there anything else I can do?'

'No thank you, dear, we'll be fine. You get back to Steph in the kitchen.' Paula left the room in a hurry with a huge smile across her face.

Mandy looked paler than pale. I poured the tea adding extra milk to hers. 'Drink this. Weak tea is supposed to be good for shock.'

'And have a cookie.' George passed the plate. 'You're probably hungry after the long drive.'

'Thank you.' She bit into a ginger biscuit.

I couldn't help noticing her slim fingers prompting me to ask. 'May I see the ring?'

She held out her hand showing off not only a thin engraved platinum gold band but a diamond ring too.

'It's beautiful.' I fingered the solitaire stone. 'Tell me more about how you two met up again.'

123

'Through Ben and Susie, as I mentioned,' George said. 'They set us up on a blind date and you know what, it was love at first sight. Wasn't it, babe?' He stroked Mandy's long hair.

'More or less.' The colour was starting to come back into her face.

'So how long have you been together?'

'A few months,' George answered.

'And what is it you do, Mandy?'

'I'm a teacher.'

'Will you continue to work? I can't imagine my son being one of those husbands that expects his wife to stay at home doing wifely duties.'

'Yes, definitely. George said he has contacts so hopefully I'll get a position by Christmas.'

'As it's getting late, would you mind if we stayed over tonight and we'll head to the Hall first thing?' George asked.

'No problem at all. I'll let Steph know that we have an extra two for dinner. You can have the best room in the West Wing.'

'One more thing. Do you think you could come over tomorrow when I break the news to Elizabeth and Simon?'

The thought of them having a fight on their hands took me back to the day when I announced to Mother and Father I was marrying Jack. I shivered when I recalled how angry they'd been about my pregnancy, which I'd fabricated so they wouldn't stop me from getting married.

'You whore,' Father had shouted. 'How could you be so stupid? Luckily for you, I have contacts at the club to fix your mess.'

'You can't mean abortion, Charles?' Mother said. 'Surely not?'

'What's the alternative?'

'I'll speak to Cousin Victoria. Grace can stay in Devon until after the confinement and then the baby can be adopted.'

I'd felt sick. He wanted to abort my baby and she wanted it adopted.

'Grace.' George jogged me back. 'For moral support?'

'Sorry, George.' I wasn't going to be anything like my parents. 'I'll be there.' I hugged my new daughter-in-law and son in turn. They had an ally in me.

Two surprises in one day. I'd gained a new daughter and I was to become a grandmother for the first time. I smiled, cherishing my blessings. I just hoped that Elizabeth and Simon didn't come down too hard on poor Mandy.

Chapter 20

George

As we drove through the tall wrought-iron arched gates into Granville Hall, I wondered what Mandy was making of it. Was she mesmerised as I was when I first came through them with Grandmother all those years ago? I pulled up outside the mansion. Its huge grounds and the enormity of the building still entranced me. I thought back to our little two-up and two-down terrace in Wintermore and would've willingly swopped Granville for my old life with Mam, Da, Alice and Beth, the new baby.

'George. Is this really all yours?' Mandy lifted her hand and shielded her brown eyes from the blazing sun.

'It is.' I got out of the car and strode around to the passenger side by the purple and pink hydrangea borders. 'We're lucky the house is south-facing, so we get sun most of the day during the summer months.'

'Suppose they don't like me?'

'How couldn't they?' I stroked her cheek. Auburn tints from her brunette hair shone in the autumn sunlight. 'Come on, let's go in.'

We reached the top of the steps and I rang the bell.

'Incredible. You have one of those old-fashioned cast iron bells,' Mandy said. 'Have you never considered converting to an electric doorbell like normal people?'

'I suppose not. I rather like it to be honest.'

'I believe I do, too. Don't you have a key?'

'Strangely enough, no. None of us do.'

'It's all rather grand but maybe that's what scares me.'

'You'll be fine, darling. If I've learned to cope with it then you will too because I'll be by your side. That sounds like someone's coming now.'

The smiling housekeeper opened the door. Her freshly pressed turquoise apron concealed most of her black dress. 'Master George, I mean Lord Granville, you're back. Miss Elizabeth and Master Simon will be so pleased to see you.' She glanced at Mandy.

'Where are my manners? Annie, this is my wife Mandy.'

Annie put her hand to her mouth. 'Wife? Oh, my goodness. No one said. Congratulations.'

'Thank you, but listen, keep it quiet as my aunt and uncle don't know yet.'

Mandy moved to walk through the door. 'Not so fast, Missus.' I lifted her up in my arms to carry her over the threshold. 'I'm a traditional guy, you know.'

'Except when you sneak off to get married and don't tell anyone.' She giggled.

'Goodness, you're so heavy.' I joked, pretending to drop her and scooping her back up into the air.

'Oi.' She giggled again, hitting my shoulder playfully. 'Are you saying I'm fat?'

'Absolutely not. You're as light as a feather with a fantastic figure. I'm such a lucky guy.' And boy did she smell gorgeous. I couldn't wait to have her long soft hair lie across my pillow. I placed her feet back on the ground. 'Your new home, Lady Granville.'

Annie hunched her shoulders. 'Ooh that's so lovely.'

'Shh… Remember, keep it quiet until I've announced it in there.' I pointed towards the drawing room.

'Mum's the word.' Annie grinned broadly. 'It's wonderful to meet you.'

Mandy straightened the ruffles on her black spotted dress. 'You too, Annie.'

'Looks like you've got a good un there, Sir.'

'You're not wrong, Annie.'

'Should I slip my boots off?' Mandy asked revealing her thigh as she bent down to unzip her knee-high boots.

'No need,' I answered before whispering, 'Stop turning me on.'

She laughed and I turned to Annie. 'I'll come and find you later.' I took hold of my new wife's hand and led her down the hallway.

'This place is so huge. And look at all these gilt-framed paintings. They're magnificent.' She stopped at the newest one. 'Who's this?'

'My grandmother and grandfather. The late Lord Charles and Lady Margaret Granville. Maybe we should appoint someone to paint us. Do you think I look like him?'

'A little, but gosh, doesn't Grace look like your grandmother?'

'She does, only Grace is a lot kinder. Prettier too, don't you think?'

'Yes, I do. How old were they here?'

'Mid-forties, I believe. Come on, we should go in.' As we approached the drawing room I overheard voices.

'So when's he back?' Simon was saying.

Elizabeth answered. 'Today I believe.'

'Good because I need him...'

'You're not moaning about me, are you, Simon?' I said laughing, on entering the room.

'Not at all.' Simon turned towards me, frowning. 'But these papers are urgent' – he held up a file – 'and need your authorisation.'

'Welcome home, George.' Elizabeth nudged Simon, her eyes glued to Mandy.

'Thank you, Aunt Elizabeth. Well, I'm back now, Simon, but let's sort out the paperwork later because first' – I steered Mandy towards my aunt and uncle – 'I've someone I'd like you to meet. Amanda, meet my Aunt Elizabeth and her husband Simon. Elizabeth. Simon. Meet my wife. The new Lady Granville.'

'What?' Simon shot up to his feet. 'You've got to be kidding. How and when did this happen?'

'A couple of days ago,' I said. Mandy backed away but I clung on to her hand to keep her close.

'But George,' Elizabeth said, 'our clients, family and friends will have expected to have been invited to your wedding. And for it to have been a big occasion like Alice's. Bigger, even.'

'That wasn't what we wanted.' I led Mandy to the couch and sat her down next to me.

'So, Amanda, tell us about your family.' Simon asked staggering over to the sideboard and pouring himself a Scotch. 'Drink, anyone? I certainly need one.'

Elizabeth stood up and walked over to Simon. 'Darling, don't…'

'Don't what, Elizabeth? Are you telling me when to have a drink now?'

Elizabeth shook her head and slowly moved back to sit down.

What the hell was going on with Simon? He'd always been so courteous to my aunt and by the looks of him he hadn't had a shave for days. 'Don't speak to her like that? Aunt Elizabeth, how long has this been going on?'

Elizabeth went to answer but Simon cut in. 'Don't talk about me as though I'm not here.'

'Can't you see you're upsetting her?' I frowned.

129

Simon swayed towards Elizabeth. 'Sorry, darling.' He bent down with his face close to hers but she backed away. 'Suit yourself.' He slurred, 'Amanda, would you like a drink?'

'No, thank you,' Mandy answered in almost a whisper.

Simon shrugged his shoulders. 'Well, if no one's going to join me.' He zigzagged back to the bar, drank back his Scotch and poured himself another. 'Now, where were we? Ah yes, Amanda was about to tell us about her family.'

'My parents are dead.' Mandy shrunk into herself.

'Stop it, you're upsetting my wife.' I stroked Mandy's arm. 'It's all right, darling, you don't have to answer any of his questions. I'm ashamed to say he's drunk.' I sighed. 'To think, Simon, I was so proud to bring my wife to meet you both. I thought you might have some reservations but this... I was foolish enough to think that you'd be pleased I'd found happiness. Happiness like I thought you and Aunt Elizabeth had.' I gripped Mandy's hand. 'We'll come back later once you've sobered up.'

'Don't be like that, George.' Simon swigged back his drink. 'I'm just showing interest in your lovely wife's background.'

'It's not interest. It's interrogation. My wife's tired and she doesn't need this.'

'I bet she doesn't...' Simon stomped back over.

Elizabeth sat with her hands over her face not saying anything.

'She's obviously a gold digger,' Simon continued, 'probably a nobody that saw you coming.'

'How dare you?' I shot up from the arm of the couch and charged towards Simon, putting my fists up ready to lamp him one.

'Don't, George.' Mandy ran from the room.

I lowered my hands. 'Look at the state of you, Simon. Half-cut and it's only lunchtime. What the hell's got into you?' I stormed out of the room after my wife.

Mandy buried herself in my arms, sobbing. 'I told you they wouldn't like me.'

'I'm embarrassed to say he's drunk. I sighed. 'I've never seen him like this before.'

Elizabeth joined us in the hallway. 'Amanda, please accept my apologies. I'm quite sure it's not the welcome you were expecting. Please excuse my husband's behaviour. He's been under the weather of late. I'm sure he didn't mean any of it.'

Mandy stepped away from my arms and wiped her eyes. She stared at Elizabeth. 'It didn't seem that way.'

'Sober him up, Aunt Elizabeth,' I said, 'otherwise he'll be looking for a new job and somewhere else to live.'

Elizabeth put her hand over her mouth. 'Surely you don't mean that?'

'Sort him out. I'm not putting my wife through this. Grace will be along shortly.'

Elizabeth touched my shoulder. 'I think maybe he's ill.'

'Whatever's wrong, get it fixed.' I took a deep breath. 'Meanwhile I'll take my wife to meet our staff where she'll get a better reception.'

'I'll do what I can.' Elizabeth disappeared into the drawing room.

'I'm sorry, darling.' I took Mandy into my arms. 'I really wasn't expecting Simon to behave that way.'

'He hates me.' She started crying again.

'No, no, he doesn't, darling. It'll be fine, I promise. He's half-shot. And by the look of him he was well on the way before we arrived. I'm sorry you had to go through that. Something must have happened to upset him. Maybe Elizabeth's right and he is ill, but I promise whatever it is, it has nothing to do with you.' I took a clean handkerchief from my pocket and gently caressed her face, drying the tears. 'Come on, let me see that lovely Mandy smile.'

'I'll try,' she said.

Chapter 21

Grace

I walked into the drawing room and hadn't even closed the door when Simon spat his words at me. 'And I suppose you knew all about this shotgun affair?' He pushed greying hair away from his face.

Good God, they must have told them. I thought they were going to wait for me. 'They told me last night but what are you talking about? She'd have to be pregnant for a shotgun wedding and she's not.'

'How do you know?' Simon sneered. 'It seems strange to me that no one had an inkling he was seeing someone and then he rolls up with a wife.'

'Where are they now?' I asked.

'Who the hell knows and who cares? They disappeared a couple of hours ago after announcing their bombshell and we haven't seen them since.'

I slipped off my mac and hung it over an armchair. 'I hope you haven't upset them. George wanted to marry quietly and I understand that. We all know only too well how he feels about being in the limelight. Amanda, Mandy, seems a nice young lady to me. You should give her a chance.'

Elizabeth stood up from the chaise longue to greet me. 'You've got to admit, Grace, it was a bit sudden and Simon's right, what do we know about her?'

'Well, instead of making waves, why don't you try getting to know her?' I said as George and Mandy entered the room. I made my way towards them and brushed my lips against his new wife's cheek. 'Hello, dear. I hope you're okay.'

'Hello again, Mrs Gilmore,' Mandy said.

I should've been here when they broke the news as I'd promised. She was such a lovely girl, how could Simon not have liked her? Her dark hair heightened her pale complexion and the red around her eyes confirmed she'd been crying. What the hell had Simon said to her? I squeezed her hand. 'Call me Grace, please.'

'I'll try,' Mandy answered timidly.

She was like a different girl to the one I'd met at my house last night although still showing exquisite taste in fashion with a jersey rah-rah dress embracing her tiny waist. Her long hair shone under the light. How could anyone not take to this attractive young lady? Simon must have knocked her confidence. I turned to George and kissed him. 'I see you've told them then. I'm sorry I got held up.' I was back in this room all those years ago when I'd lied to Father saying I was pregnant in order to be with Jack. Mandy looked like I'd felt then.

'Arriving later was probably a blessing because he was four sheets to the wind earlier.' George glared at Simon. 'The main thing is you're here now and hopefully can talk some sense into him. I see he's still moaning about my wife.'

Simon crossed his arms. 'I was just saying we don't know anything about her.'

'But I do. I've known her since I was five years old. We used to be in the same class at school. Didn't we, darling.' He held his arm protectively around his wife. 'Just ignore him and sit down with Grace. She'll look after you while I organise refreshments.'

Mandy eyes pleaded. 'I'll come with you.'

I patted her hand. 'It's all right, sweetheart, he won't be long. I'll look after you. George. You go.' George left the room and

Mandy sat back down, fiddling with the rings on her wedding finger. I was about to try and defuse the situation when Simon followed George out of the room, returning a couple of minutes later waving his cheque book.

'Now, Amanda, how much for you to leave?'

'What?' Mandy rose from the chair.

'Simon?' My stomach felt heavy.

'Five thousand pounds? Six. That's my limit?'

'You're trying to buy me off?'

Before I had the chance to say anything George stormed back into the room. 'What the hell's going on?'

'He's trying to buy me off.'

'That's right.' Simon leaned on the sideboard with the pen and chequebook in his hand. 'She's just a little nobody who you've knocked up.'

'How dare you?' George raised his fists ready to punch Simon when Elizabeth stepped in.

'Simon, what's got into you?' Elizabeth scowled.

'He gets more like his brother every day,' George said.

Elizabeth flicked her head back slightly, stuttering, 'What do you mean by that?'

'He thinks he can use and discard women whenever he chooses. And after what Richard did to Grace…' George sighed, shaking his head.

'George, don't.' My heart pulsed faster.

'What?' Simon's eyebrows narrowed. 'What did he do?'

George jabbed a finger at Simon. 'Tell him, Grace. Tell them what his dear brother did to you.'

'Elizabeth, take Mandy to meet Vikki,' I said.

'No, I want to know what happened.' Elizabeth stared at me. 'What did Richard do?'

'It was nothing.' A tightness formed in my throat.

135

'Nothing?' George raised his voice. 'She was dozing under a tree up on Meadow Hill, minding her own business, when his' – he pointed to Simon – 'his brother climbed on top of her and tried to rape her.' George stiffened. 'She was asleep for God's sake.'

Mandy and Elizabeth turned to me and back to George as he carried on. 'If she hadn't had the strength to fight him off, God knows what might've happened.'

'Grace, please, tell me this isn't true?' Simon blinked.

'What kind of animal does something like that?' George continued, 'And you… You have the cheek to belittle my lovely wife.'

I felt sick with the reminder. Waking up to that monster's clammy hands wandering over my breast. I shivered.

'I don't believe it.' Simon shook his head holding his temples. 'Grace, tell me this isn't true. Surely he wouldn't do that?'

'He did,' I answered quietly. 'You must have noticed the scar on his cheek?'

Simon slumped into an armchair. 'You did that? I remember at the time he had some excuse but I can't even remember what it was.'

'Well, now you know.' I coughed. 'If you'll excuse me for a minute.' I stood up and took myself out into the hallway and along to the bathroom. Why did George have to bring it all up again? Now everyone knew and it was back in my head after I'd buried it. I swilled my face with warm water and patted my skin dry with the towel. Taking a deep breath, I made my way back to the drawing room where Simon rushed towards me. 'I'm sorry, Grace. I'll bloody kill him. You should have told me.'

'I didn't want anyone to know. I just wanted to forget it ever happened and George saw to it that your brother wasn't allowed back on the land. I need a drink.' I headed to the sideboard and poured myself a Scotch, drinking it back in one go.

'Look, George.' Simon's chin quivered. 'I owe you and your wife a big apology. I thought you were being difficult not allowing Richard on the grounds and it was your way to force me out. And so, I became resentful... And then when you turned up earlier with Amanda, well, I can't excuse my behaviour and I don't know what got into me, but it seemed like you were trying to kick me out.' Simon clasped his hands to his face.

'Save it for someone that cares. Come on, Mandy, let's get out of here before I do some serious damage.' George took hold of his wife's hand to leave the room, turning back momentarily to stare at Simon. Sighing, he led Mandy out. 'Come on, darling.'

I rested my hand on Simon's shoulder. 'You should've known George would never force you out.'

'He threatened it this morning,' Elizabeth said, 'and I told Simon.'

'And I'm quite sure that's all it was, a threat. He was angry'– I shook my head – 'and to be frank, I don't blame him.'

'What an awful reception I offered her. I'm ashamed.' Simon bent his head.

'And so you should be. Now I suggest we all sit down as I'd like to talk to you both.' I moved towards the couch, Elizabeth and Simon followed.

'What about?' Elizabeth said in almost a whisper.

'You said he's been drinking a lot of late?'

'He has. And every time I tried to bring the subject up he snapped at me.'

'Did I, darling? I'm sorry. I hadn't realised. You're right though I have been drinking far too much. I was concerned George had changed his mind about the estate and no longer

137

needed me. Especially when he exploded a few weeks ago when I asked if Richard and his family could come over. I thought he was going to punch me.' Simon fidgeted with his hands. 'Now it all makes sense. You should have told me, Grace.'

'I don't want to talk about that now. We need to talk about you. You obviously have a drink problem. I can make some phone calls and get you admitted to a rehabilitation unit in Hooley, if you're in agreement.'

'I'm not sure. What will that entail?'

'It will be residential and for the first couple of weeks, at least, you'll not be allowed visitors and even when you are, it isn't a suitable place for children so we're going to have to come up with something viable to tell Vikki.'

Elizabeth leaned on Simon. 'Please darling, say yes. I want my husband back.'

Simon lifted his head, eyes filling. 'Yes, absolutely I'll do it. I hate this monster I've become.'

'The hospital will offer therapy to get to the bottom of what's making you drink.' Simon's appearance had gone downhill. The immaculate groomed man had been replaced by an unshaven, slovenly dressed individual. And had he even showered? 'I believe you're depressed but I'm not a doctor.'

Simon stroked his chin, reminding me of Father. 'You're right. I think I am depressed.'

'I'll make those calls.'

'Thank you, Grace.' Elizabeth squeezed my hand. 'What shall we tell Vikki.'

'A business trip. We'll tell her I've got to go overseas. That will work, won't it, Grace? I don't want Vikki to be worried. I'm sure she wants her daddy back too.'

Chapter 22

Grace

Max wandered into the drawing room, he and Charlotte had arrived last night. He brushed his white hair away from his forehead revealing fine lines. 'They'd better hurry up, hadn't they? It's almost midday. What time's the unveiling?'

'Three o'clock. There's still time, but I agree, Nancy's cutting it fine.'

'How about Alice, is she coming here first?'

'No. It's easier for her to go direct.' High heels clicked along the hall. I turned to see Charlotte coming through the door.

'Grace, darling.' She leant forward, touching my cheeks and kissing the air. She'd picked that up on her regular trips to Paris. She hadn't changed much since the first day she'd strolled into *Grace's*, my first shop. Her blonde hair was fastened into the same immaculate French knot. The colour out of a bottle nowadays. Black eyeliner widened her cornflower blue eyes and burgundy lipstick plumped up her lips. Her diamond cluster stud earrings reminded me of Mother.

'Good morning, Charlotte. Did you sleep well?' I asked.

'Fabulous darling. I love sleeping in that comfy bed. How are you coping this morning?'

'I'm all right. In fact, I'm better than all right.' I rested my hand on my chest. 'It may seem silly but it's like Adriéne's with me. I can't believe it's a year since he died.'

'I know, dear.' Charlotte gripped my hand. 'And it's not silly.'

'That sounds like the doorbell now.' I pulled the net curtains across the window to look out. 'There's a taxi pulling away. It must be them.'

'Are they staying?' Charlotte asked.

'That's the plan.' I moved away from the window. 'It'll be wonderful for us all to be together again for a few days. I miss you folks.'

'We miss you too.' Max took me into a hug. 'But look how well *House of Grace* is doing with us all branching off in different towns or countries.'

'Who'd have thought it? And according to Father, it was all frivolous nonsense.'

'It was kind of George to donate the land, wasn't it?' Charlotte scratched her nose.

'The right thing to do, considering it should always have been hers.' Max lit up a Marlboro. 'Charlie?'

'Yes darling. Light one up for me.'

Max drew on the two cigarettes and passed one to Charlotte. 'Have you still given up, Grace?'

'Yes. Over ten years now. Going back to George, he didn't have to give me that land. He's never been one for words and I think this was his way of showing me that I'm forgiven for the past.'

'You're not still beating yourself up over that, are you?' Charlotte put her hand on mine. 'You did everything you could.' She puffed on the cigarette letting out a smoke ring. 'Even I, with all my contacts, didn't have the power to stand up to the mighty Lord Granville.'

'I know. I know.'

Footsteps echoed from the corridor and Nancy came through the door entrance and into my arms. 'It's so good to see you, Grace. I've missed you so much.' My friend looked tired. I smiled to myself remembering the day Alice suggested she style Nancy's hair the same as mine and let me design her clothes. Nancy now had her own look. Copper tones lifted her light brown hair. She brushed it away from her face.

'And I you.' I gently pulled away.

Nancy unbuttoned her bottle-green velvet maxi coat. The one-button fastening hugged her waist. Despite being married, she'd held on to her independence, and had taken to the textile business well. She embraced Charlotte and Max in turn. 'And how fantastic to see you two lovely people have made it here too. How long are you over for?'

'A fortnight.' Max looked around the room. 'Where's Kevin?'

Nancy turned to me. 'I'm really sorry, Grace, he's not well at all. He's got flu. To be honest I didn't want to leave him but he insisted. Rebecca volunteered to stay with him because they both said it was more important I should be here with you. If he's well enough he'll follow up in a couple of days.'

'If he's not well, are you sure you want to be away from him for that long?' I rested my hand on Nancy's arm.

'He said he'll ring if there's a problem. I'm sure, he'll be fine. Anyway, enough of that. I'm looking forward to a good old chinwag and catch up. I want to know everything that's been happening.'

'You heard about George, didn't you?' Charlotte said.

'That he's designed the glasshouse?'

Charlotte tipped her head back and laughed. 'That's old news, darling. He's only gone and got himself hitched without telling anyone. We only found out last night, didn't we, Max?'

'We did indeed. But Charlie, don't you think that was Grace's news to tell?'

'Oh dear, yes, I'm sorry.' She looked at me. 'I didn't think.'

141

'Don't worry.' I turned to face Nancy. 'His wife's a nice young woman. You may remember her. Mandy Brown. Elsie and Brian's girl from Wintermore.'

'I do. How come George ended up marrying her? I knew he was in touch with Ben but…?'

'Ben set them up on a blind date apparently.'

'Wasn't she an only child? And how's Elsie?'

'She was. Her parents are both dead unfortunately. Apparently, George used to sit with Mandy at school.'

'He's certainly taken himself back to his roots, hasn't he? Jack would've been proud of him. And how's he coping as Lord of the Hall?'

'Okay considering. I think Alice would've felt more comfortable there than he does. She's become so materialistic. Well you saw what her wedding was like, and then there's George who gets married with only four guests, and two of them witnesses. At Wintermore Registry Office, would you believe?'

'That brings back memories. John and I were married there. You and Jack too.'

'Yes.'

Max stumped his cigarette out in the ashtray and clapped his hands. 'Right, sorry to break up your trip down memory lane but is everyone ready to leave?'

'Yes, you're right of course. I've already phoned George to say we're on our way. He'll be worried if we don't arrive on time.'

Max scanned the hallway. 'Where are the children? Aren't they coming?'

'No, they're with Joan and Ted.'

'How are the old girl and boy?' Max asked.

I laughed. 'I believe you're older than them, aren't you?'

'Possibly.' He grinned. 'How are they doing, anyway?'

'They're fine. Enjoying their retirement. And I love having them so close by. They're like real grandparents.'

'I look forward to seeing them later.' Max took Charlotte's arm. 'Michael's out in front with the Rolls.'

Nancy and I followed. I was blessed with my friends. Thank goodness for the day Charlotte walked into my shop, and Uncle Max had been like a father to me since I was sixteen, and Nancy a sister from the day we both became widows. These friends were my family. They'd been with me through everything. Losing Jack, Beth and Adriéne.

The main road was fairly quiet. I imagined the cold weather was keeping people indoors. I was excited to unveil the memorial for Adriéne. It was to be a small affair but I was looking forward to my family and friends seeing it. George was a great architect. I was pleased he'd managed to fulfil his dream as I had mine.

Driving along the icy lane my mind slipped back to a year ago today, travelling down the same road when the car accident happened and Adriéne was killed outright.

The road had been deserted. Adriéne was singing, 'We wish you a Merry Christmas.'

'You're happy,' I said.

'And why not, my darling? I have the world. I have you, our beautiful girls, and we've just had a wonderful couple of days with Elizabeth, Simon and Victoria. How could I not be happy?'

'Me too. The sun's trying to come out,' I said, 'maybe it will melt some of this snow.'

'Let's hope so. I'm glad we're not driving in the opposite direction though. It would be blinding.'

'Small mercies. I don't say it enough, Adriéne, but I love you.'

'And I love you too, my precious princess. Close your eyes if you like for a while.'

'No, I'm okay. I'll keep you company.'

Adriéne carried on singing 'We Wish you a Merry Christmas'.

'Look out,' I shouted.

A lorry from nowhere was veering across to our side of the road. Adriéne swerved and the next thing I knew I was waking up in hospital.

I squeezed my eyes shut. Charlotte gripped my hand. She always could read my thoughts. 'I'm okay,' I whispered.

Nancy took my other hand. 'You know you always have us.'

'I know. Thank you. I'm extremely fortunate to have such a wonderful family.' A family that I'd built myself, most who weren't blood related but family nonetheless, more than my own mother or father had ever been.

Chapter 23

George

Grace had phoned to say they were on their way for the unveiling, so where was she? Today was a proud day, not only for her but for me too as we opened the Palm House memorial for Adriéne. All would be revealed at three o'clock. The staff from Granville Hall and Grace's home waited outside in the crowd chatting. Alice hadn't arrived yet either.

I turned to take in the view from where I stood at the south end of the glasshouse. Sun reflected on the lake far below where geese cackled, making me smile. Grace had known what she was doing when she chose this spot. Where were Elizabeth and Simon? I hoped Simon hadn't had a setback. He'd been doing so well since his discharge from the clinic. It looked as though he had his drink problem under control and seemed happier in himself. If I had told Simon what his brother had done at the time, we might have avoided that ugly situation.

Mandy tapped my arm and I turned to her smiling face.

'They'll be here.' She pointed to the palm house. 'This building is wonderful, George. Has your mam seen it, yet?'

'Only a sneaky peep from outside last week but I can't wait until she sees inside. By the way, did she mention to you that she's thinking of having a fashion show in the spring?'

'No, she didn't.'

'Well when she does, I think she's going to ask you to model.'

'I don't think I'd feel comfortable walking across a catwalk.'

'That's a shame as you'd be perfect. Come here.' I cuddled her. 'I feel privileged to have a wife with such a fabulous figure.'

Holding me at arm's-length, she held her stomach. 'Not for much longer. Well at least not for another seven months.'

'Darling, you're pregnant?' I took her back into my arms. 'My dream coming true. What about the new teaching job?'

'I'm not sure. I thought we'd sit down and talk about it. I didn't mean to tell you right now. I was saving it for Christmas Day but it just kind of slipped out. Best not tell anyone else yet.'

'How am I supposed to keep that quiet?' I picked her up and swung her around.

She giggled. 'Because you have to. Now hurry up and put me down before anyone sees. That looks like them now. Isn't that Alice with Grace?'

'Yes, it is. Wait until you meet Uncle Max, Charlotte and Nancy. You're going to love them.'

'I'm sure I will but remember, don't tell anyone.'

'Okay, I promise.'

'What's going on?' Alice said.

'What do you mean?'

'You were twirling Mandy around. What's that all about?' Alice grinned.

'Just happy to have such a lovely wife and I'm excited about the unveiling.'

'Oh okay.' She sighed. 'I thought something must have happened.'

'It has. This is a special day. Anyway, cutting it fine, aren't you?' I asked.

'Sorry. My fault.' Nancy hugged me. 'You're looking well, George, and I hear congratulations are in order?'

Mandy and I glanced at each other. She mouthed, 'How?'

'Fancy sneaking off and getting married without your family,' Nancy continued.

We breathed a sigh of relief. Naturally, she was talking about the wedding.

Charlotte greeted me and Mandy the French way. 'Congratulations to you both. And welcome to the family. Mandy, isn't it?'

'Yes, yes, it is.' Mandy's eyes twinkled.

'Hello, dear.' Grace kissed her daughter-in-law first and then turned to me. 'Hello, darling.'

I kissed Grace. 'How are you?'

'All right, considering...' She turned back to my wife. 'Mandy, these are my oldest friends.'

Max brushed Mandy's cheek and shook my hand. 'If we'd known we could have bought a wedding present.'

'We didn't want any fuss. Anyway, Mandy'– I turned towards my extended family – 'This is Uncle Max, Charlotte, and Nancy. Nancy used to be our next-door neighbour in Wintermore.'

'I did indeed,' Nancy said, 'I remember your mam and pa well.'

'You knew my parents?' Mandy blushed and I guessed she was concerned that Nancy knew how her dad had come home drunk every night and beat her mam up.

'Well I knew your mam more. She was my friend.'

'I'm sorry,' Mandy said, 'but I don't remember you.'

'No, you wouldn't,' Grace said, 'you'd have only been eight or nine when we left the village after the tragedy.'

'I remember the coal mining accident, and then George disappeared.'

'A trying time for everyone,' Nancy said.

'Everyone in school wondered where George had gone. Our teacher asked the whole class if anyone knew. Who'd have thought I'd find him all these years later? Miss Jones too.'

147

'She's a lovely woman. I got the chance to get acquainted with her and John when they came down to stay with George. What do you make of the mansion up there?' Nancy pointed towards the Hall.

'I keep getting lost. It's huge.' Mandy laughed.

'Yes, it is. I find it a bit on the cold side. Unlike Grace's homely place. I used to live there, you know?'

'She did indeed.' Grace smiled. 'And it's still your home whenever you want.'

'Sorry to interrupt,' I said. 'Sweetheart, I'll leave you with Nancy and the others while Grace and I start the ceremony. Will you be okay?'

'I'll be fine.'

'Are you ready?' I took Grace's arm and escorted her up to the man-made stage in front of the three-tier domed glass house.

'Simon and Elizabeth should've been here by now.'

I looked at my watch. 'I wonder where they've got to.'

'You don't think Simon's fallen off the wagon, do you?'

'I hope not. He seemed perfectly fine last night and he's been doing so well since he came out of hospital.'

'As everyone's waiting, I think we should get started.'

'Yes, you're right. I'm sure they'll turn up soon.' I picked up the handbell from the stone wall and shook the bell three times. At the sound of the ringing our audience of friends, family and staff from Granville Hall, and Grace's home, stopped conversing and watched with eager eyes. It was a shame that Joan and Ted weren't here yet but Grace didn't want Joan standing out in the cold so suggested they bring Lori and Annalise along later.

The crowd watched as Grace walked elegantly towards the microphone. For a woman nearing fifty, she still had a good figure and looked trim in the black trouser suit. She coughed. 'I

148

have my son to thank for this beautiful building. Not only did he donate Granville land but he designed this monument for my late husband who, I'm sure you all know, died exactly one year ago today.' She cut the ribbon. 'I now declare the Adriéne Palm House officially open.'

Before unlocking the entrance, I turned to Grace and whispered, 'Are you all right?'

'Yes, I am. All day I've been feeling as if Adriéne is watching over me.'

'Da too, I reckon.'

'You're probably right. Look, here comes Alice and Mandy.'

'I see Robert hasn't bothered turning up.'

'No, probably not his thing. It's not like he really knew Adriéne.'

'Even so. He should have been here.'

'Yes, he should have been here for Alice, but shh now because I don't want to upset her. Those who are important to me are here and that's all that matters. Well except Elizabeth and Simon, goodness knows where they've got to.'

Alice clung on to Mandy's hand. 'Hello George, your wife and I have been getting acquainted. Haven't we, Mandy?'

'Yes, we have. It's nice to know I've got a mate living around the corner.'

Max rushed up behind. 'Right, are we going in? I'm rather parched and could do with a nice cup of English tea. One of the things I miss most in the States.'

As we entered, everyone gasped at the glittering lights around the windows and a twelve-foot Christmas tree standing in the centre.

'This place is amazing, much bigger on the inside than you think it's going to be. A bit like a Tardis. Adriéne would have loved it.' Nancy gazed around the area.

'It's lovely, George,' Charlotte said, 'you're very talented. I'm glad that you decided to stick out the schooling. Where's Elizabeth and Simon? Aren't they coming?'

'They're supposed to be here. Grace and I were just saying that we hope nothing's happened to them.'

Alice clasped Grace's hand. 'I'm sure they've just been held up, Mum.' Alice knew nothing about Simon's recent stay in the rehabilitation unit. Thankfully, we'd managed to keep it from everyone.

'Panic over.' Alice signalled to the couple and child running towards the entrance.

'Is everything okay,' I mouthed to Simon, who nodded and pointed to Vikki.

'I'm so sorry.' Elizabeth kissed Grace. 'It's this one's fault.'

'And what has this young lady been up to?' Grace looked at Vikki.

'She got bubblegum in her hair.' Elizabeth lifted Vikki's hair. 'She knows she's not allowed that rubbish. God knows where she got it from. We had to cut the gum out and then have her hair washed again. If I find the culprit that gave her that muck...'

Everyone laughed, particularly Grace and I, mainly with relief. Elizabeth and Simon couldn't see the funny side though. 'Well never mind that now,' Grace said, 'we've only just come inside so no one's had a proper inspection yet and Max is gasping for a cup of tea.'

Tea urns and a buffet were set out on a long table. Annie and Steph were hurrying around removing cling film from cheese and ham salad sandwiches and sausage rolls. Max was the first in the queue. He picked up a large mug and poured tea from the urn.

'Aunty Grace.' Vikki nudged Grace. 'Where's Annalise and Lori?'

'I'm sorry darling, they're not here yet but they'll be along later hopefully with Grandma Joan and Grandpa Ted.'

Vikki's mouth dropped.

The place was filling up with people and the air began to feel humid. I was concerned about Mandy but she looked fine; it was Alice whose face had turned white. She held her hand over her mouth.

'The bathroom's just over there on the left.' I pointed.

Mandy tapped me on the shoulder. 'I'll go with her to make sure she's all right.'

'Shall I get you a drink?' I asked.

'Just water please.' Mandy caught Alice up and ushered her through a side door.

'I wonder what that's all about,' I said.

'Who knows.' Grace smiled. I took her arm and toured around the palm house.

*

Mandy stood by the fireplace trying to warm up.

'It is cold.' I shivered. 'They've forecast snow. At least it kept off for the memorial opening. I don't know about you but I'm totally worn out.'

'Yes, I am, but I think that's due to my condition more than anything else. Apparently, Alice was telling me, you get very tired in the first trimester. Something to do with hormonal changes.'

'What does she know about it? And how come you were talking to her about it?'

'Oops. Look, George, if I tell you, promise not to give the game away.'

'I promise.'

Mandy sat down next to me, picked up her cup of hot chocolate and took a sip. 'Well, I'm sworn to secrecy but…'

151

'Out with it.'

'Alice is expecting too. She's coming up for thirteen weeks and was saying how exhausted she's been, like I have, but she's been throwing up since around four weeks. All day too. I'm lucky I haven't had any of that. Just a bit of nausea first thing in the morning. Poor Alice.'

'Ah, now I understand. That explains Grace's reaction when I asked what that was all about when you and Alice went off to the Ladies. She obviously knows.'

'Yes, she does.'

'Did you tell Alice about you?'

'No, I wanted to, but I didn't want to rain on her news.'

'Come here.' I pulled my wife towards me. 'You're always thinking about others.'

'Alice reckons she might have hers on your birthday. Imagine that?'

'It's fantastic news. And our little one' – I patted Mandy's tummy – 'will have a special friend to grow up with.' Life was getting better all the time. Grace had coped well today and it seemed like she'd turned a corner. And now she was going to become a grandmother to not one, but two children.

Mandy yawned. 'Let's go to bed. I'm shattered.'

Chapter 24

Grace

27th December 1981

I stared out of the window at sludge, the snow had finally started to thaw. Sun shone on the winter jasmine creating different shades of yellow. Purple and orange crocuses stood proud, sprouting up in the lawn. Almost New Year. Time moved too quickly these days. I wondered what nineteen-eighty-two would have in store for us as a family. I imagined poor Nancy would have a bad year ahead.

A touch at my shoulder made me jump.

'Sorry, darling, I didn't mean to give you a fright. Not quite the Christmas we were expecting, was it?'

'No, it wasn't.' I moved away from the window to sit down on the couch.

Charlotte followed and sat down next to me. 'All a bit of a shock,' she said, 'whatever got into the man?'

'There were no signs, either. Well except for him not coming to Adriéne's memorial. Seems his man flu was fake flu. Just an excuse.'

'Poor Nancy. And to find out on Christmas Eve.'

Max plodded into the drawing room. 'Good morning, ladies. Are you talking about our Nancy?' He plonked himself down on the armchair adjacent to Charlotte. 'It's a good job we're going back to the States today, otherwise I'd be down there sorting him out. How could he do this to our Nancy? Do we know who the other woman is?' Max poured himself a coffee from the pot next to a plate of toast on the coffee table.

'His secretary. Years younger too. Been going on for months apparently and poor Nancy completely unaware.' Charlotte scooped out a packet of Marlboro from the pocket of her mauve and cream silk kimono. 'Do you mind if I smoke?'

'No, go ahead.' I stood up and headed over to the sideboard to get an ashtray. I picked up the Murano glass which had been a gift from Nancy and Kevin. Nancy had been so proud announcing how Kevin had chosen it when they were in Italy. Poor Nancy.

She'd charged into the drawing room on Christmas Eve, around four in the afternoon, and ran straight into my arms. 'Grace,' she spluttered, 'he's left me.'

'What do you mean he's left you?' I tilted her head to see her pale face, and eyes red from crying. Her long hair, hidden under a silk, purple-patterned, headscarf reminded me of the turban-like scarf she wore back in Wintermore.

'Kevin. He's gone off with another woman.' She sobbed. 'Please can I stay here?'

'By all means, darling.' When I'd said it was always her home a couple of weeks ago, I hadn't anticipated this. I let her sob into my chest.

'Are you bringing that ashtray over, Grace, or should I come and get it?' Max said.

'Sorry.' I carried the ashtray over and sat it down on the coffee table.

'Are you okay?' Max asked as he flicked his ash into the tray.

'Yes, I was just thinking about Nancy.' I wiped my eyes. 'Sometimes I think I tempt fate.'

'Grace, what a strange thing to say? Why would you say that?' Charlotte puffed on her cigarette, blowing out a silvery smoke ring.

154

'I was thinking how good she looked at the memorial. Glowing in fact.'

'So?' Charlotte flicked the ash into the amber glass.

'Well perhaps if I hadn't thought how good she looked then maybe this wouldn't have happened.'

'Good God, Grace, you're sounding like a melodramatic schoolgirl. It's Queen's Park stone sentinels all over again. You can get those stupid thoughts out of your head, now.' Charlotte softly slapped my hand.

'Naturally, you're right.' I picked up the coffee pot. 'More coffee, Max? Charlotte?'

'Yes please.' Max passed me his cup.

'No more for me, thanks. Not when we've got the plane later. Now if you're offering a G&T.' Charlotte laughed.

'I wasn't.' I half laughed back. 'Not at this time of day, anyway.' Having so recently seen what drink could do with Simon there was no way I was encouraging Charlotte to start drinking this early. She drank too much anyway. I poured the hot liquid into Max's cup and added a dash of milk. 'Here.' I passed him the Royal Albert china before sitting down opposite him. 'I'll let you add your own sugar.'

'Ta, darling.' He scooped three teaspoons into his drink.

'I don't know how you keep so trim having all that.' I poured a black coffee for myself.

Max patted his stomach. 'Exercise, dear. Exercise.'

For a man of his age he looked marvellous but this visit I'd noticed signs that he needed to slow down. 'Do you have to go back to the States?' I asked. 'I don't want you to go. You're not getting any younger.'

'Grace.' Max leaned across and took my hand. 'No need to worry about me. I might be seventy-five but I'm still twenty inside.'

'That's as maybe but your physical self is arguing. You look like you've lost weight, particularly in your face.' He was starting to look gaunt.

'Tell her.' Charlotte nudged Max's knee.

'Tell me what?'

Max took a deep breath.

'You're not ill, are you?' Oh my God I didn't know what I'd do if I lost him.

'No, pet. I'm not ill but you're quite right, I'm far too old for this game, flying backwards and forwards from the States and that's why we're selling up and coming to live in England.'

I put my hands to my face. 'That's incredible news.' Finally, something good was happening. First Alice's pregnancy, George's marriage, and now this. 'Where will you live?'

'Well, I've still got the old house up in Chorley Road, although Charlie's not sure how she feels about living there.' He turned to Charlotte. 'Are you, dear?'

'No, I think it will hold too many ghosts.'

'I hadn't realised you still had that?' I was back in that house in Chorley Road with my best friend Katy. I wondered what she'd look like if she were here today and if she'd have married that rogue. I couldn't even remember his name. That house was always filled with love, a place where Jack, my first husband, had spent so much of his youth too.

'Am I talking to myself here, Grace?'

'Sorry, Max, it was the talk about that house. What did you say?'

'I said, I never sold it. Had long term tenants but unfortunately the widow died a couple of weeks ago leaving the property empty.'

'So many memories,' I said.

'Too many,' Charlotte interrupted.

'So, we've been looking around St Anne's.' Max chewed on a slice of toast from the plate.

'That must be pretty cold and soggy by now,' I said.

'Don't mind me, girlie, it's just the way I like it. Anyway, as I was saying, if we get a place in Lytham St Annes, I'll still be close enough to the factory in Bolton.'

'But Max, you need to retire. Put someone in sole charge of the factory or better still, sell it. I'll buy it from you and put in a manager.'

'Oh, Gracie.' Max laughed.

I hadn't been called that name for a while. Jack used to call me that. What would he say to his Uncle now? 'I mean it, tell him Charlotte. Come and live here. There's ample room.'

'That would be lovely darling, but I do think we need our own home,' Charlotte said. 'But Grace is right, Max, maybe we should look closer. There's that little village by the sea, Storik Sands, you remember?'

'Sorry?' Max frowned.

'That place where we had afternoon tea on the seafront last August.'

'Oh yes, I remember that. Quaint little place. We were lucky to find that. So hidden.'

'We could see what that has to offer.' Charlotte lit up another cigarette.

'I'll think about it,' Max said as Nancy wandered into the room.

'Are you talking about me and my failed life?' She pulled out a tissue from her pink satin housecoat and wiped her nose.

'Not at all, darling.' Charlotte stood up and brushed her lips against Nancy's cheeks. 'We were talking about Max and I returning to England.'

Nancy's eyes brightened for the first time since she'd arrived on Christmas Eve. 'That's great news, isn't it, Grace? Will you come and live here too?'

Charlotte laughed. 'That's what Grace was asking, but no, we're looking at a little beauty spot down the road from Worthing. Imagine waking up to the sound of waves every morning.'

'Err. Charlie?' Max nudged Charlotte. 'Don't get carried away.'

Ignoring Max's comment, Nancy carried on, 'Anything specific?' She sat down on the window seat with her back to the garden.

'Nothing's been decided yet,' Max answered. 'Now I hate to be a killjoy, Charlie, but we'll miss our flight if you don't get a move on. How about whipping upstairs and popping some clothes on?'

Charlotte looked at her watch. 'Ten o'clock. Sorry, darling, I hadn't realised it was so late. Shame we can't stay another day.' She rushed out of the drawing room, coughing while still puffing on a cigarette. I was sure she'd turned into a chain smoker.

Max sloped over to the window seat and eased himself down next to Nancy. 'Now, my dear'– he patted her hand – 'what are we going to do about you? Would you like me to get someone to sort that man of yours out?'

'Good God, Max,' I said, 'you're sounding like the Mafia.'

Nancy almost laughed.

'It cheered her up. Seriously, Missy,' he said to Nancy, 'it's his loss. Now upstairs, wash that pretty face and get dressed before we leave.'

'Yes, Dad.' Nancy wiped her eyes, wrapped her arms around Max before getting up, then disappeared out of the room.

Max heaved himself up, trudged across towards me and pressed my hand. 'Don't worry about her. She'll be fine. She managed to come through after losing John, and this time she not only has you but a good career. And we'll be here to help her through it too. Give us a couple of weeks and we'll be back.'

'So, you'll seriously consider moving down here?'

'Absolutely. Have you ever known Charlie not to get her own way when she puts her mind to it?'

I laughed and hugged this man who was, and had been for thirty years now, a father to me.

Chapter 25

George

Using charcoal, I added the final touches to my design.

'You've finished?'

I span around. Mandy was leaning over my shoulder looking at the easel. 'Morning, sweetheart, I didn't hear you come in. I was planning to bring you up a cup of tea. You're looking better.' Her pallor of the last few weeks was replaced with a bit of colour in her cheeks.

'I'm feeling better too. In fact, I feel better today than I have done for ages. Maybe this is the turning point.'

'I hope so, darling. Now maybe you can start to enjoy your pregnancy.' I touched her slightly swollen stomach and led her to the cushioned window seat to sit down.

'At least I haven't been sick like poor Alice. She's really suffered, throwing up day and night.'

'Don't you think it's time we told everyone before they start to guess?'

'Yes, but we don't want to tread on Alice's toes. Dreadful news about Nancy, wasn't it? Do you think she'll be all right? She looked wretched.'

'I'm sure she will. At least she has her work.'

'She's good at it too. These cushions are quite exceptional.' She tugged at the green, orange, and pink abstract design.

'They are.' I took hold of Mandy's hand and got as far as, 'What do…' when the rain splattered on the outside windowpane.

'Goodness, where did that come from? She released her hand, stood up and stared out onto the patio. 'It's like the heavens have opened. At this rate, those puddles will be ponds. First snow and now heavy rain, whatever next? I'm glad we don't have to go out today.'

'Torrential rain was forecast. Listen Mandy, what do you mean about treading on Alice's toes?'

'Well we don't want to steal her limelight, do we?'

'We can't help it if we're expecting close to her date. It's not like we copied, is it? And she'll be ecstatic that her little one will have a cousin to play with, just like we will be.'

'Maybe we should tell her before anyone else?'

'I can't tell her before Grace. She'll never forgive me.'

My aunt wandered into the conservatory over towards the window and gazed out. 'That's some rainstorm.'

'I was just saying that to George.' Mandy eased herself back down on to the window seat and crossed her legs.

'Ah, so that's what you young people were chatting about.' Elizabeth hovered near the bamboo chair opposite Mandy.

'I was thinking of inviting Grace over tomorrow for afternoon tea,' I said to Elizabeth. 'Would you like to join us?'

'That would be lovely. Simon has a meeting so I won't have to worry about him but Vikki has a dance lesson after school. However, I should be free around four if that isn't too late?'

'I'm planning on asking Grace around three but you could join us when you're ready.'

'Are Max and Charlotte coming too?'

'No, they're not back from the States until next week.' I stood up and moved towards my easel. 'What do you think now I've finished it?'

Elizabeth leaned towards the drawing and studied it. 'Judith's going to love it.'

'I hope so. I'm meeting her and Sir Ranklin later in the week.'

'How could they not love it? A bungalow with a lake view. I can see it now, lilac wisteria and climbing red roses covering the walls either side of the front porch.'

'You sound like you wish George had designed it for you,' Mandy said.

'In another life, maybe. Granville Hall will always be my home. But I've just had an idea.' Elizabeth sat down next to Mandy. 'George, didn't you say Max and Charlotte are looking for a new place to live?'

'That's right.' I folded my arms and smiled.

'You know what I'm going to suggest, don't you?'

'Yes, and I don't know why I didn't think of it myself. Absolutely, I should offer to design their new home. I'm sure they won't have much trouble finding a plot of land and getting planning permission, especially with my contacts on the Council.'

Elizabeth turned to the window. 'At this rate we're going to have floods.'

'That's what they're predicting,' I answered.

Vikki bolted into the conservatory and darted over to Mandy, grabbing her arm. 'Are you coming for breakfast?' Her blonde pigtails bobbed backwards and forwards. 'Mum and Dad said I can play the piano for you afterwards. Didn't you, Mum?'

'Yes, we did.' Elizabeth rolled her eyes and chuckled.

'Please come, Mandy.'

'What are you going to play for me on the piano?'

Vikki giggled. 'Fur Elise, silly.' She'd been playing the same piece day after day for the last few weeks. She pulled on Mandy's skirt. 'Come on.'

'You go,' I said to Mandy. 'I'll be along in a minute, I'd like a quick word with my aunt' – I turned to Elizabeth – 'if that's okay with you?'

As Mandy was dragged out of the conservatory, I mouthed to her, 'Talk later.'

Elizabeth stood up, smoothing down her straight skirt. 'Will this take long, George, only Simon's waiting?'

'No, not at all but sit back down for a minute.'

'What's this about?'

'I wanted to ask how Simon's really doing? Christmas can't have been easy for him.'

'What are you talking about? He's absolutely fine.'

I thought back to what Mandy had told me about her dad. She'd lost count of the drying-out units he'd been in. Her poor mam had an awful life never knowing if he'd come home drunk and batter her. She'd usher Mandy up to bed but Mandy would hear her da lashing out and her mam begging him to stop.

'It doesn't quite work like that, Aunt Elizabeth.' I touched her hand. 'I think he's drinking again. Is he still going to the AA meetings?'

'He isn't drinking. I'd know and no, he's not going to the meetings. He doesn't need them anymore.'

'Who said that, you or him?'

'Both of us. You worry too much. Come along, they're waiting for us.'

*

Annie cleared the dishes from the table. Elizabeth had invited family over for Sunday lunch and promised the girls they could do a concert afterwards.

Vikki stood up away from the table and made her way towards the door. 'Ladies and Gentlemen, the concert will begin at half past two in the music room.' She beckoned Lori and Annalise. 'Come on you two. Let's get ready.' Lori and Annalise ran from the room. Vikki turned to her father. 'You are coming, Daddy, aren't you? You promised?'

'We'll see. I need to sign some urgent papers first.' Simon was fidgety, moving about on the chair, playing with his hands, putting his hand to his chin.

'But you promised...' Vikki put her hand up to her eyes.

'I said, I'll see.' Simon pushed his chair out, stood up and stormed out of the room.

I knew he wasn't fine. This was the third day he hadn't shaved and it wasn't the first time he'd snapped at Vikki since Christmas.

'I'll be back in a minute,' I said to Mandy, before charging after Simon who was heading into the drawing room as I reached the hallway. When I followed him in, he was reaching for a bottle of Scotch.

'What are you doing?' I asked.

'I just need a small one.'

'You know you can't do that.'

'But I don't have a problem. They got it all wrong. I'm not an alcoholic. Ask your aunt, even she said so.'

'How long have you been back on it?'

Simon brushed hair away from his face. 'Sorry, back on what?'

'The drink? When did it start again?'

'I'm not sure what you're talking about. This is the first time and I just need a small one to calm my nerves.'

'Don't lie, Simon. I think you've been drinking since Christmas. You're snappy, unkempt and your clothes are dishevelled. I can't believe Aunt Elizabeth hasn't noticed.'

'Nothing gets past you, does it, Hercule Poirot?' He sneered.

'It's not a funny matter, Simon. This is serious. Grace went to all that trouble to get you into the rehabilitation unit and this is how you repay her?'

'I'm fine. I just need a small one here and there to help me through the day.'

'Why haven't you been going to your meetings?'

'Because I don't need to.'

'You do.'

'What's it got to do with you, anyway?'

'A lot.' I took the bottle out of his hands. 'Ring your sponsor.'

'I can't' – he slumped into an armchair – 'your aunt's worried someone will recognise me.'

As I thought, Elizabeth had stopped him going. 'I'm sorry, Simon, but on this occasion, sod Elizabeth. You need those meetings. Every night if necessary. You can't do it alone. Ring your sponsor?'

Shamefully, he nodded his head. 'You're right, I know. And I am trying. Really I am but Elizabeth doesn't understand.'

'It's confidential isn't it?'

'I believe so.'

'Then phone your sponsor straight after the girls have done their show and get yourself back on track. Come on, let's go and find the others.' I offered him my hand and helped him out of the chair. 'We'll get through this, Simon, but like I said, you can't do it alone.'

'You're right. I'll make that call now. You go on and I'll be along in a minute. Make some excuse.'

'I'm not sure that's a good idea.'

He slammed his hand done on the bar counter. 'For Christ's sake, George, let me do this. Leave me with some dignity.'

'If I trusted you, I would, but I'm sorry, I don't.'

165

Simon rubbed the back of his neck and frowned. 'Let's get this bloody show over with then.' He marched into the dining room as Grace and Elizabeth were walking out.

'There you both are,' Elizabeth said, 'we were just about to send out a search party. The girls will be waiting.' Elizabeth linked her arm in Simon's. They waited for Grace to walk on ahead.

As we approached the music room, I held Mandy back. 'Before we join the others come in here.' Holding her hand, I led her into the conservatory.

'What's this about, George?'

'I just caught Simon about to pour himself a drink.'

Mandy put her hand up to her mouth. 'Do you mean a real drink? Alcohol?'

'Yes, a Scotch. And it isn't the first time he's helped himself since Christmas, either. Elizabeth seems to be having a problem understanding what it means to be an alcoholic.'

'Why Elizabeth?'

'She doesn't want him going to meetings. I wondered if you'd have a chat with her, that is if it isn't too painful for you. Talk to her about your mam and dad.'

'Sure. If you think it will help.'

'It's worth a try.'

'What did you want to do about telling Grace our news?'

'I don't think today is the time but we'll tell her tomorrow.'

'Sounds like a plan.'

'And once Max and Charlotte are back, we tell the whole family?'

'Okay. If you're sure that's the right thing to do.'

'I am. We can't keep it to ourselves for much longer. Everyone's already asking questions about why you haven't taken up that position at school.'

'We did agree to wait until after Christmas before we told anyone, anyway. To make sure I was past twelve weeks.'

'We did. But the holiday period is over and the family needs some good news. I can't wait to be a dad.'

'And a great dad you'll be.'

I tilted Mandy's chin and placed a kiss on the tip of her nose. 'Have I ever told you that I love your nose?'

'Frequently.' She chuckled.

'It's such a cute nose, like a little button.' I kissed it again. 'Let's get to that concert and listen to 'Fur Elise' being slaughtered yet another time.' I laughed.

Chapter 26

George

The dining room table was set for ten adults, with wine, jugs of orange juice and iced water placed in the centre. I was excited to tell everyone our news. I couldn't believe how life was finally going my way. Like Mandy had said, I was going to be a great dad. After all I was changing my baby sister's nappies when I was only nine.

Elizabeth entered the room. 'This all looks very pretty. What's the occasion?'

'Wait and see.' I tapped the end of my nose before looking up at the clock. 'Almost eight. Everyone should start to arrive any minute. Did Vikki go off to bed okay?'

'Yes, but she wasn't happy. She knew something was going on and you know how she hates being left out of things.'

'Poor kid, but she needs rest with school in the morning.'

'You're quite right. It's lovely to see you so happy these days. Amanda is good for you.'

'You never say much about your first marriage, Aunt Elizabeth?'

'What can I say? He was much older than me and it was arranged.'

'But Simon's a lot older than you?'

'Nowhere near as much. I was sixteen when I married Gregory and he was in his fifties. Repulsive to look at, and repulsive in nature.' She turned away trying to hide her distaste.

'Sorry, I didn't mean to bring back memories and make you cry.' I wiped my white cotton handkerchief across her wet cheek.

She pressed my hand. 'The memories are always there, George. Just not spoken.'

'And Simon?'

'Simon's lovely. We had that slip-up with his drink problem but now that's under control with the help of him going to regular AA meetings. And he's the exact opposite to Gregory, and this time I married for love. Simon's always looking out for me.'

'I'm glad he's managing the alcohol thing but' – I clasped her hand – 'you know we need to watch him, don't you?'

'Yes, Amanda made me see I was being blind to things. My eyes are now wide open. And he's been talking to me when struggling.'

I looked towards the wine on the table. 'Do you think I should replace that with orange juice?'

'Good God, no. Don't do that. That will start questions and cause him embarrassment. That in itself will take him down the drink route more than a bottle on the table.'

'Well so long as you're sure.'

'You always did worry too much.' Elizabeth tapped my arm. 'Now enough about that. I think that was the doorbell. Your guests have started to arrive. Where's Amanda?'

Mandy entered the room right on cue. 'I'm here.' Her brunette hair covering her bare shoulders shone under the light of the glass chandelier.

'You look ravishing,' I whispered, 'do you know how horny you're making me right now?'

Giggling, she murmured back, 'You'll have to wait.'

'George, darling.' Grace entered the room and came straight towards me. After kissing me on the cheek she focused on

Mandy. 'You're looking radiant my dear. The dress is a perfect fit.'

'Thank you. I love it. How did you know emerald's my favourite colour?'

'I didn't, but I knew it would enhance those beautiful green eyes. By the way, it's a one-off design. I don't intend making it available for anyone else.'

'Thank you.' Mandy wrapped her arms around Grace.

I was just about to ask where Nancy was when she entered the room. 'Ah there you are. I thought we'd have to send out a search party.'

'Sorry, I had to wash my hands.' She headed over towards us and turned to Mandy. 'You look stunning? That colour suits you so much.'

'Thank you. Who'd have thought it? Me in a designer dress. Wish me mam could see.'

'She'd be proud.' Nancy kissed Mandy on the cheek.

'How are you feeling?' I asked Nancy. 'Have you heard from Kevin?'

'Better than I was, pet. Yes, I got a letter via his solicitor. He wants a divorce.'

'I'm sorry.' I grasped her hand.

'My tears are spent. Onwards and upwards. His loss.'

'That's the spirit.' Max strode in with Charlotte on his arm.

'Hello again, Mandy.' Charlotte blew a kiss either side of my wife's cheek.

'What's with the mystery?' Max asked. 'You do know we've had to cut our house hunting short to get here this evening. I hope it's worth it.'

'It will be.' I glanced at the doorway as Alice wandered in on her own. 'Where's Robert?'

'He sends his apologies but had a prior engagement.' She put her hand on her raised stomach. 'You didn't give us much notice.'

'Sorry about that. But look at you? You're totally glowing. I reckon you've got twins in there.' Her face had filled out too.

'Don't, George. The midwife thinks there may be. I'm booked in for an ultrasound scan next week to see if I've got my dates wrong or possibly, he or she is a big baby. I know my dates are correct though.'

'A scan?' Mandy frowned.

'Apparently the nurse uses soundwaves to build a picture of the baby in the womb.'

'That sounds incredible.' Mandy eyes brightened with interest. 'To be able to see your baby or babies before they're born. How clever. Does every pregnant woman get one?'

'No, it isn't routine. They only do it if they're concerned or think there may be more than one baby. Like for me.'

'Wow, that will be amazing if you have twins.' I smiled at Alice before turning to Mandy.

She mouthed, 'I think we should leave it.'

I mouthed back, 'It will be fine.' It was just like Mandy to worry about outshining Alice's news.

Simon charged in. 'Sorry I'm late. Vikki was playing up a little.'

I watched him closely for signs he may have had a drink, but apart from being rushed there was no evidence to suggest it. He was clean-shaven and smartly dressed. 'You're all right,' I said, 'we were just about to sit down.'

He scanned the room. 'No Robert?'

'No' – Alice kissed Simon on the cheek – 'I was saying to George how Robert had a prior engagement and with such short notice it was too late to cancel.'

'Let's get rid of one of these seats then. We don't want an empty space.' Simon pulled a mahogany chair away from the table and evenly spaced the others. 'Alice, you can come and sit next to your favourite uncle.'

'Oi,' Max said, 'I'm her favourite uncle.'

Laughing we all sat down. I placed myself between Grace and Mandy.

Annie waddled around the table serving soup into the bowls. She'd gained weight since taking over the role as housekeeper, looking older too. Tammy, a young trainee, had been brought in to help her and Donna. Simon must have noticed Annie struggling because he stood up and offered to serve drinks. He poured Saint-Emilion into crystal goblets for Grace, Charlotte, Max and me. Nancy and Elizabeth preferred Chardonnay.

'This onion soup is delightful, Annie,' Grace said. 'You'll have to pass the recipe on to Steph.'

'I'm happy to, Mrs Gilmore.'

'Orange juice, M'lady.' Simon positioned the jug towards Alice's glass.

She giggled. 'Yes please, Parker.'

'And how about you Lady Granville?' Simon waited a few seconds for a response. 'Amanda,' he said when Mandy didn't answer.

'Oh, that's me. I keep forgetting.' She chuckled. 'Orange juice for me too, please.'

After pouring everyone's drinks Simon returned to his seat and tipped iced water from a jug into his own glass. He was in good spirits and not being able to have an alcoholic drink didn't appear to be bothering him. It looked like the AA meetings were helping. 'So, how's the house hunting going?' Simon asked Max.

Max shook his head, tutting. 'Don't ask. It's a nightmare. We haven't managed to find our little haven yet.'

'I did,' Charlotte said, 'but it wasn't right for Max. Was it darling?' She smiled at him.

Tammy cleared the empty dishes, while Annie placed steak, chips, and peas in front of us all in turn.

'Thank you, Annie,' Nancy said, before turning back to Max and Charlotte. 'No rush, at least it means we get more time to spend with you while you're staying at Grace's.'

'George may have a proposition that could answer your problem.' Elizabeth grinned at me. 'Isn't that right?'

'Possibly.' I coughed.

'Ah, now it makes sense.' Max cut into his steak. 'So that's what this evening's about? What are you up to this time, young man?'

'No, that's not the reason. We'll talk about that later.'

Simon sipped his water as Tammy collected the plates. 'So, come on Lord Granville…'

Simon only ever referred to me as Lord Granville in jest. There was no longer any animosity between us and the estate was ticking over nicely with him at the helm and Elizabeth working part-time. I was lucky. He'd given up his own career as an equestrian to allow me to fulfil my dream to become an architect. I had a lot to be thankful for. So often I'd blamed Grace for giving me up but if she hadn't then I'd never have got to know my grandparents and this place would never have been mine. And as much as I often hated being Lord Granville, I'd most likely have ended up down the mine like Da, which had always been my dread.

'George.' Simon waved a hand.

I looked up. 'Sorry, Simon. I was miles away for a minute there.'

'I was wondering if you're going to put us out of our misery?'

'What do you think, Mandy, darling?' I put my arm around her. 'Should we?'

'I'm not sure.' She looked towards Alice and back to me before shrugging her shoulders. 'If you think it's the right time.'

Secret smiles followed around the table. 'Is it...?' Charlotte asked.

'Yes.' I nodded. 'You've guessed. We're having a baby. So, Alice, your little one or little ones are going to have a cousin to play with. Mandy's due end of June.'

'You don't seem surprised, Grace?' Charlotte said. 'Did you know?'

'I did.' She grinned. 'They told me a couple of weeks ago and I can tell you it's been a tough job keeping it quiet.'

'Congratulations' came at us from every direction around the table.

'This deserves Champagne,' Max said. 'Annie, will you do the honours?'

'Certainly, Sir. I'll just get some. Congratulations, Lord and Lady Granville. That's wonderful news. It will be lovely having a new baby around the house again.'

'Thank you, Annie.' I smiled.

Annie toddled to the sideboard to retrieve a bottle of bubbly as Alice rushed from her seat and out of the room.

Mandy shook her head. 'I told you it was the wrong time.'

'Don't worry, I'll go after her. You keep our guests entertained.' I kissed Mandy on the forehead as I stood up away from the table.

Grace was at the door before me. 'I'll come with you.' On our way out to the garden she said, 'I didn't think she'd take the news like this.'

'Me neither. Look she's in there.' I pointed. 'At least she wasn't stupid enough to have gone outside in the cold.'

Alice was staring out of the window when we walked into the conservatory.

'Well that wasn't quite the reaction I was expecting?' I said.

Grace put her arms around, Alice. 'What's the matter, darling?'

She pushed Grace away. 'Him, that's what. He always has to be in the limelight.'

'George?' Grace frowned. 'Nothing could be further from the truth.'

'Well he's always stealing mine.' Alice turned towards us. 'First he goes off and gets married straight after my wedding and now he's having a baby too. Very convenient.'

'I'm sorry that upsets you. Grow up, why don't you? For goodness sake, we didn't do it to copy you. We were completely unaware of your pregnancy when Mandy first found out we were expecting.' I sighed. 'And I'm sorry, I really didn't think it would take any attention away from you when I got married. It was one of the reasons I got married in secret.'

'Rubbish.' She slapped my hand. 'You knew exactly what you were doing.'

Glaring, I looked at Grace. 'What the hell's the matter with her?'

'I suspect it's her hormones.' Grace put her arms around Alice again. 'This is exciting news. Not only am I going to be a grandparent for your child or children but for George's too. And both your children will always have a playmate.'

Alice pushed Grace away and turned back towards the window. 'Trust you to be on the golden boy's side. It was always George, wasn't it? Right after Dad died, all you ever thought about was George. Got to get George back. No time for me. Never any time for me.'

'That's not true.' Grace tried to pacify Alice.

Was she right? Had Grace spent all her time trying to get me back at the cost of Alice's childhood? And I'd been making Grace suffer all these years for her neglect. I pressed my fingers against my forehead. This was such a mess.

Sighing again, I moved closer to my sister. 'Look Alice, I'm really sorry. I didn't mean to upset you. This was supposed to be a happy day. It seems I've been rather selfish and never considered how things were for you.'

Alice's eyes stayed fixed on the windowpane. I turned her towards me. 'I said I'm sorry but you know what' – I felt rage creeping up inside me – 'I don't think this is anything to do with us announcing our baby. I think you're jealous of the intimacy and love that Mandy and I have.'

'Don't be so bloody stupid.' Alice's face turned red.

'I know you're having problems with Robert.'

'What problems?' Grace looked at Alice.

'Nothing. Why don't you both just leave me alone?' She stormed out of the conservatory.

'I should go after her,' Grace said.

'No, wait.' I put my hand out to stop her. 'There's something you should know.'

'Don't start this again, now, George. I need to find your sister.'

Part II

Chapter 1

Grace

2nd July 1986

I was gazing out into the garden at the burnt-orange cactus dahlias in full bloom when I heard the front door close. I greeted George in the hallway. 'Lovely to see you, darling,' I said. 'Mandy and Jack not with you?'

'Not today. I needed to speak to you alone.'

'What's up?'

'I'd like to talk to you about Alice but let's sit down first.'

'What about Alice? She's okay, isn't she? Oh god, has she had an accident?'

'Nothing like that.' He placed his hand on my shoulder. 'Sorry, I didn't mean to make you panic. How long before she gets here?'

I checked my watch. 'It's just coming up to two now. She should be here by half past. Does that give us enough time to discuss whatever?'

'Should do. How about we go in there?' George pointed to the summer room.

We sank into the flowery cushions on the cane-framed sofas. 'What's this about, George? It's no good telling me not to panic.'

'It's about Alice and Robert.'

I stood up, strode across the room, and sighed. 'Not this again. I don't believe you, George, you've got me worried silly thinking something awful must've happened, and lo and

179

behold, it's your gripe with Robert again. When are you going to accept the fact that they're married? It's been five years now.'

'Sit back down and give me a few minutes to explain.'

'Very well. Let's get some air in here first.' I opened the French doors wide and sat back down next to George. 'Go on.'

'I've been watching her closely. She has bruises.'

'Darling.' I squeezed his hand. 'I know you worry about your sister but we all get bruises. Alice is like me and bruises easily.'

'It's not just me. Mandy's seen the bruises too.'

'But like I said, Alice bruises easily, and with the twins' rough and tumble I'm surprised she's not black and blue.'

'I hear what you're saying, Grace, but Mandy tackled Alice.'

I took a deep breath. 'And…'

'He's abusing her.'

I tutted. 'George.'

'No.' George raised his voice. 'You're not listening.'

'I am listening but let's be honest, you've had it in for Robert since your schooldays. This grievance needs to be put to bed.'

'It's nothing to do with grievance.'

'Then what?'

'When Mandy spoke to Alice, she admitted it but swore Mandy to secrecy. So, we need to tackle this delicately.'

'What exactly did Alice admit?'

'That sometimes Robert hurts her but she reckons it's her own fault.'

'Are you sure Mandy couldn't have mistaken what she heard?'

'No. And this is why we must confront Alice together. It can't go on. I'm worried about those girls too. You saw what he was like at Jack's birthday party when he slapped them. Sanders is nothing but a bully.'

'You could be overreacting here. Lots of parents slap their children. It's not uncommon.'

George stood up and took a deep breath before raising his voice again. 'I'm not overreacting. I'm telling you, Grace, he's a bully and he's been physically abusing your daughter, my sister, and you and I need to put a stop to it. Now.' He wiped a handkerchief across beads of sweat on his forehead.

'Okay, but calm down. Sit down and start again.'

George poured a glass of water from the jug on the table and took a mouthful before sitting back down. 'Apparently it was after the party.' He licked his lips. 'Robert, it seems, was mad because I intervened when he smacked the girls and later that evening when alone with Alice, he took it out on her.' George folded his arms. 'You can't argue with that.'

'Are you sure Mandy heard right?'

'Yes. I've already told you that. It's not something Mandy would invent. Alice swore her to secrecy but Mandy couldn't keep that secret. She felt it was important to tell me and now I'm telling you.'

Had there been signs and I'd missed them? Those looks Robert had sometimes given Alice but I dismissed thinking they must've had a row, but had there been more to it? What kind of mother did that make me? I put my hand close to my mouth and shook my head. 'I can't believe it. How could I have been so blind?'

'Because Alice is good at covering it up and he acts the perfect gentleman in public giving no reason for you or anyone else to be suspicious.'

'But you warned me and I didn't listen. I swear I'll kill him.'

'Not if I get there first.' He held his finger to his lips. 'Shh. That sounds like her now.'

'Mum.' A voice came from down the hall.

'In the summer room,' I called back.

181

Alice came in puffing and panting.

'Come in, darling,' I said. 'You're looking pretty in lemon. That skirt suits you.'

'Thanks, Mum. I love the gypsy tiers. I'm lucky to have a mother who's a designer.'

I stood up and poured her a glass of ice water from the jug. 'Sit down and get your breath back. You look hot.' Her face was red. 'Here, drink this. It will help cool you down.'

'Thanks.' She drank half the contents in one go. 'You two looked cosy. What were you talking about?'

'George was telling me what Jack's been up to with the new puppy.'

Alice slumped down next to George on the bamboo sofa and nudged him playfully. 'And how's my big brother?'

'Good thanks and you?'

'Okay but finding this heat a bit much.' She waved her hand like a fan.

'I'm not surprised.' George tugged at the sleeve of Alice's knitwear. 'I'd take that off if I were you.'

I inhaled a breath and frowned at George.

Alice smoothed down her cardigan. 'I'm all right, thanks.'

'You just said you were hot and you're right, it's a scorcher today.' George laughed. 'Seriously, Sis, you'll melt. Why not take it off?'

'I said I'm fine. Tell him, Mum.'

'George, don't badger your sister, but Alice, he's right about one thing. It's too hot for long sleeves. You look quite flushed and I'm concerned you'll pass out at this rate. Maybe we should sit outside for a while.'

'No way,' Alice said, 'it's hotter out there than in here. I'll be okay once I get a glass of Steph's iced lemonade.'

George pulled at her sleeve. 'Are you sure you're not trying to cover something up?'

Alice slapped George's hand. 'Stop it.'

'George, for goodness sake, leave your sister alone.' What had got into him? This tactic would never work.

'I just want to know what she's hiding.'

'I'm not hiding anything.'

'Behave yourself, George. In fact, why don't you pop to the kitchen and organise refreshment? It will give Alice and I a chance for a mother and daughter catch up.'

'That sounds like a good idea.' George patted Alice on her arm. 'Sorry, Sis.' He stood up. 'Any special requests?'

'Steph's homemade lemonade, please. With ice. Bring a jug.'

'I think I'll have a lemonade too,' I said.

'A jug of lemonade and three glasses coming up.' George picked up the water jug from the table and left the room giving me a thumbs up.

'I'm exhausted.' Alice wiped a handkerchief across her forehead. 'The twins can be a nightmare at times.'

'Where are Beth and Nicole now? I was hoping to see them.'

'Mother-in-law wanted them today.'

'And Robert?'

She sighed. 'Down the golf club, again.'

'How are things with you both?'

'Fine. Why are you asking?'

'Just checking as Robert appeared a bit riled at Jack's birthday party.'

'Well the girls were misbehaving. What with Jack getting that puppy, Beth and Nicole started whining they wanted one too. And you know how Robert hates dogs. And then when the girls started rolling around the grass with the thing. Well you know Robert. He likes his girls to be perfect little angels. Sitting and smiling. Never running around, and keeping their pretty dresses immaculate. Who gives a child a puppy for their birthday, anyway? What a stupid idea.'

'Jack loves Ginny, darling, as do Mandy and George, therefore it was the right gift for him. But never mind that, going back to Robert…'

'What now?'

'From the tone in your voice you didn't agree with the way he disciplined the girls?'

'I don't disagree with the way he disciplines them. A slap never hurt anyone but I don't agree they should be little angels all the time and never get dirty. They're four-year-olds and need to play. Just like I did.' Alice laughed. 'Do you remember when I used to sing o*n the good ship lollipop* and you said I looked like Shirley Temple?'

'Not something I'd forget, darling. Especially that day you nearly fell down into the railway track.'

'Oh yes. I'd forgotten about that. Poor Nancy. She was in charge of me, wasn't she? She must've felt really bad. Supposing I'd fallen…'

'Exactly.' I stood up at the door to take in some air before turning back around to Alice. 'Where's Frances taken the girls?'

'Up to town to see a show.'

'Aren't they a little young?'

'Not according to her ladyship but at least it means I get a bit of a break.'

George wandered back in holding a tray laden with refreshments. 'What do you mean a bit of a break? Don't you have a nanny?' He put the tray down and passed each of us a glass of iced lemonade in turn and placed a jugful along with a plate of rock cakes onto the coffee table.

'Well yes, but she doesn't work full-time, you know.' Alice gulped her drink. 'Ooh, that's gorgeous. Pour me another, will you, George, while you're still up?'

'Sure.' He refilled her glass. 'Here.' He passed the drink to his sister. 'I can't understand you wanting a nanny. Mandy insisted on looking after Jack herself. Anyway, that's not what Grace and I wanted to see you about.'

I scowled at George and took a deep breath. 'Can you leave this to me, George?'

'Sorry. I'm just trying to help.' He shrugged his shoulders before sitting back down opposite Alice.

'What's he on about?' Alice blinked.

'Are you feeling a little cooler now, darling?' I asked.

'Yes thanks, Mum.' Her cheeks looked less flushed.

I walked across to the sofa to sit next to her. 'You know you can tell me anything, don't you?'

'Yes.' She frowned.

'I want you to be honest with me.'

Alice looked confused. 'This is all beginning to sound very ominous. What's this all about? I feel like I'm being attacked.'

I held my daughter's hand. 'Not at all darling. It's just we were wondering…'

'Yes?'

'Darling, is Robert hurting you?'

'Certainly not. Why would you ask that?' She looked at George. 'It's him, isn't it?'

'Alice.' George lowered his voice to almost a whisper. 'Mandy told me.'

'Whatever she's told you, she's lying.'

George glared at Alice. 'She's not lying and you know it. You can't hide it anymore.'

Alice burst out crying. 'Mandy had no right. I told her in confidence and anyway, like I told her, it's my own fault.'

I shook my head. 'It's not your fault, darling.' I rubbed the top of her arm.

She jerked away, wincing.

'Is that what he tells you?' I touched the sleeve of her cardigan. 'May I?'

She nodded, sniffling.

I gently slipped off the sleeves from her cardigan revealing both arms covered in hideous purple-black bruises. I gasped. 'My poor baby.' She winced again as I hugged her. 'What else has he done? May I?'

'I suppose so.' Alice turned her face away.

I raised her blouse exposing more monstrous bruises. 'Goodness. We need to get you checked out.'

'No need. Robert took me to the hospital.'

'He's nothing more than a monster.' I hugged her gently and let her sob into my chest.

'It's my own fault,' she kept repeating over and over, 'I make him cross. Like if I ask why he's late home or doesn't come home at all or why he has to shout at the girls...'

'Is that why he hurt you the other night?' George asked. 'Because you stuck up for them?'

'No. It was because of you. He said you're always on his case. That you've never forgiven him for all those years ago on your first day at his school.'

'That's a load of codswallop. And what about all the other times?'

'He says I shouldn't get upset when he goes out and he's right. I shouldn't.' She sobbed.

'And why is that?' George raised his voice. 'You know, don't you?'

'Know what?' I asked.

'He's seeing other women, tell her, Alice.'

'I don't know what he's talking about.' Alice pulled out a handkerchief from her handbag and blew her nose.

'Yes you do. You confided in Mandy. And she didn't want to betray your trust but she's worried. We all are. And the way he treats Beth and Nicole...' George sighed.

Alice's face paled.

186

George took a deep breath. 'You don't have to put up with his unacceptable behaviour any longer. Come and live at the Hall.'

'No, George. If she's going anywhere, she'll move in here with me. Alice?'

'He'll never let me go or if he does, he won't let me take the twins.'

'Oh, he will. Don't you worry about that because if he doesn't, I'll damn well make sure the whole world knows what he's been doing to my sister.'

'Stay here tonight,' I said. 'I don't want you being in a house with that monstrous man one minute longer. Are the girls out for the night with Lady Sanders?'

'That's the plan.' Alice sobbed.

'Then you don't need to worry about them. Will you stay?'

'Okay. Just for tonight.' She picked up her glass and sipped the lemonade.

'Tomorrow, I'll go over to the Sanders' and bring the twins back here.'

'No, Mum. I will get my girls. There's no way I'm staying here without them.'

'Don't worry, Alice, I won't leave without them. You stay here where you're safe.'

'You promise?'

'Yes, my darling.'

'Thanks, Mum.' She hugged me as she had done many times before. I'd missed that intimacy with Mother.

George brushed blond curls away from his forehead. 'I'll come with you.'

'I don't think that's a good idea,' I said.

Alice wiped her nose before announcing in an uneven voice, 'What if I don't want to leave him? Why should I give up my status when I've got the chance to be Lady Sanders one day?'

'Seriously? You're unbelievable.' George took a deep breath before raising his voice. 'You won't be anything if he ends up killing you.'

'Don't be so melodramatic, George,' Alice said.

'I don't think he is being, darling. You hear of these battered wives ending up dead.'

George looked at his watch. 'I need to whizz off as I have a meeting but I'll be back tomorrow after work, about six.' He patted his sister on her arm. 'Don't worry, Sis, everything's going to be okay.' He kissed me on the cheek. 'See you tomorrow,' and before I could say anything else he was gone.

Chapter 2

Grace

George tooted his car horn.

I rushed down the steps of the house to meet him standing by the passenger side of his Ferrari.

'How's she been?' he asked.

'Not good. She's barely stopped crying and she's still saying it was her own fault. One thing I do know is that monster isn't coming near my daughter ever again. I should have listened to you.'

George opened the car door. 'Are you getting in then?'

I squeezed his hand. 'I know you only want to help but I think it's best if I go alone.'

He pushed away my hand. 'No way. I'm coming too.'

'And that's exactly why I want you to stay here with Alice. You're already getting heated and we haven't even moved from my drive. Anyway, I need you to stay with your sister to make sure she doesn't run back to him the moment my back's turned.'

George slammed the door shut. 'Very well, but I can't say I'm happy about it and if you have any problems…'

'I'll be fine.'

'If you do, phone me, and I'll be straight round to sort out bloody Sanders and his father.' He passed me his car keys. 'You may as well take the Ferrari as she's all warmed up.' After kissing me on the cheek, he marched off grunting under his breath.

I climbed into the car, started up the engine, drove out of the drive, onto the main road and headed towards Stonesay Manor. It was only a short distance from my house since I'd moved last year to be closer to George and Alice. The traffic was light and ten minutes later I arrived at the Sanders' estate, steered through the gates, and parked outside a mansion similar to Granville Hall, although not quite as grand.

I rang the brass bell beside the porch entrance. While waiting, I glanced around the front garden to admire the marigolds and alyssum in the lawn border trying to take my mind off what lay ahead. I took a deep breath. *I can do this*. It wasn't the same as all those years ago when I'd stood on the steps of Granville Hall. This time I had power.

A young maid opened the door. 'Good evening, Mrs Gilmore, are Lord and Lady Sanders expecting you?'

'Hello, Candy. They're not expecting me but are they home?'

'Yes. Do come in.'

I followed her into the house and down the hallway until she stopped and turned to me. 'If you could wait here please, Mrs Gilmore, while I announce you.'

To distract myself from my trembling knees, I looked up at the gilt-framed family portraits on the wall. This place could be Granville Hall except for different faces in the pictures.

The maid came out from the drawing room. 'Lord and Lady Sanders will see you now.' She opened the double doors wide.

As I entered, Lord Sanders came towards me and shook my hand. 'Good evening, Grace. This is an unexpected pleasure. Candy, organise tea for our guest.' He looked at me. 'Or would you prefer coffee?'

'Tea will be fine.'

'Sit down, please.' He signalled to the black leather suite.

'Thank you.' I sat down on an armchair as Frances was sitting on the sofa.

'I heard you're opening a new shop, Grace?' she said.

'Yes, that's right. Over in Croydon…'

She looked thinner. Her frown lines appeared more prominent but that could be because she'd snatched her hair back into a bun showing silvery strands.

'Frances, Grace didn't come here for small talk. She came here for a reason, let her speak.'

'Thank you.' I hated the way he spoke to his wife. No wonder his son was a bully. Neither Jack nor Adriéne would ever have spoken to me that way.

Donald Sanders frowned. 'So, Grace, to what do we owe this honour?' he asked.

I sat up straight. 'I'd like to speak to you about your son.'

'Robert? Shall I call him?'

'Presently, but perhaps we could talk first.'

'Certainly.' He took out a cigarette case from the inside pocket of his waistcoat, strode towards me and offered up the open container.

'No, thank you. I don't smoke.'

He took out a cigarette, dabbed it on the case, and leaned forward to the table lighter on the side table. The lighter sprang into flame. He inhaled on the cigarette and took a puff. 'Ah, here's tea.' He sat down next to his wife as the maid poured the beverages and passed me a cup. 'Now, what's this all about?' he asked.

I waited for Candy to leave before speaking. 'I'm not sure how to tell you this…' My cup rattled on its saucer.

'Just spit it out, woman. It can't be that bad.'

I coughed. 'I'm sure this will come as a shock but…'

'But?' he prompted.

'It's come to my attention…'

'For pity's sake, woman, if you've got something to say, just say it.'

'Your son's been abusing my daughter.' My words became hurried. 'She's covered in bruises and last week he broke a couple of her ribs. It seems Robert has been using Alice as his punch bag.' I took a deep breath. 'I'm also concerned for the twins safety.'

Donald Sanders tipped his head back in laughter. 'Don't be ridiculous, woman. I've never heard of anything so outrageous. And as for the girls being in danger…' He stubbed out his cigarette into the glass ashtray on the coffee table.

With Alice and Robert in the east wing and their own private entrance to the house, no wonder Lord and Lady Sanders didn't have an inkling. 'I can understand you're shocked. I was too, but…'

Donald Sanders stood up, raising his voice. 'Outrageous accusations. How dare you?'

Robert swaggered in. 'What's with the loud voices?' He glared at me. 'Grace. Where's Alice?'

'According to Mrs Gilmore' – Lord Sanders stomped over to the bar, poured himself a whisky and took a swig – 'apparently you're a wife beater.' He took another mouthful from his glass and stared at his son.

'What a load of rubbish, Father.' He turned to me. 'What's Alice said? And where the hell is she? She didn't come home last night.'

'I'm afraid Alice shan't be coming home. She's staying with me where she's safe.'

'What the hell.' He looked at his father. 'You know how melodramatic Alice can be.' He turned to me. 'Is she at yours now? I'll go and bring her back home where she belongs. The twins need their mother.'

'Yes, they do. Which is why I'm here to collect them.' I checked the time on my watch. 'If you tell me where the girls are, I'll get them ready.'

'No one's taking the twins anywhere.' Donald Sanders reached for a cigar from the wooden box on the bar. He picked up the cutter and applied light pressure as he pushed the cigar backwards and forwards. 'As Robert mentioned, Alice has been known to be melodramatic on more than one occasion.' He lit the cigar and took a puff. 'In fact, I've even heard you say that about her yourself.' Lord Sanders stroked his whitened beard. Frances Sanders sat in silence nodding her head in agreement.

'You're welcome to come and visit Alice, Lord Sanders, and see the bruises.' I hoped to wipe that smirk off his face.

Donald Sanders sighed as he leaned his arm across the bar. 'Woman, you're deluded. As is your daughter.'

'I can arrange access to the hospital records showing her visit from last week, and I might add, your son drove her there. My daughter will give her consent, but it would be much better if we could get a confession from your son instead.' I took a deep breath. 'Let me take the girls for their safety, please, Donald. Only last week he was slapping them in public.'

'The woman's talking garbage, Father.'

Lord Sanders stumped out his cigar in the ashtray on the marble counter, and moved towards me, hissing. 'I think it's time you left, Mrs Gilmore, don't you? The twins are going nowhere.'

I had to hold my ground. There was no way I was going back to Alice empty-handed. She'd never forgive me. 'I'm not going anywhere.' I stared at Lord Sanders.

He raised his voice, 'If Alice returns home in a reasonable time, I will contemplate letting her stay but she'd better not take too long to decide.'

'Alice will return here over my dead body.'

'Then so be it. Now are you going to leave?'

'No. I'm not going anywhere without my granddaughters.'

'Oh, but you are.' Lord Sanders rang a bell.

A butler entered the room. 'Yes, Sir?'

'Mrs Gilmore was just leaving. Please can you see her out.'

'I said, I'm not going anywhere.'

'Please don't make me use force. Jenson…'

'Mrs Gilmore.' The butler took my arm.

'Let go,' I said, shaking him off. 'Very well, I'll leave but don't think I won't be back. You won't get away with this. No wonder your son has turned into a wife abuser when his father is such a bully.'

'Mrs Gilmore, please.' Jenson held his hand out.

I pushed it away. 'I don't need any help thank you.' I turned to Donald Sanders. 'I'll be back with Lord Granville.'

Lord Sanders threw his head back and let out a roar of laughter. 'Don't make me laugh, woman. You think that whippersnapper has more clout than me?' He shook his head. 'He's a lord in name only. He doesn't have the respect his grandfather had. Now, will you leave quietly or must Jenson throw you out?'

'Don't make the mistake, Lord Sanders, of underestimating me or my son.' I stormed out of the room and out of the house. My legs shook and my heart pounded. Alice would never forgive me returning home without the twins but what else could I do? We'd have to go down the legal route and I just hoped we had more influence than Lord Sanders credited us with.

*

I drove up to Adriene's memorial at Granville Hall and sat down on the bench outside the palm house. Would going down the legal route work this time? It hadn't all those years ago when

I'd tried to retrieve George. What if Lord Sanders was right and George didn't have the influence Father had. But I had influence. I may not have a title but I was respected and people listened to me. I gazed out onto the lake. Watching the swans glide by and the geese chevron over the water was calming.

'Jack,' I said out loud, 'What am I going to say to Alice?' Although this was Adriéne's spot I always felt Jack was close by too. Jack was my first love and had always held that special place in my heart, and Alice was his little girl. The sky reddened as the sun came down. I shivered from the chilled breeze. It was time to go home and face Alice but I wasn't looking forward to it.

*

'What do you mean you haven't got the twins?' Alice grabbed her handbag and headed for the door.

'We'll get them back, don't worry,' I said.

'What, like it took you six bloody years to get George back? Well I'm not you, Mother, and I want my girls and I don't care if that means I get beaten black and blue, I'm going back.'

George went after Alice. 'We can't let you do that. Come back in and let's sit down and talk about our next step.' He turned towards me. 'I told you to ring if you encountered a problem.'

'And what then? You punch Robert and his father and end up in court. How would that look? Lord Granville up for assault. We have to do this properly. Call the Granville lawyer and we'll get advice.'

'I hate you both.' Alice started punching me in the chest as she sobbed.

'We'll get your babies back,' I whispered, stroking her hair, 'I promise.' Somehow, we would.

195

Chapter 3

George

Jack woke up as we were ready to pull off the M6.

'Are we there yet?' he asked.

'Nearly,' I said.

Ginny stood up, filling my rear-view mirror. She arched her back and wagged her huge, fluffy tail. Her long tongue hung from her mouth as she panted.

'Lie down for a bit longer, girl,' Mandy said.

I'd bought a Ford Escort estate to accommodate the red setter. Jack wanted a blue car so I chose a magnificent shade of cobalt blue. I added a guard in the back for the dog to travel safely.

'I wonder if Ginny and Kerry will look like twins,' Jack said.'

'I'm sure they will.' I flicked the indicator to turn into a road a couple of miles away from Betty and John's.

Jack unclipped his seat belt. 'We're nearly there. I remember.'

I pulled the car over and stopped. 'Put your belt back on right now, Jack, and it doesn't come off until Mum or I tell you. Is that clear?'

'Sorry, Daddy.'

'He's just excited.' Mandy frowned.

'I don't care. We can't go easy on him about things like that. It's too important.' I started the car up again and as I pulled back out, the rain started to come down. I could see Jack sulking from the driving mirror.

Mandy touched my hand as if to say I'd been too hard on the child.

'Just make sure he doesn't do it again,' I told her. 'I can't watch him and drive the bloody car. It's bad enough Ginny getting up and blocking the rear screen.' I sighed. 'Now, rain.'

'Well we're here now.' Mandy rested her palm on my leg. 'Just lighten up a little.'

I pushed her hand away. 'Don't tell me to lighten up. Jack's done wrong and he needs to know it. If that had been me, my da would've given me a hiding with a slipper across my backside once I got in. It's not like I've ever hit him. Is it?'

'I know. You're right of course.'

I signalled left to pull over outside Betty and John's.

Mandy grabbed the mini umbrella from the glove compartment, climbed out of the passenger door and leaned into the back seat to unfasten Jack's seatbelt. 'Come on, Jack.' She put the brollie up. 'Get under here quickly. Your dad will sort the dog.' She slammed the car door shut and marched off up the path with Jack huddling close under the umbrella.

The front door was open by the time I got our overnight bags and Ginny from the back of the car. 'Hi Betty.' I pecked her on the cheek. 'Can she go straight out to the garden?' I signalled to Ginny on the lead. 'She's been cooped up in the car far too long. We stopped a couple of times but she needs a good runabout.'

'Sure, I'll get John to open the side gate. You might as well come in that way too.'

*

I sipped my coffee. 'I needed that. It wasn't an easy drive. I thought we'd miss most of the traffic, leaving when we did, but there'd been an accident on the motorway.'

197

'Well at least it's stopped raining now so the boys and dogs can have a good runabout. Here, have a biccie.' Betty passed me the plate of biscuits.

I bit into a chocolate digestive not really wanting it. 'My favourite,' I said for manners. I stood up and went over to the window. Nathan and Jack ran around the lawn with Kerry and Ginny bouncing across the grass. John was so patient throwing balls to the dogs in turn. It was hard to believe that he and Betty were now our closest friends. It seemed a long time ago when Betty, Miss Jones, was my schoolteacher. I moved back to Betty and sat down.

'So, how's it going with Ginny?' Betty asked. 'Is she settling down?'

'Err, what do you think? And how about you old girl?' I stroked Tassles who had curled up on the floor by my feet.

'Poor girl doesn't know what's going on with Kerry bounding around her all the time. 'You're getting old and tired, aren't you, girl?' Betty gently ruffled Tassles' ear.

'She's still a beauty though.'

Mandy came back into the room. 'That's better.' She sat next to me. 'I feel a bit more human now. I hope I haven't used all the hot water.'

'I'm sure it will be fine,' Betty said. 'I switched the immersion heater on before you arrived. So, tell me what's been happening since we came up for Jack's birthday party? You said something about Alice and the twins. What's that all about?'

I clenched my fists. 'Robert's been beating the living daylights out of her. That's what.'

'You're kidding?'

'I kid not. And if it hadn't been for Mandy tackling her, we may never have got to the bottom of it. The bastard cracked her ribs of all things.'

'George.' Mandy shook her head.

198

'Excuse my language. But would you believe my stupid sister still wants to stay with him? Blames herself.'

'They say that happens a lot. But at least she hasn't gone back to him.'

'No but she wants to. Before it was just her being more interested in becoming bloody Lady of the Manor than her own health but now...'

Mandy touched my hand. 'Okay, George. Calm down.'

I pushed her hand away. 'I am calm. For Pete's sake, Mandy, stop going on at me. Actually Betty, do you mind if I take a bath. See if I can get rid of this rotten headache?'

'No of course not. Dinner won't be ready for at least another hour and as you've seen, the boys and John are having a good time out in the garden. Would you like some painkillers?'

'No. I'll try without first.'

'Use the Radox,' Betty said. 'It'll help you relax.'

'Thanks.' I kissed Mandy on the forehead and whispered, 'Sorry,' before trudging up the dark-brown carpeted stairs.

I ran the bath, picked up the box and tipped the pine salts into the running water, before climbing in. I had been a bit of a grump of late, I lay back and tried to relax. It was all too much with this business of Alice, and Simon. I'd make it up to Jack and Mandy later. I closed my eyes.

*

Blazing sun shining through the curtains disturbed me. I turned over in bed to find Mandy had already gone. I picked up my watch to check the time. Nine o'clock. Why hadn't anyone woken me? I slid out of the sheets and slipped on a robe from the back of the door. Betty and John were always so considerate making sure we could travel light. As I stepped out onto the landing, I listened for sounds of life downstairs but it was silent. I quickly showered and brushed my teeth before slinging on a

T-shirt and jeans. The aroma of bacon crept upstairs. I headed down towards the kitchen.

'Where is everyone?' I asked Betty.

'They've taken the dogs to the park.'

'Mandy should've woken me. I'm really sorry.'

Betty came towards me and patted my shoulder. 'It was obvious you needed to rest. Now sit down, have some breakfast and then you and I can have a chat.'

I pulled a chair up to the table.

'Pour yourself coffee and orange juice.' Using a fish slice, Betty scooped three rashers of bacon and two eggs onto a plate. 'Here get stuck into that.'

'Thanks, Betty. You're so good to me.'

Two slices of toast popped up in the toaster. Betty padded back over to the counter, returning with a rack of toast. She eased herself down on a chair opposite me and poured out a cup of black coffee just like I drank mine.

I dipped the toast into the egg yolk. 'This is great. Thank you. I hadn't realised how hungry I was.'

'I'm not surprised, you didn't come down after your bath last night so missed dinner.'

'I'm sorry about that. My head hurt too much and I needed to close my eyes in a dark room.' I put my knife and fork down in the finished position. 'That was delicious. Thank you.'

'Now while we're alone, would you like to tell me what's going on with you?'

I shook my head. 'Honestly, Betty, you don't want to know.'

'I do and that's why I asked. So, while we're alone, spill.'

I sighed. 'Where to start?'

'From the very beginning as they say in the song.'

I shook my head. 'Well…'

'Go on.'

'What did Mandy tell you last night?'

200

'Not a lot.'

'I mentioned Robert had been abusing Alice but what I didn't get to tell you was the girls are still with the Sanders.'

'My God, poor Alice.'

'I know. Grace went to collect them but bloody Lord Sanders wouldn't let them go. Said Alice was making up the whole saga. Practically threw Grace out. I wanted to go round there but Grace said it's got to be done legally. I tell you, Betty, I reckon it's only a matter of time before Alice goes back to him. They're having mediation.'

'Is the mediation to get a reconciliation?'

'Not if I or Grace can help it but you know what? Who could blame Alice for going back with him? If I had the choice of risking my own health or not seeing Jack again, I'd choose Jack every time. Yet we're preventing Alice.' I tutted. 'Grace should have let me sort out Sanders in the beginning. It's just like when she left me at Granville Hall. Now the twins have been left at the Sanders.'

'I think you're underestimating your mother. What could you have done that she couldn't?'

'I could have given Sanders a good thumping for starters.' I gave a half-hearted laugh.

'And what would that have achieved? You up in court. How would that have helped your sister or the girls?'

'That's what Grace said. I've failed Alice.'

'No, you haven't. You'd have failed her if you'd gone up there causing a scene. And don't underestimate your mother's influence. Grace Gilmore has clout worldwide. She'll get Alice her children back.'

'Even if you're right about that there's still Simon…'

'What about Simon?' Betty poured us another cup of coffee.

201

'I think he's drinking again. He's on edge just like last time.' I pressed my forehead. 'I just don't know how much more I can take.'

'Gosh what a mess. No wonder you're having headaches. I'm sure if Simon is drinking, with your patience and guidance, he'll beat the demon drink again.' She took a sip from her cup. 'So, tell me, George, how long have you been having these headaches?'

'I didn't say I had, other than last night.'

'George?'

'All right. A few weeks. I take painkillers but they don't touch it.'

'Have you seen your GP?'

'Hell no. It's just a headache.'

'A headache that you've had for a few weeks and hasn't been relieved by medication. It could be migraine brought on by stress. You need to sort it out. You can't go on speaking to your wife like that. Mandy's a good woman. Loyal and hardworking. And she doesn't deserve to be treated the way you spoke to her last night.'

'I know. I'll make it up to her.'

'See that you do.' Betty poked my arm gently. 'And talk to her. She's not a mind reader. Look why don't you take her out later? Jack and Ginny will be fine with me and John. Give you a chance to talk. What do you think?'

'Thanks. That sounds like an excellent idea.'

'Maybe arrange to meet Ben and Susie too. A little bit of relaxation and socialising is what you both need.'

'Yes, it would be good to see the old mucker again. It's been a while as they didn't make Jack's birthday party.'

'Make sure you allow some alone time for you and Mandy beforehand. Book a table somewhere for dinner and meet Ben and Susie later.'

'Thanks, Betty.' I squeezed her hand. 'What would I do without you?'

Chapter 4

George

Mandy looked stunning. Her new dress showed off all her curves and she had her hair down over her shoulders. I'd forgotten how gorgeous she was. I was a lucky man. I itched to kiss her neck just above that cameo choker. Avoiding the lit candle, I stretched my arm across the table and took her hand. 'I'm sorry for being such a misery guts lately.'

'That's okay,' she said.

'No, no, Mandy, it isn't. I shouldn't have spoken to you or Jack like I did yesterday. Everything's just been getting on top of me.'

Mandy gripped my hand. 'I understand. This Alice business hasn't been easy on any of us.'

'You're right but Simon's been on my mind too.'

'Simon? He's not drinking again, is he?'

'I think so. I've no proof but some of the signs are there. I should've told you.'

'Yes, you should have.' She squeezed my fingers lightly. 'But you're telling me now, that's the main thing.'

The waiter came across with our order. We moved our hands away from the table. 'Madam.' The waiter placed a plate of moussaka down for Mandy and one for me. 'Your side salads will be here in a moment.' He picked up the bottle of rosé from the ice bucket and poured wine into each of our glasses.

'Thank you,' Mandy said, taking a sip.

'And here are your side salads.' The waiter signalled the waitress to put them down on the table before they both left.

'This is a lovely surprise, George. Thank you.'

'It's the least you deserve. I really am sorry.'

Mandy ate a forkful of moussaka. 'This is delicious. My favourite dish.'

'I know, that's why I booked here. It's the best Greek restaurant in Wintermore.'

Mandy laughed. 'It's the only one, isn't it?'

'Well yes.' I chuckled. 'But that's beside the point.' I drank a mouthful of wine. 'Betty seems confident Alice will get the girls back.'

'Let's hope so.'

'And you know how I've been blaming Grace. Betty made me realise Grace made the right decision choosing the legal route, and with her influence and my status Alice should regain custody before too long.'

Mandy placed her hand on mine. 'I think Betty's right.'

'Betty also thinks I should be able to help Simon get back on track too. That is, if he is drinking.'

'Sure you will, just like last time. And remember, you can always talk to me. I don't understand why you didn't.'

'You've had a lot going on. What with Jack, and your new teaching post. I didn't want to worry you.'

'School and Jack aren't an issue but I must admit I've been feeling pretty guilty betraying Alice like I did. If I hadn't told you then she'd still have her girls.'

'And she could be dead so don't feel guilty for speaking out.' I bit into a cherry tomato that squirted onto the tablecloth. 'Oops.'

Mandy laughed as she mopped it up with her napkin. 'I think it's only a matter of time before she goes back to him. She's been seeing him, you know?'

'For the mediation, yes.'

'Not just that. They've met up a few times for a drink.'

'What?'

'Shh. Only in public places. She needs to find a way back to her girls. And please don't tell her that you know, she's barely speaking to me as it is. If she finds out I've told you' – Mandy let out a deep breath – 'she'll never speak to me again.'

I gritted my teeth. 'I promise I won't let on.'

'Thanks. And from now on you and I are going to promise to tell each other everything. It worries me when you lose your temper and I don't know why. I thought you'd gone off me.'

'Never. You're my world. I'll never tire of you.'

*

We pushed open the door to *The Woodcroft* and looked at each other in surprise.

'Good Lord,' I said, 'it's like stepping into a different world.'

'I hope the Ladies is still in the same place. I'm dying to go.'

I glanced up towards the right-hand wall. 'Yes, it is. Look.' I pointed to the sign. 'Toilets.'

'Phew. I'll just be a minute then. Can you order me a lager and lime, please?' Mandy practically ran across the loud patterned carpet.

I made my way over to the bar where a woman with long blonde hair approached me.

'Hi,' she said, 'what can I get you?'

'Oh.' I looked around for the landlord. 'Where's Bob?'

'He retired some time ago.'

'I see a lot has changed.' I tapped the rich mahogany counter. 'This is very smart.'

'Sheila and John did a complete refurbishment when they took over. It's their night off so you're in luck, you have me.' She held her arms out wide and laughed. 'So, Mister, what's your poison?'

'Two pints of John Smiths, half a lager and lime and...' I spotted Mandy coming out of the toilets. I mouthed, 'What does Susie drink?'

'Woodpecker,' she called. 'I've left my coat in the loo. I'll be two ticks.' She disappeared again.

'And a pint of Woodpecker,' I added to the barmaid. Susie was the only woman I knew who drank pints. Mandy wouldn't dream of it.

'Coming up.' The barmaid took a glass and pulled the first pint from the beer cask.

'So, when did all this happen?'

'The takeover? A year ago. Are you from round here?'

'Originally, yes, but moved when I was a child. And you? I've not seen you in here before.'

'Grew up in Wintermore but moved to London. Things didn't work out so now I'm back.'

A hand touched my shoulders. I turned to see Mandy. 'I didn't hear you creep up on me. Did you know Bob's retired?'

'No. Oh that's a shame. How would I know, anyway?'

'I wondered if Susie had mentioned it when you've been on the phone.'

'No, she didn't. Maybe she didn't think it was significant. I can't believe Bob's retired, I thought he'd be behind this bar until they carried him out in a box.'

'Yeah, me too.'

The barmaid placed the final drink onto the bar. 'That will be...'

'Kathleen Meadows,' Mandy said in a high-pitched voice, smiling, 'it can't be.'

'If it isn't my old mate Mandy Brown?' The barmaid flicked her long blonde hair away from her face. 'Well I never.'

'It's Mandy Granville now.'

'You two know each other?' I asked.

'We were best friends until Kathleen disappeared one day without telling anyone where she was going.' Mandy turned to the barmaid. 'Why didn't you keep in touch?'

Kathleen shrugged her shoulders. 'You know how it is.'

The pub door swung open. Footsteps alerted me to turn around and I spotted Ben heading our way. When they reached us, I clasped Ben in a bear hug. 'Where's Susie,' I asked. 'I've got your drinks in.'

'She'll be here in a minute.' Ben took out a packet of Embassy. 'Ciggie?'

'No thanks,' I said. 'Why don't you take a pew? I'm not sure how long I could be waiting. Mandy seems to know the barmaid. They're having a right chinwag.'

'They were bessie mates at school. Susie too, although I think she felt a little left out at times.' He picked up his and Susie's pints and headed for the new bench seats across the room.

The barmaid moved towards me. 'Can I get Mister Mandy anything else?'

'A couple of packets of cheese and onion, please. Call me George, by the way.'

'Kathleen.' She leaned towards the back of the bar and grabbed the Golden Wonder crisps.

I handed over a ten-pound note. 'Keep the change.'

'Cheers.' She turned to Mandy. 'You married a millionaire or something?'

Mandy laughed.

I picked up our drinks. 'Mandy, we're over there' – I pointed to the window on the right – 'don't be long.'

'I won't.'

On reaching the table I placed our drinks down and sat on a chair opposite the bench seat. 'Mandy will be over in a mo.'

'So how are you, me old mate?' Ben asked.

'Good thanks. So, tell me about this Kathleen Meadows.'

'She was at school with us. Maybe she joined after you'd gone. She and Mandy were thick as thieves until Kathleen disappeared out of the blue. No one really knew why, or heard from her, and then last year she turned back up. Still don't know what the story is. Maybe your Mand will find out.'

Susie burst in. 'Sorry, George, Ben's mam collared me as I was going out the door. Where's Mandy?'

'Talking to the barmaid.'

Susie looked towards the bar and frowned. 'Oh. She's on tonight, is she? I'll tell you what, I'll whip up there and drag Mandy back.' Susie marched up to the bar.

Ben ripped open the crisps. 'What's the occasion for dinner then?'

I took a mouthful from the John Smiths and wiped my lips. 'Nice. I'd forgotten how good this stuff is.'

'Don't you drink at home?'

'Not beer. Only wine or spirits in our house.' I looked towards the girls at the bar. 'They look like they're hatching a plan, don't they?'

Ben laughed. 'Yeah. They were always like that. That Kathleen's a good-looking woman. I'm surprised she's not been snapped up. And with tits like that. Cor...'

Ben was right. Kathleen was quite striking. Looked more in her twenties than thirties but then so did Mandy. I was glad Mandy didn't hang her breasts out for all and sundry to ogle, or wear that heavy make-up. 'Here they come now,' I said.

Mandy and Susie waltzed over chatting and giggling. It was good to see Mandy carefree for a change.

'You were saying about the special occasion?' Ben said.

'No special occasion. I've just been neglecting my wife lately.'

'I see. Where did you go?'

'That new place in the High Street. *Olives and Meze*. Do you know it?'

'Too posh for the likes of me.' Ben picked up his pint, slurped the beer back and burped. 'Excuse me. See what I mean? You can't take me anywhere.'

'No, we can't.' Susie took a gulp of cider before slumping down next to Ben. She wiped her lip. 'So how come you guys are up this way?'

Mandy was standing behind me. She placed her arms around my neck. 'Things were getting a little heavy at home and George needed a break. We both did, really, didn't we, love?'

I reached up and touched her hand. 'We certainly did.'

'Well it's good to see you both,' Ben said. 'You staying at Betty's tonight?'

'Yes. It was Betty who suggested I take Mandy out. It's been a while since we've had time, just the two of us. Hasn't it, darling?' I said as Mandy sat down.

'It has.' Her eyes sparkled when she smiled.

'What have you girls been cooking up?' I asked.

'Never could get anything past you, could I George Granville?' She picked up her glass and took a sip. 'Mmm.'

'Come on then, tell me.'

'Well...'

By this time Mandy had the attention of Ben too.

'Go on,' I said.

Mandy laughed. 'I've invited Kathleen to Granville Hall. We've not set a date yet but I thought Ben and Susie could come too.'

'That sounds nice,' I said, hoping things had settled down a bit at home before the visit.

'We thought we'd go to a show,' Susie said. 'And you and Ben can look after Jack. You don't mind, do you, George?'

'No, of course not. I think it's an excellent idea. Is there a Mr Kathleen?' I nibbled on a crisp, not because I was hungry but because they were there.

'Not at the moment, apparently. I can't believe how we lost touch. We were like the three musketeers at school. Weren't we, Susie?'

'Well… To be honest sometimes I felt a little left out.'

Mandy frowned. 'I don't know why. You never were. Oh, I've just remembered my mac's on a stool up there.' She disappeared to the bar for a few seconds and was back again with Kathleen in tow. Mandy laid her coat on a spare chair.

'Room for a little 'un for five mins?' Kathleen asked.

'Sure. Grab a stool,' I said.

'Well, Mand, are you going to introduce me to your old man properly?' Kathleen smiled as she sat down, crossing her long legs. Ben couldn't take his eyes off them.

'Sorry. That was very remiss of me,' Mandy said, 'George, Kathleen. Kathleen, George or I should say, Lord Granville.'

'No way. So you really did marry a millionaire. You lucky bitch. I love your dress by the way. Looks expensive but then I suppose money's no object for you anymore. That red really suits you. Crimson, I reckon. And I love that halter neck. Ideal in this heat.'

'My mother-in-law designed it.'

'Wow. Some mother-in-law.'

'Grace Gilmore,' Susie said.

'Not *the* Grace Gilmore?' Kathleen stared wide-eyed.

'Yes, Mandy's mother-in-law is the designer and founder of *House of Grace*.' Susie smirked, sitting back, self-assured. 'Grace has designed me a couple of outfits too. In fact, she designed what I'm wearing now.'

211

'No way. I love your culottes. They make you look really trim. I'd love a *House of Grace* designer dress. Way out of my price range though. How did you afford yours, Susie?'

'They were a gift from Grace.'

'Wow. You lucky cow. You know, I've always wanted to work in fashion. I'd love to meet Grace Gilmore. Do you think something could be arranged when I come down to yours?' Kathleen looked at Mandy and Mandy looked at me.

'I'm sure something can be sorted,' I said.

'Kathleen,' Susie said in a loud voice, 'you've got a customer at the bar.'

'So I have.' Kathleen stood up. 'I'd better go. Nice meeting you, George, and wonderful to see you again, Mand. Lord Granville, I look forward to coming up to Gerrard's Cross and meeting your mam.'

'See you soon.' Mandy got up and kissed Kathleen on the cheek.

'Nice meeting you too.' I took a gulp of beer.

Susie muttered something incoherent under her breath before turning to Mandy. 'Shall we have some girl time while the men catch up?'

'Sure.' Mandy swapped places with Ben. She stroked the fabric on the seat. 'I love this pink-velvet. So posh.'

Susie brushed her fingers through the pile. 'Better than that drab stuff they had before.'

Ben and I caught up on small talk for the next couple of hours while the girls giggled about old times and then Mandy swapped places again.

'How's your mam doing?' I asked Ben.

'She's fostering now.' He shook his head. 'I've no idea where she gets her energy from.'

'We find it hard enough looking after one. And, of course, not forgetting the dog.' Mandy giggled.

'How you getting on with the dog, Jenny, isn't it?' Ben brushed crisp crumbs off his shirt.

'Ginny,' I said. 'All right but she's a bit of a monster travelling in the car. She keeps standing up and blocking the rear-view mirror.'

'She'll settle down soon.' Mandy stroked my arm.

I took a deep breath. 'My wife's right. Ginny's just a puppy and will calm down soon.' I added under my breath, 'At least I hope she will.'

Kathleen rang the bell. 'Last orders.'

'That time already. We should make a move.' Mandy got up, took her mac off the spare stool, and hung it across her arm.

'You're right.' I stood up. 'It's been great seeing you guys. We'll sort out you coming up to the Hall in the next few weeks.' I kissed Susie on the cheek and patted Ben on the back.

'Time we made a move too.' Ben swigged the rest of his pint. He arched his back rising from the chair. 'Are you ready, Sues?'

'I'm ready.' Susie put her jacket on.

'Bye Kathleen,' Mandy shouted as we opened the door. 'I'll be in touch.'

Outside the pub, Susie said to Mandy, 'It's been fab seeing you. I'll leave you to organise the show.'

'Sure,' Mandy answered, 'although... if Kathleen wants to meet Grace, we may not have time to do both.'

'Oh okay. Do you still want me to come?'

'Absolutely, silly.' Mandy hugged Susie.

We waved Ben and Susie off and waited for them to disappear from view. Mandy shivered. I put her coat around her shoulders before taking her into my arms. 'It's got a little nippy, hasn't it? Have you had a good evening?'

'Lovely, thank you.'

'I love you, you know?' I kissed her full on the lips. 'I don't say it enough and I know I take you for granted but you're my world. Thank you for putting up with a miserable old chap like me.'

Mandy kissed me back.

Chapter 5

George

September 1986

Ginny ran into the conservatory from the garden leaving her muddy footprints on the white marble tiles. Wagging her tail, she puffed and panted, hanging her tongue out.

Elizabeth entered the room, glared at the dog, and sighed. 'Really?'

'Sorry, Aunt Elizabeth.' Jack bent his head. 'She escaped before I could clean her up.'

'That's okay, Son' – I rose from my chair – 'no harm done, chuck me the towel.'

Jack threw the psychedelic rag. I got down on the floor and wiped the dog's paws. 'There you go, girl.' I patted her on the back. 'You'll do.'

'For heaven's sake, George, look at the floor.' Elizabeth tutted. 'I told you keeping a dog inside was a big mistake. She should be in a kennel.'

Jack squeezed his eyes shut. 'Dad, please... Ginny hasn't got to live outside, has she?'

'No. She hasn't.' I turned to my aunt. 'It's not a big deal. Jack, take the dog and go and find Mum.'

He hooked his hand in the dog's collar and ran from the room.

I raised my voice. 'You know you've upset Jack?'

'I'm sorry if I upset your son but really…' Rain pelted down on the window. 'Good Lord look at that.' Elizabeth moved to stand next to me by the French doors.

'Jack got in just in time,' I said. 'Listen, if it's the extra work you're worried about, I'll clean the bloody floor myself.'

'Hardly an example to the staff seeing Lord Granville mopping floors. Is it?'

'You know me. I've never been one to have airs and graces.' I shook my head. 'You know, Aunt Elizabeth, everyone in this household gains pleasure from Ginny except you, and let's face it, you're just stubborn.'

'I've got enough to deal with at the moment.' Elizabeth stared out of the window.

'What are you talking about?' I placed my hand on her shoulder. 'Something's upset you. Sit down and tell me about it.'

Elizabeth eased herself down onto the window seat. 'I think he's drinking again,' she said in a soft voice.

My suspicions had been right after all. I sat down next to my aunt. 'Go on.'

'The signs are there. His appearance. He's been snappy. Will you speak to him?'

'Do you think he'll listen to me?'

'He did last time.'

'Then I'll have a word, but you lighten up a bit and get to know the puppy.'

'I'll try.'

'Where's Simon now?'

'In his office.'

I patted her hand. 'I'll go now.'

'Thanks, George. I knew I could depend on you.'

I left the conservatory and wandered down the hallway. There always seemed to be something these days, as one problem was sorted another started. At least my headaches were under control since visiting the doctor.

At the right of the study door, I stopped to admire the commissioned painting hanging on the wall. It had arrived yesterday and was a good likeness of my family. Mandy and I stood behind Jack who was sitting on a chair hugging Ginny.

I took a deep breath and tapped on the study door before pushing it open. Simon sat at his desk, his head bent over a ledger.

'Hello, Simon,' I said.

'George. Take a seat.'

'Thanks.' I grabbed a chair and placed it at the side of the desk. 'How's it going?'

'Hmm…'

'What does that mean?'

'I've been meaning to speak to you?'

'About what?' The room reeked of whisky.

Simon mumbled. 'The estate.'

'What about the estate?'

'I think we're losing money.'

'I see. Since when?'

'A while.'

'Why are you only mentioning it now?'

'Because you've had enough on your plate. I planned to tell you after Jack's birthday but then all that business with Alice.' He put his pen down and looked at me. 'There just never seemed to be the right time.'

'Let's get the accountant in to check the figures and if there's a problem we'll come up with a solution. To be honest, Simon, right now I'm more worried about you.'

'In what way?'

'I'm concerned you may have been tempted to take a drink.'

'What? Definitely not.'

'Are you sure?'

Simon frowned. 'Of course I'm bloody sure.' He stood up, sloped across to the window, and peered out.

I got up and went over to him. 'Come off it, Uncle, I can smell it on you. It was like entering a brewery when I walked in here.'

'I don't know what you're talking about.' He kept his back to me.

'I think you do.'

'You're talking rubbish. Don't you think I've enough to worry about without your absurd accusations.'

I turned him to face me. 'Simon,' I said in a soft voice. 'We know.'

'What do you mean?'

'Elizabeth asked me to speak to you.'

He put his hand to his forehead. 'For Christ's sake, there's nothing to know. I'm not drinking and that's that.'

'How bad has it got?'

'Stop nagging. I've had the odd one here and there, that's all.'

'Don't give me that. It's never that.'

'What the hell do you know? Get off my case.' Simon knocked a batch of binders from the bookcase.

'Look at the state of you.' I bent down, scooped up the files, and returned them to the shelf. 'And when was the last time you had a shave or combed your hair?' No wonder Elizabeth was suspicious. I shook my head. 'Do we need to get you into rehab again?'

'Leave it out.' He pushed me away and stormed out of the office.

I followed him down the hallway and out to the garden. When he almost tripped on the outside step, I said, 'For crying out loud man, you can't even walk properly. How many have you had?'

'I told you. Just the one. I also told you to fuckin' leave me alone. Can't a man have a bit of peace?'

'No. Not when you're like this. I promised Elizabeth I'd talk to you.'

'Well now you have, so you can bugger off.'

'I'm not going anywhere. Vikki gets home in a few days, do you really want her to see her father like this?'

'Like what?'

'Like a drunken slob.'

'Fuck off.'

I shoved his arm. 'Whatever, Simon. There's no point trying to reason with a drunk.' I left him slumped on the step in the rain.

*

'George, do you have a minute?' Elizabeth asked as I saw Mandy and Jack off to school.

'Yes, sure.' I closed the front door.

'How did you get on with Simon yesterday? He didn't come to bed last night.'

'There was no reasoning with him but I'm off to see him now, hoping he'll be sober so I can try and get through to him.'

She clasped my wrist. 'Thank you, George. I've just seen him charging into his study about five minutes ago. I called after him but he ignored me and banged the door shut.'

'Don't worry, I'll go and see him.'

I walked down the corridor and stopped outside the closed door. I knocked and waited. When there was no answer I turned the handle and entered the office. Simon had a decanter of Scotch in his hand and was about to pour some in a glass.

'Don't,' I said.

219

He looked up. His hand was shaking. 'I just need a little one to steady my nerves.'

'Put it down and let's talk.'

'What's there to talk about?'

'Your daughter and your wife for starters. Put the bottle down and sit.'

He placed the decanter on the desk and slumped into the chair, putting his hands to his face. 'What about my family?'

'If your daughter sees you like this she'll be heartbroken. You know she has you up on a pedestal.'

Simon glared at me. Was I getting through to him?

'Seriously, Uncle, this isn't going to go away on its own. You need help. And what about the state your poor wife's in?'

'What do you mean?'

'I've just left her almost in tears and we both know it's unheard of for Elizabeth to show her emotions. What are we going to do? Do you want me to speak to Grace about getting you into rehab again?'

'No.'

I pulled up a chair next to him and placed my hand on his arm. 'What then? It's not going to go away on its own,' I repeated.

'I can sort myself out. I just need to remedy this estate problem.'

'I told you before not to worry about the estate. There are plenty of options to increase revenue if need be. For example, open up more of the grounds, add a crazy golf or something. The maize has been successful. Maybe we can do kids' parties. Horse riding. Lots of potential. Right now, my main concern is to get you back on track.'

Simon lifted his head and looked me in the eye. 'I saw my brother the other day.'

I frowned. 'Really.'

220

He ran his tongue across his lips. 'It's agony not being able to see him. His wife's left him, you know? And she's taken the children.'

'No, I didn't know. Probably not before time.'

'But, George, he's remorseful about what happened all those years ago. And he's dry now. I know I promised Grace I'd have nothing else to do with him but do you think she'll allow Richard back here?'

'What. You've got to be fuckin' joking. That man will be allowed back in this house over my dead body. Never mind what Grace thinks.' I shook my head. 'After what he did.'

'Release me from my promise then? So I can see him, away from the house. Neither you nor Grace would have to see him.'

'I doubt it.'

'Please, George. I miss not having him around. Twins should be together. It's tearing me apart knowing he's in pain and I can't help him. If I'm honest I think that's the trigger... you know...'

'Emotional blackmail now, Simon? I never credited you with that.'

'Sorry.' He lowered his head. 'I didn't mean... I just meant... Look please... Can you at least think about it? I promise I won't allow him on Granville property at all.'

'I'll consider speaking to Grace.' I put my arm around my uncle. It must've been tough for him not to have been able to see Richard. And Richard was Vikki's uncle after all.

Chapter 6

Grace

Alice had gone for mediation and the twins were still at Stonesay Manor with the Sanders. I had the house to myself which was a rare occasion these days. I'd recently discovered that Alice had been seeing Robert outside of the mediation sessions and I intended to do everything in my power to prevent a reconciliation. It was a hard fight with the legal system, but under no circumstances would I allow the doors to close like all those years ago when I'd lost George. This time I was confident we'd win.

I peered out into the garden at the burnt-orange cactus dahlias. They'd one week left of bloom at the most before the tubers needed to be brought inside to protect them from frost. I'd loved that flower for so long. It prompted me to think back to Katy, Jack, and what was Katy's boyfriend's name? Eddy. That was it. I wondered what Katy would have been like if she'd lived. Would she have married? Had children? Such a waste ending her life like that. And so young. *Stop it Grace. Stop being so melancholy.* I didn't know what the matter was with me these days. Maybe it was all this to-do with Alice and Robert. And what was it George wanted to discuss with me today? Hopefully not more problems. The clock in the hallway chimed midday. He'd be here any minute. I wandered out of the drawing room into the corridor just as he walked through the front door.

'Hello, Grace.' He looked at me closely. 'Are you okay?'

Just a little tired. Too much has been going on. I hope you're not the bearer of bad news. I don't think I can take much more.'

'No. Well err...'

'What is it?'

'Nothing. How do you fancy going to that new pub down the road for lunch? You look like you could do with getting out of the house for a while.'

'New pub?'

'*Japonica Arms*. I've heard they do a nice cheese quiche and chips on Fridays.'

'That sounds like a lovely idea. You're right, it will do me good to get out for a while. I've been trying to complete the designs ready for the spring fashion show but haven't been able to get them right.'

'Maybe you should have a separate workplace away from the house? Too many distractions here I imagine.'

'You have a point.'

George smiled. 'I've an idea but we'll discuss it in the pub.'

'You're not going to leave me in suspense?'

George nodded his head. 'I am. How soon before you're ready?'

'A couple of minutes to freshen up. The sooner we get to the pub, the sooner you can tell me your idea.' I left George sitting on a chair in the hallway with his head buried in *The Times*.

I dabbed a bit of powder on my face and traced a line of plum gel across my lips, reminding me of the first time I wore lipstick. I was sixteen again. Katy's mum was giving me my first ever makeover. *Stop it, Grace*. What was with me today? I left the bathroom and grabbed my burgundy trench coat from the wardrobe and rushed back to George. Maybe his idea would help me out of these doldrums.

The pub was empty apart from three staff members. A woman in her thirties wiped down the tables and added beer mats.

'Why don't you choose a seat and I'll pop to the bar,' George said. 'Quiche and chips twice.' He grinned.

I opted for a table by the window with a good view of a small pond with ducks swimming. I laughed to myself as a couple of mallards ducked their heads into the water, sprang back up and flapped their wings. Oh no, I was sixteen again and Jack was introducing me to feeding bread to the ducks for the first time.

'What is it?' George asked as he joined me. He placed a pint of beer and half a lager down on the table. 'Are you unwell?'

'I don't know, George. I can't put my finger on it but I keep slipping back to the past. I keep wondering whether today's significant or what. I'm just...'

'You're not falling back into depression, are you?'

'No, I don't think so. Like I said, earlier, I think I'm just tired. There's been far too much worry of late. Anyway, tell me about your idea. I hate being left in suspense.'

'You know I've been working on that farm down the road from Granville?'

'Yes, how's it going? Barn conversion, isn't it?'

'It's going well. Should be finished in a couple of weeks.'

'Wonderful. I imagine the developer will put it up for sale.'

'It would be perfect for you. Plenty of room for everyone.'

'George.' I laughed. 'You're not suggesting I move again? It's only a year since you got me to move last time.'

'But you've never been happy there.'

'You're right. It's never felt like home. Not like the house in Cheam which was filled with warmth.'

A pub-hand in a red-striped uniform stood close to our table and asked, 'Two quiche and chips?'

George put his hand up. 'Yes, that's us thank you.'

The lad smiled as he set the plates in front of us. 'I'll get some cutlery. Would you like any sauces?'

'Mayonnaise and ketchup would be nice,' George answered. 'How about you, Grace?'

I looked up at the young man and smiled. 'Just vinegar for me, please.'

He disappeared from our view but was back in no time with cutlery and condiments. 'Enjoy your meal,' he said before leaving us alone.

'Come and see it.' George cut into his quiche. 'Mmm… the rumours are true. This quiche is delicious.'

I took a bite. 'They have a good cook. Good service too.'

'Well… Will you?'

'Will I what?'

'Come and view the property.'

'Tell me more about it.'

'It's got three barn conversions.'

'Three?'

'Yes. An eight-bedroomed house with four bathrooms, a two-bedroom bungalow, perfect for Joan and Ted, and the final one is a house with four bedrooms. Ideal for Alice and the twins.'

'It does sound perfect. Yes, all right, it can't hurt to take a look.'

'You're going to love it. It's got a stable block conversion too which will make a perfect working space, and wait for it… it has another stable block so you could keep a couple of horses.' George beamed.

A group of couples ploughed into the pub. 'Quick, get that table over there,' one of the men said.

225

Three women headed off to the back of the pub giggling while the men queued at the bar. Tobacco stench travelled from the stocky man's Tom Thumb cigar.

George looked at me. I sniffed and held my hand over my mouth.

'If you're going to smoke a cigar for goodness sake at least smoke a proper one,' George whispered.

'Shh. They'll hear you.' I chuckled.

'Well at least I made you laugh.'

'They must've been to a wedding or something as they've got carnations pinned to their leather jackets.'

'I think you're right, but never mind them. How's Alice doing?' George took a drink from his pint. Before I had a chance to answer, the man with a ponytail up at the bar asked the barman in a loud voice, 'Have you got any darts, mate?'

I glared at the barman. He said something to the guy who turned around to face us. 'Sorry, Missus. Didn't mean to disturb you.'

I smiled before switching back to George. 'Alice. Well…'

'Yes…'

'She's not doing as well as we'd hoped. She's talking about going back to him.' I sighed.

'Hmm.' George bit his lip. 'I had a feeling it might come to that. You can't really blame her, though, can you? If it were me and the only way I could be with Jack... Well, I'd move heaven and earth.'

The group at the bar started singing and one yelled out towards the women. 'Jane, was yours a vodka and lime?'

'Look,' George said to me, 'why don't we head over to those armchairs near the fireplace when we've finished our meal. Hopefully, it'll be quieter so we can talk.'

'I'm pretty much finished now, anyway. To be honest I wasn't that hungry. Do they do coffee in here?'

'I'm sure they will if I ask but why not have a liqueur instead?'

'A much better idea.' I stood up away from the table. 'What would you like?'

'Surprise me.'

'Grab that table before someone else does. I'll go and order.'

I managed to claim a table with two armchairs seconds before another couple came along. The young woman tutted. They were obviously looking for a quiet place too as the pub had filled up. It was dimmer in this corner, tucked out of the way, and not close to any windows but the glowing fire was welcome. I found the amber flames calming. I thought about the property George had mentioned and it did indeed seem perfect. And it sounded like a home for Alice and the twins once she gained custody. There was no way I'd allow her to go back to him.

'Here you go.' George placed a tumbler of Baileys and ice in front of me, and a small flute of something for himself. 'Cheers.' He raised his glass.

'Cheers. What's in yours?'

'Cointreau. Would you have preferred that?'

'No, you got it exactly right. Baileys is my favourite.'

'I thought so.' He took a sip. 'Now, where were we? Ah yes. As I was saying before we were rudely interrupted by that rowdy lot, you can't blame Alice for wanting to go back with Robert if it means getting her kids back. She must be missing them like hell. It's been over two months and while I know she's been allowed short visits those girls must wonder what is going on.'

'I agree. However, with a bit of luck the court should decide in a few weeks and I'm confident they'll favour Alice. Particularly as they've had access to her hospital records.' I sipped the liqueur.

'I hope you're right.'

'How's young Jack anyway?' I asked changing the subject. 'And that gorgeous puppy?'

'They're both doing fine. Jack loves her. He's such a good boy. I do wish we had a brother or sister for him though. But then…'

I put my hand over his. 'There's still time.'

'Maybe.'

'Is everything okay with you and Mandy?'

'Oh yes, better than fine in fact.' He brushed his blond fringe away from his face.

'Shouldn't you get that cut?'

'Why?'

'It's rather long. Your grandfather would have had a fit.'

'A good job he's not here anymore then isn't it?' He rubbed his upper lip. 'Listen, Grace, there's something else I need to speak to you about.'

'Really? What's that then?'

'I'm not sure how…'

'You're making me worry now. For god's sake, just tell me.'

'It's Simon.'

'He's not ill, is he?'

'No. Well not that way. He's fallen off the wagon again and reckons he can get through it on his own without rehab but…'

'But?'

George chewed his lip and frowned. He took a big sigh. 'I promised him if he agreed to rehab that I'd speak to you.'

'You'd like me to sort it out? Why didn't you just say so instead of being cagey?'

'Well yes, but it isn't just that.'

'Then what?' I sipped the Baileys.

'I'm not quite sure how to bring this up so I'll just come out with it.' George looked straight at me. 'He's missing his brother.

Richard's wife has taken the children and left him. He needs Simon and I think Simon needs him and Simon was wondering…'

'Yes?'

George sighed again. 'He asked if you'd be willing to let Richard back on Granville property…'

'He asked what?' I said raising my voice.

'Don't worry, I told him in no uncertain terms what I thought about that idea.' He took a deep breath. 'However, I know this is still asking a lot from you, Grace, but…'

'Spit it out, George, for God's sake.'

'Do you think you could find it in your heart to release Simon from his promise not to see Richard again?'

I shivered remembering that man's hands all over me. 'That's still asking a lot. I thought we'd all agreed that man was to be out of our lives for good.'

'I know and I agree but… Simon says Richard's dry and he's not the same man who attacked you. You know how I feel about what he did to you but I understand where Simon's coming from. He says he's worried about the estate, but that's just an excuse. The estate is doing fine. The problem lies with him not seeing his brother. That's what's pushing him over the edge.I do think he needs Richard in his life.' George gripped my hand. 'Will you at least think about it?'

'I'll think about it, yes.'

'That's all we can ask.' George drank the dregs from his glass.

*

Max slammed his hand down on the arm of the couch. 'He's asked what? What the hell was he thinking?'

'I know.' I shrugged my shoulders. 'I could hardly believe it when George told me. However, his second request was to

229

release him from his promise not to have anything to do with the man. I can see where he's coming from. Maybe I should let bygones be bygones and it's not like I'll have to see him.'

'But after what he did to you?' Charlotte perched on the wing of my chair. 'Are you sure, darling?'

'No. I'm not sure. I don't know what to think.' I burst out crying.

'Darling.' Charlotte put her arm around me. 'This isn't like Grace Gilmore?'

'Well that's it,' Max said. 'Look what the thought of it has done to you. You tell George or Simon, whoever. You tell them *no*.'

'Oh, Max. It isn't as simple as that. I was like this before George brought up the subject. I don't know what's the matter with me. I keep breaking down, and I'm frightfully tired all the time.'

'I think a trip to the doctor is in order, don't you?' Charlotte turned towards Max, 'Sort out some coffee will you, darling?'

Max grunted. 'Ah, yes.' He stood up. 'I see, girls' talk.' He rubbed his hands. 'I'll go and chat to Steph in the kitchen for a while.'

'You're probably right,' I said to Charlotte as Max left the room. 'I'll ring the surgery tomorrow morning.'

'It sounds like the change to me. I was exactly like you. Hormones up the creek. Are you having trouble sleeping?'

'Yes.'

'And battling with the old weight gain?'

'Strangely enough, yes. I've never had to worry about carrying extra pounds in my life before but I've noticed a couple of extra inches around my midriff.'

Charlotte nodded her head. 'Hmm. I'll be surprised if the doctor tells you different. A good dose of HRT and you'll be right as rain. As for Richard. What do you really think?'

'I don't know. Life seems too short to hold grudges and it's not like he actually raped me, is it?'

'But he might have done if you hadn't woken up.'

'Simon's promised not to bring him to the Hall, or the grounds. I remember how hard I found it being estranged from my family and Simon has no one else but Richard. And if it's going to lessen the risk of him drinking…'

'What does Elizabeth say about it?'

'She was outraged at the thought of Richard being allowed back in the house, but considering the affect it's having on Simon not seeing his brother, she thinks I should agree to the twins seeing each other away from Granville. "After all," she said, "it won't have any impact on you at all." And maybe she's right?'

'Maybe. Don't rush into a decision though. Give it some more thought. And maybe wait until after you've seen the doctor.'

'I will.'

Charlotte lit up a cigarette. 'What's happening about Alice and that dickhead Robert?'

I shook my head. 'George thinks it's only a matter of time before they have a reconciliation.'

'And what do you think?'

'If I have my way he'll never set foot in my house again. I'm positive Alice will win the case. Particularly now they have proof of what he did to her.'

'I'm sure you're right, darling.' Charlotte placed her hand on top of mine. 'You've had a lot to contend with. I'm not surprised things are getting on top of you. Do you think she'll have the girls back by Christmas?'

'Oh yes. I'd say before October is out.'

'That soon?'

'I'm hoping so. She needs to be with her twins and hopefully that will put paid to any talk of reconciliation.'

'Fingers crossed. And how's our Nancy doing?'

'Buried herself in work. She's aiming to have a new textile line out in time for the Spring fashion show. I'm so behind on that.'

'Maybe you could do with some help?'

'I was thinking the same. Vikki's shown an interest. I thought I'd see if she fancied coming to work for me a couple of evenings after school and Saturdays. I'd need to check Elizabeth and Simon are okay about it, though.'

'Knock knock,' Max whispered as he tapped on the open door. 'Is it safe to come in yet?'

'It's safe.' I laughed as he peeped his head around the door.

Max pushed a hostess trolley into the room laden with coffee and scones. 'Afternoon tea.' He smirked.

Already I felt much better. Of course, Charlotte was right. It must be the menopause. I didn't know why I hadn't thought of that myself.

Chapter 7

Grace

October 1986

George shuffled a new pack of cards. He'd invited us all around for the evening but Alice had declined as she wanted to start planning the furnishing of her house on my new property, Appleyard Farm. She was positive the court would soon award her custody of the girls following the first hearing. I left her flicking through homeware catalogues. Nancy was meeting a client and Max and Charlotte didn't fancy driving all the way from Storik Sands. Therefore, apart from myself, it was George, Mandy, Elizabeth, Simon, and Charles sitting around the table. Charles, George's business partner, was in his fifties, distinguished with silvery hair, and stunning sapphire blue eyes that matched his tailored shirt. I wanted to be annoyed at the obvious fix-up but strangely I was drawn to this man who was nothing like Jack or Adriéne. In fact, rather than their slim physiques, Charles carried a little extra weight around his girth.

'Is Alice looking after your girls?' Mandy asked as we all sat around the table.

'She did offer but Joan and Ted had already jumped at the chance of coming over when they heard I was going out. Although Annalise pointed out they don't need babysitting as she's eleven.'

'How are Joan and Ted?' Simon took a sip from his glass of water.

'They're not getting any younger but keep themselves busy and fit. Ted's been painting the cottage ready for the sale while Joan makes lots of jam with whatever fruit is in the garden. I've brought a couple of jars this evening and passed them to Annie.'

Simon rubbed his hands. 'Thanks, Grace. I love Joan's jam. What flavour?'

'Raspberry.' I smiled.

'My favourite.' Simon licked his lips. 'I'll have that on my toast for breakfast.'

'If we've finished with the small talk, shall we begin?' George continued to shuffle the cards. 'Does everyone know the rules to Canasta?'

I nodded as did Charles. George didn't wait for the others to respond because he obviously already knew the answer. As he dealt thirteen cards to each of us, I noticed he looked more relaxed than I'd seen him for weeks. I was too, after my doctor had confirmed the menopause. He offered me HRT, which Charlotte vowed by, but I declined.

'Grace, you're with Charles. Is that okay?' George asked.

'Sure.' I smiled at Charles.

'Fine with me too.' Charles winked at me.

'Elizabeth and Simon are partners which leaves me with my lovely wife.' George grinned.

*

'Can I get you a coffee, Grace?' Charles asked heading to the sideboard in the drawing room and pouring himself a cup.

'Yes please. That would be nice.'

Charles passed me a cup and saucer. 'M'lady,' he said acting the perfect gentlemen. 'May I?' he asked pointing to the seat on the couch.

'Please do.' My stomach gave a slight flutter at the thought of him sitting next to me.

'I understand you're moving into the old Appleyard Farm.'

'Yes, that's right. It's perfect for me and my family. Closer to here too.'

'Excellent. George was so pleased when you agreed. It's been a grand project to work on. I bet it was a surprise when you discovered the title deeds were already in your name?'

'A complete surprise. I've told George, though, I can't accept it as a gift, I must pay him back as soon as the sale on my property has gone through.'

'You're an independent woman.'

I laughed. 'My father was a Charles.'

'Really? Mine too. I was named after him. He was a likeable old man.'

'I didn't get on that well with mine, in fact, we became estranged when I was only eighteen. He didn't like the choice of my first husband, Jack, who was a coal miner.'

'George mentioned that. You were happy though?'

'Very. Are you married?'

'Widowed.' He gave a little laugh. 'I don't want to unnerve you but I've a feeling someone's trying to do a bit of matchmaking.'

'I had worked that one out.' I looked up and noticed Simon and Elizabeth heading towards us. 'Charles, do you mind if I have a word with my sister?'

'I'll get us more coffee. Unless you'd like anything a bit stronger?'

'What are you having?' I asked.

'I thought I'd have a brandy.'

'Make that two then.' I smiled.

Charles got up and went to the bar.

'Elizabeth, Simon. Do you think I could speak to you both for a few minutes about Vikki?' I asked.

'What's she been up to now?' Elizabeth sank down into the adjacent brown velour sofa and placed a tumbler of orange juice on the marble table. 'I've no idea why that girl takes after you as a teenager rather than me.'

I laughed. 'Whatever do you mean?'

'Disobedient. Wilful. She even looks like you.'

'Come on, darling.' Simon joined Elizabeth and put his arm around her. 'We have a wonderful daughter.'

'I might know you'd say that. She can't put a foot wrong with you. I'm always the one in the wrong.'

'Never mind that now,' I said, 'I hadn't meant to cause a row between you two.'

George coughed to get our attention. 'Mandy and I need to disappear for half an hour to walk the dog.' George pressed his hand on the top of my arm. 'Are you all right with that?' he asked in a soft voice.

'I'll be fine. Don't worry.'

'We won't be long.' George caught up with Mandy by the door and they left the room.

Charles returned with our drinks and sat back down. 'Grace.' He clinked glasses with me.

'Now,' I said to Elizabeth, 'Vikki's done nothing wrong. In fact, she's quite a delight. I'm not sure whether you've noticed or not but she's shown a huge interest in fashion design and is very talented.'

'Has she? Is she?' Elizabeth said. 'That's the sort of thing I mean. Why couldn't she have told me that?'

'Shh, darling.' Simon put his finger to his lip. 'Let's listen to where Grace is going with this.'

'I'd like her to come and work for me a couple of evenings a week and one day at the weekend.'

Elizabeth frowned. 'What about her exams?'

'She's finished her 'O' levels. And I shan't let the hours interfere with her study for 'A' levels. Going one step further, if Vikki's interested, and naturally, you both agree, I'd like to offer her an apprenticeship with *House of Grace* once she's finished college.'

'I'm not sure, Grace.' Simon flicked his lighter and lit up a Marlboro. He stood up and passed the silver cigarette case to Charles. 'Help yourself.' As Simon sat back down, he said to me, 'I kind of hoped Vikki would come into the estate business. I could do with a hand. After all I'm not getting any younger.'

Charles puffed on a cigarette. 'I know it's not really anything to do with me but I think it's a great idea. If she were my daughter and had an opportunity to make something of herself in the design business...' He winked at me again. 'Personally, I'd snap it up.'

'What does Vikki think about the idea?' Elizabeth crossed her shapely legs. She was wearing sheer black tights this evening accentuating her slim calves and ankles.

'Vikki would like to give the casual hours a try.' I took a sip of brandy.

'Again.' Elizabeth shook her head. 'She's not mentioned a word to me.'

'Can we give it a go?' I put my glass back down on the table.

'Simon?' Elizabeth turned to her husband.

'Why not? There's still plenty of time for her to decide whether to join in the family business and then, looking to the distant future, I suppose there's always Jack.' He laughed. 'I know George...'

'Did I hear my name mentioned?' George ran his fingers through his damp hair. 'Any of that coffee left?'

'Plenty. I'll get it,' I answered, 'unless you prefer brandy?'

237

'Now you're talking,' George said, 'it's damn cold, and wet, out there. Mandy, brandy darling?'

'Coffee for me.' Mandy huddled herself up on the armchair.

I strode over to the sideboard, removed crockery from the cupboard for Mandy's coffee, and poured a brandy for George. For the first time in a long time, I felt uplifted.

Chapter 8

Grace

Simon pulled up at nine o'clock prompt. He and Vikki stepped out of the bronze BMW.

'Is this a new car, Uncle Simon?' Lori asked.

'It is. I only picked it up yesterday and apart from Vikki, you and Annalise are my first passengers. Grab your coats. This November wind is biting.'

The girls ran into the house, returning in thick wool coats. The green-plaid emphasised their dark, shoulder length, wavy hair. Annalise and Lori looked so similar, both in facial features and height, they could easily have been twins. They were spending the day at Granville Hall which included a riding session with Simon while I got Vikki started in her new job as my trainee assistant. The plan was I'd pick up the girls when I took Vikki home.

Simon glanced around the plot. 'It's looking good, Grace. I can't wait for the big tour tomorrow when we come over for dinner. How are you finding having the studio away from the house?'

'Much better. It means I can switch off from work when in the house.'

'I can understand that. Although once I close my study door for the day, that's it.' He turned to my girls. 'Come along you two, get in the back.'

'Can't I sit in the front because I'm the eldest?' Lori pleaded, her huge brown eyes sparkling.

'No. Both of you in the back.' Simon ushered. 'Now say goodbye and fasten your seat belts once in.'

'Bye, Mum,' Annalise and Lori said in turn before climbing into the back of the car.

Simon moved over to Vikki and gave his daughter a hug. 'Have fun, Angel. See you later.'

'Thanks, Dad.' Vikki shivered, folding her arms.

Simon got into the car and drove out of the drive with my girls waving frantically.

'Let's get inside,' I said to Vikki. 'That wind is icy.' I rubbed my hands together to warm up. 'You must be freezing in that dress. Not that it isn't lovely.' The peach floral gypsy dress showed off her trim figure.

'I designed it myself,' she said entering the studio.

'Really? I can see I was right about you and your talent.'

'I ran it up on my sewing machine.'

I lifted the bottom part of her dress and looked at the inside stitching. 'A professional job, too.' She really was a mini me.

Vikki grinned. 'I can't wait to get started. I've wanted to be a fashion designer all my life and now it looks like it's going to happen. Thank you so much for offering me this chance.' She gazed around the workroom. 'Mum said this used to be a farm. What was this building?'

'Believe it or not' – I laughed – 'this was a stable block.' George had made a grand job of the conversions and brought me to see it once finished. I was so pleased he had. It was perfect.

'So haven't you got any stables?'

'Yes, we have another block which means I don't have to come over to Granville Hall every time I want to ride, and the girls are over the moon too.'

'What would you like me to do first?'

'How about you pop the kettle on and make us a cup of tea? That way we can get warmed up before we start. The kitchen's through there and you'll find a tin of cookies in the cupboard.'

'Okay.' Vikki hurried out of the room.

I took out an A4 sketch pad from the drawer and laid it on top of the desk, along with half a dozen different range pencils. Vikki was back in no time at all with a tray and two mugs of tea and biscuits on a plate.

'Put the tray down on that cabinet.' I pointed. 'This will be your desk and one thing to learn from the beginning is we don't have any drinks or food near the drawings. Right?'

'Right, Aunt Grace. Or should I call you Mrs Gilmore when I'm working?'

'Aunt Grace is fine.'

I directed Vikki to sit down on the small couch at the side of the room and carried our beverages across to the smoked glass coffee table. 'We'll chat while we have tea and you can tell me about your ideas.'

'This dress for starters. All my friends love it and keep asking for one. But I have lots more suggestions.' She crunched on a chocolate cookie.

241

Chapter 9

Grace

'I hate you.' Alice stormed into my studio. She stood before me scowling. Her hair dripping wet.

'Whatever is the matter?' I asked.

'You promised I'd have the twins back by October and it's November now and I still haven't.' She sobbed.

'Let's go into the house and talk.' I put down my pencil, grabbed an umbrella, and took Alice's arm. I held the brolly over us. 'We'll make a quick dash.' Although only twenty yards away, the unsurfaced road was muddy.

I pushed open the front door. 'Sit by the fire in the drawing room' – I steered Alice – 'and I'll be along in a minute.' I grabbed a towel from the cloakroom and organised hot drinks for us with Steph.

When I entered the drawing room, Alice was still sobbing, her head bent down.

'Darling.' I rubbed her hair gently with the towel. 'You're soaking wet. You'll give yourself pneumonia' – I passed her a clean handkerchief – 'now dry your eyes and tell me what's happened.'

She sniffled. 'The solicitor has just told me that the court can take months to make a decision.'

'I'm sure he's just giving you the worst-case scenario. You know there's got to be an investigation?'

'He is. But even so. At this rate I'm not going to have my girls with me for Christmas. I'm fed up with only a couple of hours twice a week at Stonesay Manor. You don't know what it's like when I have to leave them and they start crying that they don't want me to go. They don't understand why I'm not living there. You might have been happy to give up George for six years but I'm not like you. All you cared about was your new precious fashion business.'

I grabbed hold of the mantelpiece to keep myself balanced. Sick inside I was lost for words.

'How dare you speak to your mother like that?' Nancy said. I hadn't even heard her enter the room. 'All your mother has ever cared about is her family. And you, you foolish girl, you can't even see that she's protecting you.'

'Protecting me,' Alice shouted. 'How the hell is keeping me away from my children protecting me? I can't expect you to understand when you've never had a child.'

'Alice.' I touched my brow. 'Apologise to Nancy, right now. I don't care what you say about me but don't talk to Nancy like that.'

'Sorry. I didn't mean to, Nancy, I'm just furious with her.' She glared at me.

'Alice…'

'Leave this to me, Grace. You go back to work for a while.'

'I think I should stay.'

'No, Grace, please… Let me sort it. You're too close.'

'Fair enough.' I headed out of the room but took one last look at Alice, shaking my head before venturing back outside. Tears pricked my eyes. At least it had stopped raining. I trudged back to the studio, sat down at my desk and picked up a pencil, but nothing would come. My head was filled with Alice's words. I stood up, went into the kitchen and on autopilot I filled the kettle, plugged it in, and added three teabags to the pot.

*

I pulled up at the parking area for Adriéne's memorial on Granville Estate and made a quick dash to the palm house in torrential rain. It was blowing a gale. I unlocked the door and the heat from the glass house immediately hit me. I shook the surplus rain off my mac in the doorway entrance. The door banged shut from the wind and I hung my coat on a peg to dry. Alice's words still haunted me. Naturally I didn't want her to be parted from those sweet girls. Only last week she'd been so excited when showing me their newly decorated bedroom with care bear wallpaper across one wall and the rest of the walls painted in a soft rose pink. White-coloured high sleeper beds with a wardrobe and desk underneath were placed either side of the room, mirroring the image. The girls would love it. With a four-bedroom house they could easily have their own room but they were inseparable like most twins.

The girls were identical. So different to Alice at that age. Their short chestnut-coloured hair just touching their collar and big brown eyes were a complete contrast to Alice's long, blonde ringlets and blue eyes. Nicole had a beauty spot on the right-hand side of her chin which was the only way of distinguishing her from Beth.

Oh Jack. What am I to do? How could I let Alice go back into that monster's arms? Next time it could be more than broken ribs. She could end up dead.

To distract myself from my thoughts, I picked up a sprinkling can and watered some of the shrubs while looking around at the maturing plants and palms. The pink pillar and vibrant blue bougainvillea particularly caught my attention with their beauty, and the scent of the violet African lily took me back to strolls in the park with Jack where we took George and Alice.

I sat down at one of the tables and took a notepad and pencil from my handbag and attempted to sketch a new design. I sighed, got up and walked around to part of the area which was like a jungle with huge palms reaching the ceiling. I checked my watch. Three-thirty. I didn't need to worry about Lori and Annalise finishing school because Joan and Ted were picking them up and taking them back to their place for a sleepover. The day that lovely couple walked into my life was a gift as they were such good surrogate grandparents. Not only to my younger daughters but to Alice too.

It was getting hot in the glasshouse so I opened the front door. The wind had dropped and the rain had stopped. Sunshine peeped from the clouds. Up in the sky, over the lake, a magnificent double rainbow had formed. I grabbed a towel from inside, mopped up the bench, and sat down to watch the swans as they glided close to the bank. The swans, ducks and geese always calmed me. I closed my eyes.

*

'Grace, wake up.' Someone was nudging my shoulder.

I jumped.

'It's okay, it's only me.'

I opened my eyes and looked up to see George. Daylight had gone. 'What time is it?'

'Seven o'clock. Thank God you're okay. You gave me a fright when I saw you slumped here. I thought you were dead. You're shivering. Let's get you inside.'

'I must have dropped off,' I said, entering the palm house. 'How did you know I was here?'

'Nancy rang me. She's out of her mind with worry and thought you must be up here. What happened? She said something about Alice upsetting you.' On the way in, he grabbed my coat off the peg, wrapped it around my shoulders, and guided me into the kitchenette. 'Instant do?' He switched on the kettle.

245

I nodded and watched as he spooned Nescafe granules into two mugs. 'Here, this will help warm you up.' He passed me the steaming black coffee. I warmed my hands before setting the cup down on the table and buried my head into my son's chest and sobbed.

Chapter 10

Grace

Steph set a tray of refreshments down on the tiled coffee table in the conservatory. She hesitated before leaving. 'Are you all right, Mrs Gilmore?'

I turned away from the window. 'I'm fine, thank you, Steph.'

'It's just with...'

'Alice last night?'

'Yes. Joan and I have been worried about you.'

I patted my housekeeper's hand. 'Sweet of you both but there's no need. I'm sure Alice will feel better today.'

'If you're sure, I'll leave you to it as I can hear your guests coming through the front door now.' She smiled.

Before my visitors entered the summer room I heard, *this is unbelievable. I can't believe I'm actually in Grace Gilmore's house* in a high-pitched voice. I greeted Mandy and her friend at the door. 'Oh,' I said, noticing only a slim woman with long blonde hair. 'No Susie?'

Mandy kissed me on the cheek. 'Ben's mam was admitted to hospital last night so Ben and Susie have gone over there.'

'Oh goodness. I hope it's nothing serious.'

'Us too. George was all for driving up there but Ben told him to hang fire. Grace, this is Kathleen' – she signalled to her friend – 'and Kathleen, this is the one and only Grace Gilmore, founder and director of *House of Grace*.'

'Thank you so much for agreeing to meet me.' Kathleen's eyes sparkled.

'Do sit down.' I pointed to the bamboo cane sofa by the window.

'Thank you.' Kathleen eased herself down on the floral-patterned cushion and crossed her long legs. Mandy was right about her being attractive. She certainly had a good figure but her style of dress was rather revealing. However, with the right clothes she'd make an excellent model.

'Can I get you a tea, coffee?' I asked still standing by the table.

'Yes, please.' Kathleen beamed. 'Coffee would be great. Milk with sugar, please.'

'Coffee for me too, thank you.' Mandy made herself comfortable next to Kathleen.

I poured out the coffees and passed a cup to each of them. 'Help yourself to sugar, Kathleen.' I knew Mandy didn't take any.

'Thanks.' Kathleen scooped two heaped spoonfuls into her drink. I wondered how she managed to stay so slim.

'Did Mandy tell you that I've been in fashion sales?' Kathleen said stirring her drink. 'Not as big as *House of Grace* but I've got a good head for marketing.'

I sat down in the chair opposite. Alice's words from last night kept echoing in my ears. *Did she really hate me?*

'Mrs Gilmore? Are you all right?' Kathleen prompted.

I fanned my face. 'Please forgive me. I didn't get much sleep last night. What was it you were saying, dear?'

'I was asking if Mandy mentioned my experience in fashion sales. The company was only small but it's clear from my references that I'm a natural.' Kathleen's blonde hair shone.

'She did, but I'm afraid Sales isn't my department. However, I do have a big fashion show coming up in March if you're interested in that? As a model?'

'Me?' Kathleen sat with her mouth wide open. 'Me? You really mean it? I'd love to.' Her cup rattled on the saucer as she put it down on the table.

'Naturally, you'll be paid.'

'I've always dreamt about being on the catwalk. Getting paid would be wonderful too,' she added hurrying her words, 'but to actually model for *House of Grace*.' She took a deep breath and shook her head. 'I can't tell you how much this means to me.'

'The added bonus is you choose your favourite outfit to keep.'

'Really? Oh wow' – she turned to Mandy – 'won't Susie be jealous?'

'Susie's modelling too,' Mandy answered and I watched Kathleen's lip drop.

I liked this young woman, although a little rough around the edges. I loved her enthusiasm and felt she'd make a good asset to *House of Grace*. 'About a sales position,' I said, 'I'm sure my partner could do with a new recruit but she'd need to interview you. We're planning on coming up your way shortly as we have a new shop just outside Bolton in Wolford. Do you know it?'

'Oh yes, yes I do.' Kathleen sat upright on the edge of her seat. She turned and grinned at Mandy.

'She went in there on opening day, didn't you, Kathleen?' Mandy nudged her friend.

'I certainly did. I didn't want to miss out on the initial offers. I had a good browse but the only thing in my price range was this.' She stroked the mauve, velvet choker around her slender neck.

'A good choice. That's one of my favourite ranges,' I said. 'Well, I'd like you to visit the store again but this time to purchase a black pencil skirt suit and a white, high neckline, blouse.'

She just stared back at me.

'Kathleen…?'

'But…'

'Don't worry, I don't expect you to pay. It can be charged to my account. I'll give you a letter for the manager, and I'll send you a date for an interview with Charlotte, Charlotte Cunningham. If you can impress Charlotte, I'll take you on as her trainee in April.' Charlotte had kept her maiden name for work as she felt it would be too confusing with two Gilmores.

'Wow, thank you, Mrs Gilmore.'

Alice burst into the room. 'Sorry, Mum, I hadn't realised you had guests. Hello Mandy. Who's your friend?'

'This is Kathleen. We go way back. We were at school together. Kathleen, this is Alice, George's sister.'

'I can see the resemblance with the same curly hair.'

Alice looked stunning with her hair falling into blonde spiral curls and her make-up immaculate. She looked better than I'd seen her for ages.

'I hate to break up the party,' she said, 'but I need to speak to you. I've asked George to come over too and he's on his way. About half an hour?' She grinned.

'Certainly,' I said, wondering what was going on. 'Mandy, when George arrives why don't you take Kathleen for a stroll around the stables to see the horses? Help yourselves to more coffee, I'll be back in a few minutes.'

*

'What's going on?' George asked as I met him in the hallway. 'I had a call from Alice telling me to get over urgently. Are you okay? Is it Mandy?'

'Mandy's fine, as I am too and your guess is as good as mine. Alice is in a bubbly mood so hopefully that means she's over yesterday. We're in the conservatory.'

Alice was standing in the centre when we entered the room. 'Ah good, you're both here,' she said. 'Thanks for coming over, George.' She turned to Mandy and Kathleen.

'It's okay' – Mandy stood up and signalled to Kathleen to follow her – 'we're going for a stroll around the stables.'

I looked down at Kathleen's stiletto heels. 'You'll find spare boots in the cupboard under the stairs. Mandy will show you where to find them.'

As my daughter-in-law and her friend left the room, I asked Alice, 'Would you like a coffee? Tea?'

'No thanks. I'd rather get straight to it.'

'Aren't you sitting down?' I stared, watching for a sign of what was going on. She seemed calm. What had changed?

'No, I'm good, but you two can sit if you like.'

I glanced at George. 'We'll stand too.'

'You're not going to like this but…'

'What?' My pulse pounded.

'I've been meeting Robert.'

'Yes, we know,' George answered before I could, 'for mediation.'

'Apart from that we've been meeting…'

I clasped my hands together. 'So you've been lying to me?'

'Not really. I told you I was with friends so that wasn't really a lie because Robert's my friend. Anyway.' She licked her upper lip. 'We've sorted things out and decided to get back together.'

I stood speechless.

George clenched his fists. 'You've got to be kidding us?'

Resting my hand on her shoulder, I asked, 'Is this because of yesterday? I'm sure you'll get the twins back soon.'

'Actually, I will have that coffee.' Alice poured herself a cup from the pot on the table and moved to the seat by the window. 'I'm sorry I was horrid, but no, this has nothing to do with that. Sit down and I'll explain.'

251

George popped himself down next to his sister and I sat opposite.

'Yesterday, I told you I needed my kids. What I didn't say was that I need Robert too. I love him and he loves me. Look at me.' She held her hands out in front. 'I'm calm. This isn't an irrational decision. I've thought long and hard. For the first time in a long time I feel like me again. I feel worthy. Surely you can understand that?'

'Of course, but...' My daughter was right about one thing, she did look like the old Alice. I hadn't seen her look like that for months.

'But nothing, Mum. I know you're worried but there's no need. Robert's been receiving anger management and it's brought up a lot of baggage, all to do with his father.'

'Alice' – George took his sister's hand – 'I think you're making a huge mistake.'

She pushed his hand away. 'Then it's my mistake to make. Isn't it? Imagine if you were forced to be away from Mandy and Jack?'

He tapped the back of her hand gently. 'Just know I'm always here for you.'

'As am I,' I said.

'Our girls need us both,' Alice continued, 'and I belong at Stonesay Manor and one day it will be mine and Robert's.'

George jumped up and marched across the room waving his arms around. 'For Christ's sake, Alice, is that what this is about? Bloody Lady of the Manor again. Well that's not going to happen if you end up dead.'

Alice remained composed. 'I understand your concern, and thank you for it, but this is my decision to make. And no, it's not all about the manor, it's about me loving my husband and girls and needing each other.' She looked at me. 'Surely you must understand? I mean look at you with Dad?'

She was right. I'd turned my back on my family and wealth to be with Jack but then Jack was never a wife beater. Maybe Alice was right and Robert would be different following the counselling sessions. I could understand him being messed up with Donald Sanders as a father. I'd seen the way he intimidated his son. I moved across to the couch, sat down and wrapped my arms around my daughter. 'Remember, I am here for you, no matter what.'

'Thanks Mum.'

George was still marching backwards and forwards across the room. 'And what about the house Grace sorted for you?' He took a deep breath. 'And the girls' bedrooms you decorated?'

'Someone else can live there. Mum's always picking up waifs and strays.' Alice laughed.

I glared at her. 'That's not funny.'

'No it wasn't and I'm sorry, and I'm sorry about the house but…'

'We're just going round in circles.' George sat down opposite and folded his arms. 'So when's this big reunion happening?'

'Today. In a minute. I'm going back with him now. He's waiting outside. In fact, Mum, he'd like to come in and reassure you.' Alice got up and left the room.

'What the hell?' George said.

I shrugged my shoulders.

'You're not going to just let her go. Surely?'

'What else can I do? She's made up her mind and who are we to stand in her way if she loves him. You said yourself on more than one occasion who could blame her if it means she's back with her children. We'll watch him. Don't worry.' I stretched across to reach his hand.

Light footsteps came along the hallway. Alice came back in beaming. Robert sloped behind her with his head down. None of his normal swaggering. It was clear from his stance he was ashamed. George and I stood up to join them.

'Mrs Gilmore, George.' He coughed. 'I'm really sorry for the pain I've caused Alice and promise it will never happen again. I've been getting help…'

'So we've heard,' I said.

'Thank you for giving me another chance…'

'We're not giving you another bloody chance' – George grabbed Robert by the collar – 'if I had my way I'd be giving you a bloody good hiding.'

I pulled George away.

'You're right,' Robert said, 'it's what I deserve but I promise…'

I took a deep breath. 'All I can say, young man, is that you'd better keep that promise because otherwise I won't be holding George back and not only that I'll have you locked up in a cell for a long, long time.'

Robert nodded. 'I understand and I won't let you down. I promise I'm going to look after Alice. I do love her and this has been a wake-up call. Our girls need us both in their lives and under one roof. You don't have any need to be concerned.'

Alice hugged me. 'Bye Mum and thanks. And I am sorry about those awful things I said to you. I know you did your best and now I must do mine.' She took Robert's hand and led him out of the room before anything else could be said.

George was still puffing and panting. 'I can't believe you let them go.'

'There was nothing to be done but we will keep a close eye.'

Chapter 11

Grace

The rain smashed against the windscreen as I drove up to Granville Hall. I switched off the engine and made a dash up the steps and rang the bell. The mansion hadn't changed in the years since it had been my home. The brass bell on the wall was still there as were the stone columns at the side of the porch. Paint had been retouched on the black front door but otherwise all was the same as that day all those years ago. The day I'd stood outside in the pouring rain waiting for someone to answer. A hint of scent from golden winter jasmine tickled my nose. The door opened, breaking my thoughts.

'Good afternoon, Mrs Gilmore,' Annie said, 'do come in. Miss Elizabeth is waiting for you in the drawing room.'

'Thank you.' I shook my umbrella and dropped it in the antique steel stand on my way in. 'You're looking tired, Annie.'

'I'm fine, Miss Grace. It's the running up and downstairs. It can be a little hard at times.'

'Where's Donna?'

'She's gone for her break.'

'Well I hope Lord Granville's looking after you. It seems to me you've taken on too much lately, what with cooking and housekeeping duties. I shall draw it to my son's attention. Get you some more help.'

Annie's hand flew to her chest. 'Please don't mention it. I'm fine, really. I'd hate his lordship to think I'd been complaining.'

I put my hand on her shoulder. 'Don't worry, Annie, he's not going to think bad of you. I am just concerned that all this is too much for you.'

'I can cope, Miss Grace.' Annie's eyes filled.

'All right, Annie. I hadn't meant to upset you. Think no more of it. I can see myself to the drawing room.' I made my way down the hallway making a mental note to speak to George about Annie. She didn't look well. It was time he reduced her duties.

Elizabeth was at the drawing room door by the time I reached it. 'Grace, there you are.' She kissed me on the cheek. 'I can't remember the last time we got together for afternoon tea like this. Can you?'

'It's been a while.' I followed my sister into the room and sat down on the chaise longue. The roaring fire was inviting as was afternoon tea set out on the glass coffee table. A three-tier cake-stand stood with small triangular sandwiches on one level, scones and tiny pots of jam on the next, and chocolate and strawberry gateaux on the top. This was a feast.

'Are you expecting anyone else?' I asked.

'No. I just wanted to make it special. Like I said, I can't remember the last time we did this.' She sat opposite me and picked up the teapot. 'Earl Grey all right for you?'

Heavy footsteps and chatter came from out in the hallway before someone tapped on the door. 'Sorry to gatecrash, Aunt Elizabeth, but we heard afternoon tea was being served.' George laughed. 'You don't mind if we join you, do you? You remember Charles?'

'Yes of course,' Elizabeth said. 'Do come and sit down.'

Charles winked in my direction. He came over and signalled to the seat next to me. 'May I?'

'Certainly. Elizabeth's pouring tea. It's Earl Grey or would you like an alternative?' I asked.

'Earl Grey's fine. In fact, my favourite,' Charles said, sitting down.

I took my cup from Elizabeth and stirred my tea. 'What have you gents been up to?'

'We've been to Abbots Fields, a rundown farm about ten miles from here. It's up for auction so George and I are looking at putting in a bid and converting the plot to a small development of detached houses.'

Elizabeth passed Charles his beverage.

'Has the plot got planning permission?' I asked.

'Not yet but with our connections in the council we don't think there'll be a problem.'

George patted Elizabeth's shoulder. 'Do you mind if I have a quick word?'

'Certainly.' Elizabeth got up from the chair, smoothing down her bottle-green corduroy skirt. 'I shan't be long.' She followed George out of the room.

Charles coughed. 'I'm afraid that was for my benefit.'

I frowned. 'Sorry?'

'George knows I wanted to ask you something and preferably without an audience.'

'Oh.' I laughed. 'What was it?'

'I wondered if you'd like to come to dinner with me tomorrow evening?' His eyes sparkled like sapphire gems.

'I'm sorry, Charles, but I'm away on business tomorrow.'

His bottom lip dropped. 'I see. I hope I haven't embarrassed you by asking.'

'Not at all. Seriously, I wasn't trying to put you off. I'm due to go to Bolton in the morning. That's one of the reasons I've come over today to discuss the arrangements with Elizabeth as my young niece is joining me. Remember, I mentioned her training as a designer at the card evening.'

'Yes. Yes, I do. So, it's not a *no* then? Just not tomorrow?'

'I'd love to come to dinner with you. How about Friday this week?'

He took my hand. 'I'd love that and look forward to it. Now about this afternoon tea. I'm starving.'

'Help yourself.'

'Food. I'm famished,' George said as he and Elizabeth came back in. 'We missed breakfast this morning, didn't we, Charles?'

Charles nodded.

That explained his urgency to tuck in. I was about to take a bite of my cheese and pickle sandwich when Donna came into the room.

'I'm sorry to disturb you, Mrs Gilmore, but there's a phone call for you.'

I hoped it wasn't Alice. She'd only been back with Robert for a couple of weeks but we'd spoken on the phone last night and she seemed content. 'Excuse me.' I walked out to the telephone in the hallway and picked up the receiver. 'Grace Gilmore.'

*

'Is everything okay?' George asked as I headed back into the drawing room.

'I'm not sure.' I steadied my hands to stop them shaking. 'It was Charlotte. Max has had some kind of turn and been advised to rest.'

'He's all right though?' George came over to me. 'And how about you? You've gone an awful ashen colour. Come and sit down.'

Charles poured a fresh cup of tea and scooped three spoons of sugar into it. 'Sweet tea's recommended for shock.'

I took a sip and screwed my face at the taste.

'Oh dear, I hope Max will be okay. Is tomorrow cancelled?' Elizabeth asked. 'Vikki will be disappointed.'

'No. No it isn't. Charlotte's insisting I still go. Orders from Max apparently. "He'll still be here when you get back," is what she said.'

'That doesn't sound too serious then. Charlotte wouldn't tell you to go unless she was sure.' George selected a ham and tomato sandwich from the plate.

'Look, I'm sorry but I'm going to need to go. There's a lot to rearrange. I need to see if Nancy can come with me. Will you excuse me?'

Charles stood up. 'Let me drive you home, Grace. You're in no fit state to drive. George can follow behind with your car?'

'I'll be fine.'

'No arguments,' George said.

Chapter 12

Grace

We had all arrived separately at the factory but now we were ready to start the tour. Bill handed out orange earplugs to each of us.

'You'll need these,' I said to Vikki and Kathleen. 'The machines are very noisy.' I let Bill lead the tour. As we entered the factory floor the heat and dust hit us straight away. Our earplugs kept the sound at bay.

'This is the weaving room,' Bill shouted. Both sides of the area had power looms with employees weaving fabrics.

'This is so fascinating,' Vikki said, totally engrossed with the men and women at work.

We went through a double door. Steam rose as a woman in her thirties pulled down an ironing press. Vikki and Kathleen's eyes darted as we moved from one area to another. A production line of workers had men and women sitting down. Some women worked on sewing a sleeve, while others sewed on the collar or added darts into the garment. Another group stitched buttons on the cuffs and a man in a brown overall pushed a huge fabric basket on wheels along the line as he gathered up completed items.

'This is amazing,' Vikki said.

'It's huge' – Kathleen looked around – 'how many workers do you employ?'

'Around three hundred,' Bill answered. 'We're very lucky that Mr Gilmore, Max, is such a good boss. We were sorry to hear he's under the weather. Nothing serious, I hope?'

'Charlotte assures me he'll be fine. Although to be honest I shan't be entirely happy until I've seen for myself.'

'I understand.' He rested his hand on the top of my arm for a second. 'Shall we head to the laundry room next?'

We followed him into a room with huge washing machines and tumble dryers. Women washed, rinsed and stone washed denim. The stench of ammonia made me light-headed. Men and women poured water onto the floor into a cut-out drainage system as they bleached and rewashed the fabrics.

'The finished product next.' Bill took us through another door and into a large warehouse where a variety of fabrics were stored and wrapped on huge rolls.

'You can take the plugs out now,' I said to Kathleen and Vikki. 'It's nice and quiet in here.'

'The tour's been amazing.' Vikki's eyes sparkled.

Nancy removed the plugs from her ears. 'I felt like that the first time I came here.'

'Am I allowed to touch the fabrics?' Vikki asked.

'Yes,' I said. 'You too, Kathleen. Get used to what each fabric's texture is like.'

Purple, blues, reds, orange, patterned, flowered or plain hung on each roll. Velvet, corduroy, cotton, polyester and nylon. Kathleen and Vikki leisurely browsed the aisles, checking the different materials. They beamed as they touched.

Bill looked up at the clock. 'Half past one. I've organised lunch for you all in the canteen.'

'Thank you, Bill. Will you be joining us?' I asked.

'I'd love to join you all as I have time.'

'And after lunch if Nancy and I could use your office to conduct an interview with Kathleen and perhaps Vikki could sit with Gemma?'

'Yes. Yes of course.' Bill led the way along the corridor and upstairs to the dining room. Although only half-full the chatter

261

was loud. 'Most of these will be back at work shortly. I've reserved a table out of the way, over in that far corner.'

We sat down at a trestle table covered in white linen, and unlike the workers who had to queue for their meal, ours was brought to the table. The chef brought out plates of roast beef and Yorkshire pudding and a couple of kitchen girls carried dishes of potatoes, carrots, peas and gravy.

'Have the staff had roast dinner too?' Kathleen asked.

'Goodness, no.' Bill laughed. 'We'd go bankrupt in a week if meals like this were provided each day. I believe sausage, mash and beans was on the menu today. Don't worry though, they never go hungry and Mr Gilmore, Max, is very generous as the workers get free meals. There's not a lot of employers that do that. In fact, around here I don't think I know of any other. Max also provides Luncheon Vouchers as part of their wage which means they can treat themselves to a Chinese at the end of the month or stock up on groceries.'

The food was hot and tasty. I felt a tad guilty that we were getting special treatment but as Bill said, Max looked after his staff well.

I checked my watch. Three o'clock. I turned to Nancy. 'I think we should get started on this interview. What do you think?'

'Yes, I agree. I don't know about you but I'm starting to flag now. Did you sleep well at the hotel?'

'We did. Remarkably well in fact. We're booked in at *The Imperial*. The beds are very comfortable.'

Nancy rubbed her hands. 'Good. Let's get this interview done so I can go and have a nap. I'm developing a headache.'

'It shouldn't take long as it's just a formality. I like Kathleen and I think Charlotte will enjoy working with her. Look how she's getting on with Vikki. You'd never think they'd only just met and she's helping to bring Vikki out of herself.'

'She's certainly got style,' Nancy said.

I laughed to myself wondering what Nancy would have thought if she'd seen Kathleen the other week wearing the low-cut blouse and tight mini skirt. Today was a complete contrast. She looked the height of elegance in a white silk blouse showing off her slender neck and the black pencil skirt suit accentuated her slim waist. Yes, in my book she was already our new recruit.

Chapter 13

George

Jack chucked a ball across the grass. Ginny bounded across the grounds to retrieve it.

Charles walked up to meet us. 'Look at your boy, he's having the time of his life. I wish I saw more of my grandson.'

'Charles, glad you could make it. How old's your grandson?'

'Six, so a bit older than Jack. I've got a photo.' Charles took his wallet from his coat and handed me a small snap. 'Michelle, my daughter, sent it over last week.'

'He's adorable. Looks like you too. What's his name?'

'Joe.'

'Joe. That's a good name. Let's take a pew.' I perched on the nearby garden bench.

'I don't mind if I do.' Charles pulled his coat closer to his chest as he sat down. 'It's bitter today.'

'I know what you mean. Once Ginny's had her exercise, Jack can take her inside, leaving us free to chat. Where did you say your daughter lives?'

'Over in the States. Savannah. Do you know it?'

'I've heard of it but not been there. I've promised Jack we'll take him to Florida sometime. He's so eager to go on an aeroplane.'

'He'll love Disney World.'

'Fancy a hot drink? Annie made me a flask.'

'I wouldn't say no.'

I poured steaming coffee into two plastic beakers. 'Only black I'm afraid. How often do you manage to get over to see them then?'

'I try once a year, but between you and me, Michelle always makes me feel like I'm in the way. The journey's pretty rotten too. Heathrow to Atlanta, change, and on to Jacksonville. Then Michelle has to pick me up, which is a good two-hour journey. She hates it and doesn't mind letting me know.'

I blew on my drink to cool it down before taking a sip. 'How did she end up there?'

'Married an American guy. Older than her. We don't get on that well. Reckon he complains about me being there and that's the reason I'm not invited that often. He's got three older kids so they have a houseful.'

'That's such a shame. Well as I've told you before, Charles, you're welcome here anytime. And Jack loves having you around. You're like a grandad to him.'

'I love being with you and your lovely family too, and really appreciate it. Gets a bit lonely living on my own.'

Jack threw the ball in our direction. The dog raced across towards us and lurched up on Charles, standing on her hind legs.

I held my hand in the air. 'Ginny, down now. I'm so sorry, Charles.' I stared at the mud pawmarks across his coat.

He laughed. 'You're all right. It'll brush off.'

'Jack. You did that deliberately.'

Jack giggled.

'Stop that now. You knew exactly what would happen throwing the ball in our direction. What do you say to Uncle Charles?'

Jack bent his head and mumbled, 'Sorry.'

'Take Ginny in now. And don't forget to wipe her feet and yours too.'

'Yes, Dad.' He grabbed hold of the dog's collar and attached the lead. 'Come on, Ginny.' They ran off together towards the house.

'There really was no need to tell the boy off. I didn't mind.'

'He has to learn. Anyway, he needed to go inside so I can show you his Christmas present.' I shook the coffee drops from our cups and put them back on the neck of the flask before getting up.

We trudged across the grass to the stables. The groom came out. 'Good morning, Lord Granville. Have you come to check on the lad's horse?'

'Yes, John, how's he settling in?'

'He's doing fine. Come and see for yourselves.'

We entered the third stall. 'He's a beauty, don't you think, Charles? He reminds me of the first pony my grandfather bought me.' I stroked the Morgan's tan coat and thick mane.

'Jack's one lucky boy.' Charles patted the pony.

'Are you going to the States for Christmas?' I asked.

'No. Not this year. Michelle mentioned springtime.'

'You must come to Granville Hall then. We're having the whole family over.'

'Thank you. I accept your offer gratefully.' Charles' stomach rumbled.

'Have you eaten breakfast?'

'No.' He laughed. 'I tend to skip it being on my own.'

'I've not eaten either. Come and join me. Annie's cooking a fry-up.'

'Thank you, George. You're very kind.'

After washing our hands in the outhouse, we traipsed over to the Hall and through the back door into the kitchen. 'Hello Annie, got enough breakfast for Charles?' I asked.

'Certainly, Lord Granville. I'll bring it to the dining room.'

266

'No need' – I pulled a chair out from the wooden table and sat down signalling Charles to do the same – 'we'll eat here.' As a child the kitchen had always been my favourite place with its homely feeling and that had never gone away. 'Mugs will do for the coffee,' I added.

Annie set the table with cutlery before dishing up two plates of bacon, eggs, sausage, beans and a couple of rounds of toast.

Charles sniffed. 'Smells good. Thanks for going to so much trouble, Annie.'

'No trouble, Sir.'

I spiked a piece of bacon onto my fork and dipped the toast in my egg yolk. 'So, tell me, Charles, how did your date go with Grace?'

'Your mother is a fascinating woman.'

'It went well then?'

'She's great company. You don't mind me seeing her, do you?'

'No. I think you're good for her.' And I meant it. There was no one I'd trust more with Grace than Charles. He was a true gent and I had no objections if things became serious between them. I would've happily had him as my stepfather.

'I was thinking of booking a couple of opera tickets as a surprise. Do you think she'd like that?' Charles shoved a forkful of sausage and beans into his mouth and followed it with a gulp of coffee.

'She loves opera.'

'It's a good idea then?'

'An excellent one.'

'I'll do it then. I'm out of practice with this dating game.'

Chapter 14

Grace

Rain pounded on the windscreen as we pulled up outside my home.

'It's been a wonderful evening, Charles.' I looked towards my house. 'Would you like to come in for a nightcap?'

'If you're sure it's not too late. I'd hate to disturb the others.'

'Everyone's out. Nancy's away on business, the girls are staying with Joan and Ted and it's Steph's night off. It would be nice to chat about the opera over a cup of coffee or brandy.'

Charles switched off the ignition. 'I'd like that.'

With coats over our heads, we dashed to the porch and I unlocked the front door. I made my way towards the drawing room with Charles at my side. 'Do sit down.' I signalled to the chaise longue. 'Coffee? Brandy? Or would you prefer a Scotch?'

'Better stick to coffee as I'm driving.'

I flicked the switch on the prepared coffee maker and sat next to Charles. 'Do you go to the opera much?'

'I used to but this was the first time since my wife died. I'd forgotten how much I enjoyed it. The company this evening helped.' His eyes twinkled. 'Purcell was a magnificent composer.'

'Indeed he was. *Dido and Aeneas* is my favourite. As a youngster, Mother and Father took me to the opera frequently. Part of learning to become a lady and dutiful wife.'

'Dutiful wife? That sounds rather archaic.'

'Just a bit. Thank goodness I managed to escape an arranged marriage. Simon, Elizabeth's husband, and his twin brother were set up as potential suitors.'

'Ah, I see. This is where you running off with the coal miner comes in?'

I laughed. 'Yes. You wouldn't believe the plan my friends and I concocted to get me out of Father's plans. Maybe I'll tell you about it one day. Can you bear to listen again to the last act of *Dido and Aeneas*?'

'Oh yes, I'd like that.'

I got up, selected the album from the record rack, took the LP from its sleeve and placed it on the music centre turntable. Charles joined in with the sailor singing on the first track as I poured out coffee. I carried the mugs across to the chaise longue and sat back down next to him. 'You have a wonderful voice. Baritone?'

'Well detected. I used to sing in a choir but another thing I gave up when I became a widower.'

'It's hard' – I touched his hand – 'isn't it?'

'I suppose the hardest thing I find now is being in such a big house on my own. I should look at downsizing but the old place has a lot of memories.'

'I understand. I had no choice but to move when Jack, my first husband, died. We lived in a small terraced tied to the job. Mother and Father helped me get on my feet but it came with a price.' Tears pricked my eyes.

Charles squeezed my hand. 'George mentioned that.'

I wondered what else George had told him. 'Here's the lament now,' I said as Dido sang, and I joined in with the soloist.

'And you are an amazing soprano.' Charles took a sip from his coffee. 'This is nice and warming.'

Tears brewed up in me. 'Sorry,' I said, 'this track always gets to me. So poignant.'

'Hey.' He stroked my wet cheeks and brushed my hair behind my ear.

I stared into his sapphire eyes.

'You're so beautiful, Grace. I know it sounds daft, when we haven't known each other for long, but I think I'm falling in love with you.' Charles leaned forward and kissed me on the lips and I kissed him back.

My heart raced as he caressed my bare shoulders and brushed kisses on my neck. I closed my eyes, happy and content, and snuggled up close, smelling his Old Spice aftershave. I was brought back to reality with the phone ringing in the hallway. 'I'd better get that,' I said.

'Must you?'

'I think I should. It could be Alice, or Joan about one of the girls. I'll be two minutes.' I rushed up, glancing back at his dreamy eyes before leaving the room to attend to the telephone in the hallway.

I picked up the receiver. 'Grace Gilmore.' I listened to the quavering voice on the telephone.

Dazed, I walked back into the drawing room.

'What is it, Grace?' Charles was at my side.

'It's…'

'Come and sit down.' He led me to the nearest armchair. 'What's happened?'

'It was Charlotte. It's Max. He's been rushed to hospital' – I stood up – 'I need to get over there now.'

'I'll drive you.'

*

I charged through the automatic doors and headed towards the receptionist.

'Take it easy, Grace, or you'll end up in here too,' Charles said, hurrying after me.

'Max Gilmore,' I said to the woman behind the desk. 'He was brought in by ambulance earlier.'

She keyed in Max's name and looked at the screen, pushing her round spectacles up against her nose. 'Ah, here he is. He's been admitted to *Goodford*. It's on the first floor. You can use the lift over there.' She pointed to the left.

My heart was racing. *Please God let him be okay*. We got into the lift and Charles pressed the button. As we came out, I looked for *Goodford*.

'This way.' Charles guided me to the right. 'I'll wait here.'

Sister was standing behind a desk when I entered the ward. 'Can I help you?'

'I'm looking for Max Gilmore.'

'Oh yes, he's in the private room over there.' She pointed.

I hurried over, pushing open the door. Charlotte was at Max's side. He was slightly propped up with pillows and connected to leads. 'What happened?' I asked. 'Are you okay?'

Max pressed my hand. 'I'm all right, Grace. They've given me aspirin and the monitor will confirm whether I'm having a heart attack or not, although if I am, they think it's a mild one. They've been using me as a pin cushion, taking lots of bloods.'

'Thank God you're okay.'

'How did you get here?' Charlotte asked.

'Charles drove me.'

A nurse approached. 'I think it's time you ladies let Mr Gilmore get some rest. He's in good hands and' – she turned to Charlotte – 'it looks like you could do with some sleep. We'll call you if there's any change.'

Max took Charlotte's hand. 'I'll be fine, darling. You don't get rid of me that easy.' He smiled.

'I'll come back tomorrow with pyjamas and slippers.' Charlotte kissed him lightly on the lips.

'Look after her, Grace.'

'I will.' I leaned over and kissed him on the cheek.

Chapter 15

George

Christmas Day 1986

Two massive round tables covered in white tablecloths were situated close together. Staff bustled around setting places, while others hung decorations from the ceiling and around the walls. I'd given Annie and the rest of the staff the day off from their duties but gone against Grace's wishes to invite them to join us for lunch. It wasn't that I thought we were better than them but more they'd be embarrassed if asked. Instead the staff, including the stable grooms, were having their own Christmas lunch in the kitchen, where they too, would be waited on by external catering staff.

Grace, Nancy, Lori, Annalise, Joan and Ted were the first to arrive. I greeted them as they walked in. 'Happy Christmas.' I kissed them on the cheek in turn.

Grace strolled over to the huge Christmas tree in the corner. 'This is magnificent. I love the red and gold baubles.' She looked up towards the top of the tree. 'Still claiming her pride of place then.'

'Naturally,' I said, 'a little bit of Da.'

'Girls.' Grace beckoned my young sisters over. 'Come and see Tinkerbell.'

Lori shrugged her shoulders. 'No thanks, you're all right.'

'She's a teenager now. I don't think she's interested.' I laughed.

'Can we see Jack's new horse?' Annalise asked, eleven going on twenty, also not interested in the fairy or tree.

'Please Dad, can I take them to see Whisky?' Jack beamed.

Nancy laughed. 'I wonder where he got that name from?'

'Because he's the same colour as whisky, silly. You can come too if you like, Aunty Nancy.' Jack jumped up and down. 'Please, Dad. Can we go?'

'After lunch if it isn't snowing.' I turned towards the door. 'Here's Uncle Max and Aunt Charlotte.' As I reached the doorway to greet them, Betty, John, Nathan and Kathleen arrived too.

Grace nudged me. 'Where's Charles? I thought you'd invited him.'

I glanced towards the entrance. 'Here he comes now. I heard you two were getting on well,' I said, making Grace blush. I'd not seen her do that before. 'Charles,' I said, as he made his way to us. 'Glad you could make it. We were getting a little worried.'

'My apologies. I forgot to put the car in the garage last night so it took me a while to scrape ice from the windows. That'll teach me.' He laughed.

'The main thing is you're here now and just in time to sit down. I've seated you next to Grace.'

Charles's smile widened.

As the hired staff showed guests to their seats, Elizabeth and Simon entered the room. 'Look who we've found,' Elizabeth said.

It was Alice, Robert and the twins. I hadn't wanted to invite them but Grace insisted we must have Alice and the girls with us on Christmas Day, and if that meant putting up with Robert too, then so be it. I walked over to greet them. 'Alice.' I kissed my sister on the cheek. 'Robert.' I took a deep breath before putting out a hand to shake. I wished I could give him a punch

274

instead. Thankfully, Mandy had organised the seating arrangements to ensure Alice and Robert were on a separate table to Grace or us. To distract myself from feeling that way, I bent down to, Beth and Nicole, my young nieces. 'And what did Father Christmas bring you lovely girls?'

'I got a Polaroid camera and a watch.' Beth held up her wrist.

'And I got a watch too, Uncle George. Look.' Nicole pushed her Mickey Mouse watch under my nose.

'Aren't you lucky girls.' I stood up, resting a hand in the middle of my back.

'And we're going to Disney World after Christmas. Aren't we, Dad?' Nicole looked up at Robert.

'Yes, yes we are.' He smirked at me.

'Lunch is ready so if you'd like to take your seats. Alice, you and your family are over on that table.' I pointed before heading over to my own seating place.

There was a hustle and bustle as everyone pulled out the chairs to sit down. Waitresses moved around the tables serving roast potatoes, sprouts, carrots and peas, while Simon and I carved turkey. Conversation was noisy during the meal but everyone appeared to be enjoying themselves. Max, however, was looking tired. I imagined he'd be asleep in an armchair after lunch.

After the first course, a waiter brought out a large Christmas pudding and set it in front of me. I heated a ladle of brandy over a candle, let it burst into flame and poured it over the pudding. Everyone clapped. Christmas crackers snapped as guests pulled them in turn. The waiter took the pudding away to serve and returned with individual bowls of dessert and jugs of brandy sauce.

Spoons clattered on the dishes until everyone had finished.

'Can we go and see Whisky now?' Jack whispered.

'If it's stopped snowing?' I answered.

'Can I go and look?'

'In a minute. Wait until everyone's left the table.' I stood up and cleared my throat. 'I'm sure you'll all agree that was a fine meal.' I lifted my glass. 'Merry Christmas everyone.' My gaze flicked towards my wife and family as they too raised their glasses. I was a lucky man. I placed my Champagne flute back onto the table. 'Please make your way to the lounge where coffee with mince pies will be served.'

As the guests pushed back their chairs, I walked over to the window to check on the weather. Mandy came up behind me. 'Dinner was a success.'

I slipped my hand around her waist. 'It was, and did you see the way Grace and Charles were looking at each other throughout the meal?'

'I did.' She gave a small laugh. 'Do you think it's serious?'

'I hope so.'

'Why don't I take the children to see the pony while you have coffee with the guests? Alice can come too. It will give me a chance to find out how things are going with her and Robert and you can find out more about Charles and Grace.'

'If you don't mind. But wrap up warm. I'll get Simon and Elizabeth to keep Robert away from me.'

'Good idea. I'll see you shortly.' Mandy stroked the top of my arm and kissed me lightly on the lips.

I watched as she led Alice and the children out of the room before making my way into the lounge. I glanced around and spotted Kathleen, with Grace, standing and chatting to Charlotte. Max was asleep in an armchair. I made my way over to where Charles was sitting alone. 'Are you all right, mate?' I patted him on the shoulder.

'Hello there, George. I'm fine. Grace will be back shortly. She's just introducing Kathleen to Charlotte. It was a fabulous lunch' – he patted his stomach – 'thank you for letting me join you.'

'You're welcome.' I pulled up a chair and sat down next to him. 'Cigar?' I picked up the wooden box from the side table.

'Don't mind if I do.' He took a Cuban and sniffed it before preparing it to light. 'You not indulging?'

'Not today.' Although I didn't smoke, very occasionally I'd have a cigar.

The waiters circled the room handing out coffee and brandy while a couple of young waitresses offered mince pies.

Christmas carols played on the music centre turntable. This was one of my happiest Christmases for a long time. I had my family and friends around me. It was unfortunate Ben and Susie couldn't make it as they were spending the festivities with Ben's mam and she wasn't up to travelling this year, but I had Betty, John and Charles here. Charles had become a surrogate father to me and a grandfather to Jack.

Simon walked over. 'It's coming up to three. I've turned the television on in the drawing room. Will you make the announcement, or shall I?'

'You can do the honours,' I said.

Simon clapped his hands. 'Ladies and Gentlemen, it's almost time for the Queen's speech. Follow me if you'd like to listen.' He looked at me. 'George?'

'I'll be along shortly. Excuse me Charles.' I wandered over to Grace and her party. 'Anyone for the Queen's speech?'

Joan and Ted were snoring on a couch by the fire. I laughed before turning to the others. 'Are you coming?' I asked.

'Max.' Charlotte leaned over and rocked his shoulder. He slumped sidewards. She knelt by him. 'Max. Wake up. Max.'

Grace rushed to his side touching his neck with her fingers. She shook her head. 'Quick, someone phone an ambulance.'

Chapter 16

Grace

Light bounced off the dark clouds in the sky. It was almost certainly going to snow. Charlotte and Nancy came out of the front door as the hearse pulled up outside my house, two black limousines close behind. A spray of white lilies, freesias, roses and palm leaves covered Max's coffin. White carnation and red rose lettered wreaths, spelling out *Max* and *Husband*, lay by its side. The undertaker stepped out of the vehicle and tipped his hat. Charlotte headed over to him, taking care on the ice in her high heels. She looked a picture of elegance in her black-fleck wool outfit, and a matching cloche hat framed her heart-shaped face. She hadn't registered yet that Max had gone. I'd half expected her to break down when I was working on the design of her suit, but just like now, she'd stayed composed. Maybe after the funeral it would hit her. After a few moments speaking to the funeral director, she walked back to us. 'Where's Joan and Ted? They should be here by now.'

I glanced to the left and spotted them hobbling up the gravelled path, Ted in his black suit, and Joan in a dark A-line dress and jacket. 'Here they are now. You and Nancy get in the car. I'll wait for Joan and Ted.'

As I walked up to greet them, Joan wiped a tissue across her eyes. 'I'm so sorry, Grace.' She squeezed my hand, sobbing.

'Are you all right, sweetheart?' Ted asked me.

I shrugged. 'I think I'm doing okay.'

'And Charlotte, how's she coping?' Ted asked as we moved closer to the house.

'Remarkably well. Too well perhaps. Listen, we need to get going. We'll talk properly later. You and Joan are in the car behind us.'

A tear pricked my eye as we passed the hearse but I couldn't afford to break down. Charlotte needed me to be strong. We continued walking to the second limousine. The passenger doors were open ready. Joan and Ted shuffled onto the back seat. I leaned in. 'Are you two going to be okay?'

'Don't you go worrying about us, Grace. I'll take care of Joanie. You concentrate on our Charlotte. See you in the church.' Caringly, Ted rubbed my arm before closing the door.

'I'll see you there.' I waved and made my way to the first vehicle to join Nancy and Charlotte. After climbing in, I gripped Charlotte's hand and Nancy held her other.

The funeral director cut an imposing figure in his top hat and cane. He walked slowly ahead of the hearse with a procession of cars trailing behind. Once we reached the exit from Appleyard Farm, the undertaker climbed back in the vehicle and our convoy turned out on to the main road.

I was back in nineteen fifty-two, in a black wedding limousine with Max listening to my cries. My father should have been giving me away. My sister should have been my bridesmaid and why wasn't my mother there as Mother of the Bride and proud of me?

'Pull over,' Max had told the chauffeur as we approached an open field.

The chauffeur stopped the car. 'What's happening?' I brushed the wedding veil away from my face.

'We're going to get out of the car now and you're going to scream,' Max said.

'What? I can't.'

'Yes, you can. No one else is here.' He got out of the car, opened my passenger door and held out his hand to help me, lifting my long train so it didn't drag on the ground. 'Go on. Scream. I promise you'll feel a whole lot better.'

He was right. I did scream and when I got back in the car all my frustrations had gone. I was ready to get married.

Now, as I sat in this car, I was tempted to ask the chauffeur to pull over but didn't think it would be etiquette. Instead, I gripped Charlotte's hand tighter and screamed in silence.

After what seemed an age of driving along the busy road, we turned into the drive leading up to St Michael's Crematorium. I shivered. The last time I'd been here was to say goodbye to Adriéne.

Cars arriving from the opposite direction held back as we drove into the entrance. We reached the chapel and I spotted Alice and George waiting with their spouses.

Nancy stepped out of the vehicle first, Charlotte followed, and I got out last. The vicar came over and spoke to Charlotte. He was her regular vicar from Storik Sands who'd agreed to come up to do the service. I couldn't hear what was being said but Charlotte nodded and turned to me. 'They're ready.'

We stood back at the side of the porch as the pallbearers slid Max's coffin from the hearse and lifted it on to their shoulders. They held still for a moment before entering the chapel and starting the procession. Charlotte, Nancy and I followed with Alice, George, Joan and Ted behind us.

Nat King Cole's *Unforgettable* played as we walked down the aisle. I clutched Charlotte's hand. She was shaking as much as me. Max's casket was placed in position. Charlotte, Nancy and I sat down in the first pew while George, Alice, Joan and Ted took the one behind. George patted my shoulder and mimed, 'Are you okay?' I nodded, lightly brushing his fingers.

The vicar walked up to the lectern and after adjusting his round metal-framed spectacles he coughed. 'We are gathered here today to say our final farewell to our brother Maxwell Henry Gilmore.'

The chapel was packed, so much so, the doors had been left open to accommodate those who couldn't fit inside. Max was dearly loved. Even Bob and Gemma had come down from Bolton. Bob had been a loyal employee for a long time.

'We will now begin our first hymn,' the vicar continued, '*How Great Thou Art*, which you will find on the inside of the order of service.'

The organist played the introduction and, on the key to start, everyone sang. I stroked the photograph of Max on the front of the pamphlet. I smiled and cried in silence at the same time. He was such a wonderful man. He'd been a father to me. I was back at Willow Banks all those years ago when I'd gone to stay with Katy in Bolton. The first time I had met Max. Her father. I remembered his blond curls, just like Jack's, George's, and now Jack Jnr's. Katy and I were all set to go out to the palais in our posh frocks when Max emerged from the drawing room. 'What a bevy of beauties lies before me,' he'd said. That day I had flutters inside my stomach going out to my first dance, today I had them as I was forced to say goodbye to the dearest of men.

Charlotte whispered to me, 'Are you all right?'

'I was just reminiscing the first time I met Max. He was such a lovely man.'

'He was indeed. And a wonderful husband.' She gripped my hand tighter. 'Are you sure you're up to doing the eulogy? We can get someone else to read it out.'

'No. I need to do it. It will be my parting gift to a man who gave so much to me. I'm supposed to be looking after you, not the other way around.'

'I'm fine.' She smiled. 'I'm just grateful for the time we had.'

The hymn finished and the vicar beckoned me to the front. 'Grace Gilmore will now read a eulogy she's written for Max.'

Charlotte squeezed my hand. 'You can do this.'

Nancy rubbed my arm and George patted me on the shoulder. I made my way to the podium and unfolded the sheet of paper with my words. I looked ahead at the congregation. 'Charlotte, Max's wife and my closest friend, has asked me to say a few words about our dear Max.' I coughed. 'Max Gilmore was a wonderful man, a wonderful father, and a wonderful husband. He has been more of a father to me than my own ever was. I was sixteen when he took me into his home and cared for me like a daughter.' I looked up across at Charlotte as she dabbed her eyes with a handkerchief.

'Max's father and grandfather were coal miners and it was expected Max would choose this route too. Indeed, he started his working life down the pit but determined to make a better life for himself and his family, he worked hard to make that happen. After investing in a Bolton cotton mill, he prospered. Max became a fair and caring employer, loved by all his staff. So much so, a couple of his employees have travelled down from Bolton to say a final goodbye to their wonderful boss.' My eyes were drawn to the middle of the congregation where Bob and Gemma nodded their heads.

'Max was always happy to stand in as a surrogate father and giving me away when I married his nephew was no exception. Unfortunately, in the early fifties, Max's daughter, Katy, took her own life, resulting in Max and his first wife, Eliza, moving to America. Max, the ever-loving husband supported Eliza when she suffered from depression and spent time in and out of hospital.' Nancy looked up at me, smiled and mouthed, 'You're doing well.'

'In nineteen sixty-six, fate intervened and brought Max back into our lives. Once more he took up his role as my surrogate father. There for me and my family through thick and thin. After becoming a widower in the late sixties, Max began to rebuild his life and later married Charlotte, my dear friend.' Charlotte bent her head. Nancy comforted her, placing an arm around her shoulder.

'Max and Charlotte had seventeen wonderful years together which was cut short by Max's sudden death a week before his eightieth birthday.'

I wiped the handkerchief across my eyes and took a deep breath. 'If I know our Max, he'll be smiling down at us right now, along with his beautiful daughter, Katy.' My eyes filled up.

The vicar tapped the back of my hand. 'Well done, Grace. I'll take over now.'

I turned away from the congregation and dried my eyes before heading back to the pew with my best friends, Charlotte and Nancy, who were more like sisters.

'George, Max's great nephew, will now read out a poem.'

George stood in position. He brushed his curls away from his eyes. 'Do not stand at my grave and weep...' His words drifted away as I thought of Max's smiling face. I didn't think I'd ever seen him cross. Even that time Jack was in a bad way from too much alcohol after his father, Max's brother, had died. Max still smiled and told me everything would be fine. I wanted to run out of the church and let my tears go but instead I gripped Charlotte's hand tighter. I had to be strong for my friend.

George headed back to his seat as the vicar announced, 'Will you please stand for the committal?'

There was a shuffling of feet, coughing and sniffing as everyone stood up.

'It's now time to say a final goodbye and commit Max's body to be cremated and thus committing his memory to our hearts for the rest of our days.'

The congregation sang *You'll Never Walk Alone* as dear Max, my dear dad, took his last journey and I don't believe there was a dry eye left in the church.

Chapter 17

Grace

The drawing room had been cleared to accommodate several trestle tables covered in white linen tablecloths, housing a cold buffet for our guests paying tribute to Max.

Charlotte and I continued to circulate while Nancy insisted on running around providing teas and coffees, despite the fact I'd employed catering staff.

Joan and Ted sat by the glowing fire chatting to George and Mandy. George tapped Ted's shoulder before leaving them and making his way over to us. 'I've told Ted, they should go home. They look done in.'

'I was thinking the same,' I said. Joan looked like she was nodding off. It occurred to me we should do the toast for Max, so the guests would then start to disperse.

'We're all going to miss him.' George kissed Charlotte on the cheek before turning to me. 'I loved him like a grandfather.'

'I know, darling.' I stroked his cheek as Bob and Gemma headed our way.

'I am so sorry, Mrs Gilmore.' Bob took my hand and then Charlotte's. 'He was such a good boss. The factory won't be the same without him.'

Charlotte gently pulled her arm away. 'Thank you both for coming. Will you excuse me for one moment?'

'Charlotte?' I mouthed *are you okay*?

'I just need a few minutes.'

I nodded in acknowledgement.

'Look, Grace.' George touched my arm. 'Mandy and I can carry on circulating if you'd like to spend a bit of time with Bob and Gemma.'

'Thank you, I'll take you up on that offer.'

As Mandy and George left my side, hand in hand, I turned my attention to Bob and Gemma. 'Come and sit down.' I pointed to a table and chairs in the far corner. 'Have you managed to make yourselves comfortable in the house across the way?' I eased myself down onto a chair.

'Yes. Yes, thank you, Mrs Gilmore.' Gemma beamed. 'It's a lovely house. Four bedrooms. It's huge. So kind of you to let us stay rent free.'

One of the waitresses came over with a tray. Smiling, she passed us all a cup of tea and left.

'It's just sitting empty.' I noticed Alice sitting with Robert a few feet away. 'It was meant for my daughter but at the last minute she decided against it. Have you met Alice yet?'

Bob shook his head. 'No. I don't believe so, although we did meet George, when he came up to work on the factory plans. We had a nice chat with him earlier, too.'

I beckoned Alice. She came straight over with Robert in tow. 'Yes, Mum?'

'I'd like you to meet Bob and Gemma. They are employees at Max's factory.'

'Pleased to meet you. He was a great sport our Uncle Max. The world lost a diamond the day he... I can't...' She rushed away.

'Excuse me.' I stood up and hurried after Alice. Tears streamed down her cheeks. 'Hey there.' I took my handkerchief and wiped her face like I used to when she was a child.

'Sorry, Mum, I can't... I can't do this.' She rushed down the hallway towards the front door.

'Don't worry. I'll look after her.' Robert pressed my hand and, with haste, left the house too.

I made my way back to the drawing room to Gemma and Bob. 'I'm sorry about that.'

Bob laid his hand across mine. 'We understand.'

I hadn't realised Alice would be so upset but then as George had pointed out, he was like a grandfather to all of my children. I glanced up as Charlotte reached our table. She wiped a hand across her forehead. 'Sorry about that, Grace. I had to get out for a few minutes. Was that Alice and Robert I saw leaving?'

'It was. Poor darling. She's taken it harder than I thought. Robert, apparently, is going to take care of her. He'd better.'

'Now, now, Grace. Give him the benefit of the doubt. He's been trying.'

'So I understand.' My friend's silvery hair shone and highlighted her almost line free complexion. Cherry-coloured lipstick emphasised her smile. 'You look beautiful. No wonder Max loved you so much. He'd be so proud of you right now.'

She laughed, dabbing her eyes with a tissue.

'Don't, please, Grace. Don't get me started. We shouldn't have wasted so much time. You should learn from this.'

Kathleen headed our way. 'I'm so sorry Mrs Gilmore and Mrs Gilmore. Oh, this is so confusing with two Mrs Gilmores.'

'Call me Grace.'

Charlotte took a deep breath and coughed. 'At work I'm known as Mrs Cunningham, although you can call me Charlotte as we're going to be working together.'

'I only met Max a couple of times but I could tell what a kind man he was.'

'Yes, he was.' I pictured the way he used to tilt my chin when giving me a pep talk. Out of the corner of my eye I noticed a waitress pass by. 'Grab yourself a cup of tea, Kathleen, and come and join us. Gemma, Bob, do you remember Kathleen?'

'Err yes, I do, from the factory when you brought your niece.' Bob shook Kathleen's hand.

'I remember both of you too.' Kathleen withdrew her hand and twiddled a strand of hair around her finger. 'Gemma and I had a good old chit-chat about fashion, didn't we?'

'Yes. It's good to see you again.' Gemma stood up and kissed Kathleen on the side of her face.

'I'm pleased to see you're all getting on as Kathleen will be staying in the house with you tonight. I trust that's fine with you all?'

'Definitely,' Bob answered, 'it's so very kind of you to put us up rather than us having to go to a hotel.'

'It's my pleasure. Now do help yourselves to some food before they clear it away. There's plenty. Chicken, beef, salad, potatoes, and if you've got a sweet tooth there's gateaux and cheesecakes. I'll get the caterers to make you up a doggy bag for later too.'

'Charlotte' – I looked at my watch – 'it's almost six. I think we should do a toast. Shall I organise it, or will you?'

'Do you mind, darling? I think I'd like to just sit here for five minutes. My feet are killing me.' She slipped her foot out of a stiletto and rubbed her toes.

'Are you going to be okay?'

'I'll be fine. I've got these lovely people to keep me company.'

After making my excuses to the others, I made my way to one of the waitresses, whispered for her to bring champagne, and headed to the opened front door for some air. I stood outside for a few minutes in the snow. I didn't care that it was cold, or wet, I needed to feel something instead of this awful numbness.

It had been a hard day for us all saying goodbye to Max. The clock on the wall chimed seven. Thankfully the guests had now left, leaving just the three of us. Nancy had gone upstairs to freshen up when Charlotte broke down.

I rocked her in my arms. 'I know, darling, let it go.' I was surprised she'd held it together for so long.

Charlotte lifted her head, wiping her eyes. 'I need to pull myself together. This isn't me.'

'You need to grieve. Let it go. When Jack died, I was almost in the grave with him and I don't think I was much better when I lost Adriéne, was I? Thankfully I had you looking after me.' I stroked her hair. 'You look gorgeous with your hair down.'

'That's how Max liked it too.' She buried her head in my chest and sobbed.

Nancy headed into the room. 'I'd say someone needs a stiff drink. In fact, I reckon we could all do with one.' She went to the bar and poured out three Scotch and sodas, adding ice. 'Why don't we go through some old photos. That's if you're up to it, Charlotte?'

'I think that's a good idea.' Charlotte wiped her eyes.

'Grab your drinks then, and sit down.' Nancy passed us each a crystal tumbler.

'Let's have a toast first. To Max.' Charlotte clinked her glass with mine and Nancy's.

'To Max.' Nancy and I cheered in unison as we stood by the bar.

Nancy disappeared from the room and Charlotte and I sat on the settee by the fire. Moments later Nancy was back with a large cardboard box. 'Charlotte, you sit in the middle.'

We shuffled along the couch and Nancy laid an album across Charlotte's lap so we could all see.

The first photo was my wedding photograph and Max was giving me away to Jack. 'Good God.' Charlotte picked up the black and white picture, running her fingers across Max's face. 'It's like looking at George. I know you're always saying this but…'

'I know. The Gilmore men are like clones.' I flicked over to the next page.

'I wish I'd known him then. Oh no, not again.' Charlotte slid the album on to my knee and walked over to the window sniffling. She pulled back the drapes. 'It's raining now.'

Before we had a chance to answer there was a sudden bolt of thunder making us all jump and seconds later lightning flashed across the room. Nancy rushed over to the curtains and re-closed them. 'I hate storms.'

'It's okay, Nancy.' I smiled. 'That's just our Max letting us know he's landed in Heaven.'

Charlotte laughed before starting to cry again, blowing her nose. 'I'm sorry, ladies. I think I've been trying to hold it together and now it won't stop. It's just like Max to send us a sign that he's arrived.'

'Don't be afraid to cry, Charlotte.' Nancy sniffed. 'He was your husband. You can't expect to keep it together.'

I opened up the next album with photos from Elizabeth's wedding. 'Are you up to a bit more reminiscing?' I patted the seats either side of me.

Once Charlotte and Nancy had sat back down, I put my arms around them both. 'You two are my oldest friends. More than friends. My sisters. And we will get through this just like we've got through everything else. Together.' I let them go and flipped over the page. 'Look, Charlotte, it's you and Max dancing.'

'Oh yes. That's when it all started and I realised Max was the man for me.'

After a small tap on the door, Steph came into the room. 'Sorry to interrupt, Grace, but can I get you ladies anything before I go home?'

'No thank you, Steph. We can manage,' I answered.

'It was a beautiful service today.' She played with her pendant necklace. 'You did Max proud with the eulogy, and George did well with that poem. Max was a wonderful man and I'm so sorry for your loss. All of your losses, because I know he was like a father to you and Nancy as well as being a great husband to Charlotte.'

'Thank you, Steph. Are you all right getting off home in this storm?' I signalled outside.

'Yes, Roger's picking me up. He's out there now waiting.' Steph had stopped living in after marrying a lovely young man. 'I'll be off then. Good night, all.'

'Good night, Steph.' I waved and mimed *thank you* as she left the room.

Charlotte fiddled with her pearl studded earing. 'Listen, there's something I've been meaning to ask you both but I thought I'd wait until after today.'

'What is it?' Nancy took a sip of whisky.

'It's something, I think might help us get through this, that we could do together…'

'Anything.' I hugged her to me.

'After Max's first heart attack, he started talking about if something happened to him. I didn't want to talk about that but he insisted and one thing he put forward was that after he died, we three should take a luxury world cruise.'

'A cruise?' Wide-eyed, Nancy crossed her legs.

'Yes. Fly out to America. Meet up with his old friends then board a ship and see where it takes us. I don't know, maybe be away for around three to six months. What do you say?'

'Are you serious?' I frowned.

'Yes. I've been mulling it over since Max's death. It's what he wanted us to do. What do you think?'

Nancy shot up, refilled our drinks and passed them to us. 'I think it's a fabulous idea and we should have another toast.' She raised her glass. 'To Max.'

'To Max.' Charlotte and I clinked our glasses.

'I'm all for keeping to Max's wishes but…' I sighed.

'What, darling? What's worrying you?' Charlotte held my gaze.

'Well we've got the *House of Grace* fashion show in a few weeks for starters…'

'And we'll be here to see that through. I'm thinking we should go maybe, April or May?'

'And then there's the girls.'

'They could always come too,' Nancy said.

'But there's school to consider… And then there's Alice…'

Nancy put her arm around me. 'I'm sure something could be sorted out about the girls. And Alice seems happy enough with Robert now.'

'And then…' Charlotte faced me. 'Charles.'

'Well yes but… That's not the reason.'

'No, but maybe it should be. Anyway, you don't have to decide now. I'll start planning things and provisionally book the tickets.' Charlotte twisted her wedding ring. 'If you decide against it, that's not a problem, Nancy and I will still go.' She headed to the bar and grabbed the bottle of Scotch. 'Who's for a refill?' She poured neat whisky into our glasses. 'To Max and our around-the-world cruise.'

Chapter 18

Grace

I was behind the curtains of the makeshift stage with the models. The children were to go on first.

Jack looked up at me, dropping his lip. 'Grandma, why wouldn't you let me bring Ginny?'

I ruffled his blond curls. 'Because it wasn't feasible, my darling.'

He blinked his eyes. 'What does feasible mean?'

'It wasn't possible. Not do-able. We couldn't do a fashion show with a dog.'

'But Nathan and I could both have had our dogs and he could've walked one way and I walked the other. It would have worked Gran.'

I had to laugh. Jack certainly had an imagination. 'Right, young man, your grandmother needs to get everyone organised.' I clapped my hands loud enough to be heard above the chatter. 'Is everybody ready?'

Nancy squeezed my arm. 'You get yourself front of house. Betty will look after the children and I'll make sure the models come out on cue.'

'If you're sure. Good luck everyone.' I waved and made my way to the front to find Charlotte chatting to George and Charles.

The palm house had been set out like a theatre and a red carpet ran along the aisle as a catwalk.

Charlotte gripped my hand. 'Are you ready?'

'As I'll ever be.'

George kissed me on the cheek. 'Good luck. Not that you need it.'

Charles brushed his lips lightly across mine and whispered, 'Break a leg, darling.'

Charlotte took my arm. 'Okay let's get up on the stage.' She led me up the couple of steps to the platform. Chatter was loud from the seating area filled with buyers from retail outlets all over, including Europe and the States.

Charlotte tapped the microphone. 'Good evening ladies and gentlemen. Before we start the show, I will hand you over to my partner and founder of *House of Grace*, Grace Gilmore, to say a few words.' Charlotte stepped to the side.

'Thank you, Charlotte. Ladies and Gentlemen thank you for coming. I know you're going to love this year's summer lines for all the family. Refreshments will be served in the marquee during the interval and at the end of the show. I will now pass you back to Charlotte Cunningham who'll introduce our lovely models and without further ado, let's commence the *House of Grace* 1987 fashion show.'

As the audience applauded, my eyes were drawn to the back of the room to George and Charles. Charles winked and George held up his thumb.

Charlotte coughed. 'Thank you. Grace. Our first models up are Jack and Beth.'

Jack and Beth came out on to the stage hand in hand and stopped close to Charlotte who continued to speak. 'We have Jack in a red tartan jacket over dark blue trousers.' Jack did a twirl, took off his jacket and slung it over his shoulder. 'As you can see under the jacket, Jack wears a white cotton shirt finished with a red satin bow tie.' Jack walked up and down the stage.

'Jack's outfit is offered in red or green tartan and comes in an age range from four to ten years.'

The audience applauded and Jack took a couple of steps back as Beth moved forward.

'Here we have Beth in a purple tartan dress with a tiered frilled hem. The dress is finished in white lace and a black ribboned bow hangs from the yoke.' Beth did her twirl and marched up and down the stage before joining Jack. As the audience clapped, Beth and Jack stepped off the stage and made their way down the aisle, back again, and around the back of the stage as Nathan and Nicole came out, also holding hands.

'Thank you, Beth and Jack,' Charlotte continued, 'and we now have Nathan and Nicole. As you can see Nicole is wearing a turquoise T-shirt three-tier rah-rah skirt-suit and Nathan, a cornflower blue, wide-collared gingham shirt, tucked into dark denim jeans finished with a tan leather belt.'

Nicole and Nathan did a twirl and walked up the aisle and back again as everyone clapped. Charlotte smiled at the children on stage. 'Nicole and Nathan's outfits also cover an age range of four to ten years and Nicole's rah-rah suit may also be purchased in rose-pink.'

Child and teenage models we'd hired in took it in turn to make their entrance modelling various tops, skirts, trousers and baseball caps. The crowd loved it.

Charlotte looked to the left of the stage at Annalise, Lori and Vikki waiting for their cue. 'For the teenager, we have Annalise in a yellow, long knitted jumper over black ski pants, Lori is wearing snake print jeans finished with a pink T-shirt, and we have Vikki in a cream satin blouse tucked into a maroon needlecord rah-rah skirt with poppers all up the flounce. Vikki's outfit is finished with black lace fingerless gloves and a long-beaded necklace twisted to make it multi-layered.'

The girls twirled and walked up and down the stage, before heading down the catwalk showing off their outfits to the clients. The men and women in the audience clapped as they chatted and nodded to each other.

Charlotte spoke into the microphone. 'We'll now take a short interval. Do make your way to the refreshment tent where tea and coffee is being served.' Chairs creaked and chatter was loud as everyone stood up and dispersed.

I met Charlotte at the bottom of the stage. 'It's going fabulous. The crowds are loving it and the children were so good.'

Charlotte wiped the back of her hand across her brow. 'It's hot under those lights.'

'Well at least you haven't got to go up there for the second half. Why don't you go into the tent and start circulating while I say goodnight to the children so they can get off home to bed? I'll send Kathleen over too. It will be a good opportunity for you to introduce her to the buyers.'

'That's a good idea, darling, but will she have time to get changed ready for her set?'

'Yes, she'll be fine. She can come back ten minutes earlier. I'm sure the other girls will go over for a quick drink too. Go and get yourself a cup of tea. You must be parched after all that talking.'

'All right, darling.' Charlotte headed out to the marquee and I made my way backstage and greeted the children. 'You were all wonderful. The audience loved you. Well done.'

Parents of the hired young models took their children, waving as they left.

I bent down to Beth and Nicole. 'You girls looked beautiful and you were so well behaved. I was very proud of you.'

'Thank you, Grandmother.'

I took them both into a hug.

Alice checked her watch. 'It's time I got these two home to bed.'

'I'm surprised you didn't want to model this year. You usually love it?'

She shrugged her shoulders. 'Well, you know, it's difficult with the girls.'

'You've always managed it before.'

'Not such a big deal is it? I mean George didn't model for you.'

I laughed. That would be something to see. 'Is everything okay at home?'

'Sure,' – she tapped my hand – 'stop worrying, Mum. Right girls.' She held the twins either side of her and pecked a kiss on my cheek. 'I'll see you tomorrow.' She dragged the twins out of the palm house. It reminded me of when Mother had dragged George out of my house in Wintermore, only this time it was Beth and Nicole staring back at me with pleading eyes. Had Alice turned into my mother or was Robert controlling her again?

'Are you all right, Grace?' Betty came up beside me.

'Sorry, yes. Just taking a moment to think. Nathan did extremely well. Thank you for letting him take part.'

'He loved it. He'll be telling his schoolmates about it indefinitely. Mind you, Jack got him going with the idea of bringing Kerry. Jack is a real card, isn't he?'

'He certainly is. Are you coming over for refreshments?'

She turned her wrist to check her watch. 'I really need to find John and get Jack and Nathan to bed.'

'Well come and have a cup of tea first and the boys can get a squash.'

'Yes okay. I think John's probably in the tent with the other men anyway.'

As Betty took hold of Nathan's hand, I took Jack's. 'Let's go and find Mummy and Daddy.'

'Was I good, Gran?'

'You were perfect.'

*

I stepped up on to the stage and took the microphone. The audience applauded.

'Thank you. I hope you enjoyed the first half of our show. A cold buffet and champagne will be served in the marquee following the finish. Sit back and enjoy as we move on to our adult range.' I picked up a glass of water taking a mouthful. 'And first up' – I signalled to the left of the stage – 'we have our lovely models, Mandy, Susie and Kathleen in leisure wear all set for a Popmobility class. Mandy has a psychedelic leotard over pink tights with matching colourful leg warmers. Susie is donning a blue leotard over lilac tights with maroon legwarmers and Kathleen completes our trio with an emerald leotard over yellow tights and blue legwarmers.' The crowd clapped.

Next up the hired-in models took the stage with geometric design tops, striped trousers, tiered skirts and jumpers for women, while the men modelled suits, denim wear and hacking jackets.

Charlotte gave me the signal that Mandy, Kathleen and Susie were ready, having changed their outfits. I took a sip of water before announcing them on stage. 'I hope you're all enjoying yourselves. The best is yet to come. Next up we have our beautiful models, Mandy, Kathleen and Susie again. This time they are modelling dresses. First up is Mandy.'

Mandy walked on to the stage and did a twirl. 'Mandy's dress is in a silk fabric. It has a drop waist and falls loose in pleats. The white sailor collar is finished with a contrasting bow. You can order the dress in navy, red or blue. Our model is wearing natural sheer tights and completes her outfit with black kitten heels and a double string pearl necklace.' Mandy looked gorgeous. Her dark hair fell in waves and framed her roundish face. She'd put on a few pounds but it suited her.

Kathleen headed for the stage as Mandy took the catwalk. 'Every woman needs a little black number in the wardrobe and this satin dress Kathleen is wearing is this season's must. Perfect for the summer evening with its three-quarter sleeves as the evening chills slightly. The padded shoulders offer a perfect posture and Kathleen finishes the dress off with golden open-toe high heels.' The spectators clapped as the girls made an exit.

I took a deep breath as Susie stepped on to the platform looking gorgeous in a high waisted black skirt with a red satin shirt complete with braces. 'What do you think of Susie's outfit?' I asked the crowd. They cheered and clapped. 'I must tell you that this outfit has been designed by my apprentice, Victoria Anson.' I held my arm out to signal for Vikki to come. She walked on the stage and took a bow.

'Vikki is my niece and presently at college but in time she will become a full-time designer at *House of Grace*. In fact, I see the future of our designer house in her hands.'

The crowd clapped again. Vikki blushed and mouthed could she go. I acknowledged with a nod. She took another bow before leaving the stage.

Hired-in models came on showing off striped sailor dresses, paisley blouses, and tiered skirts.

'Before we finish the show, we have a final outfit modelled by husband and wife.' Ben and Susie waited in the wings for their cue. 'If you're getting married this summer but want to keep it low key, this bridal ensemble is just the ticket.' I nodded to signal to Ben and Susie they were on and they strolled across the stage, hand in hand.

'Ben is wearing a cream suit over a white shirt and a maroon silk bow tie.' Ben did a turn on stage. 'Susie models an ivory satin strapless dress. As you can see it falls from the yoke in soft pleats. She completes her outfit with a cream lace shawl, a single string of pearls around her neck, and cream sandals with a two-inch heel.' Susie took Ben's hand and they moved down the red-carpeted aisle in slow motion as if they'd just got married. The crowd loved it. They stood up, cheered and whistled. Clapping echoed throughout the palm house.

'Thank you all very much for coming. Remember a buffet is being served in the marquee. Do come and find myself or Charlotte if you have any questions. Our order list will be open from Monday morning.' I signalled to Charlotte in the wings, and all the models except for the children, came out on stage. More applause from the audience.

I took a deep breath and stepped off the stage and moved to behind the curtains where Nancy and Charlotte were waiting for me. Nancy had done an amazing job making sure everyone got out on time and were dressed in the correct costumes.

'Another great show, ladies.' Nancy took Charlotte and I into a hug.

'Right' – I rubbed my hands together – 'let's go and see what the buyers thought.'

I turned off the light, locked up the palm house, and we headed into the refreshment marquee to join our guests.

Chapter 19

Grace

The sun shone through the windscreen as I drove into the entrance of Granville Hall. Daffodils bobbed their yellow heads in the bedding borders while pink camellia flowered against the outside walls. I pulled up at the stables.

'Ah, there you are.' George kissed my cheek. 'How are you getting on with the new Merc?'

'It's lovely to drive. I can't believe this is only my second outing in it, yet I feel like I've been driving it for ages. Is that why you asked me here? So, you could see my new car?'

'Not at all.' George laughed. 'It is rather nice though. I don't think you've had a white car before, have you?'

'No. I normally go for red but thought I'd have a change. Well actually, Lori and Annalise decided I should have a change. If it wasn't to see my new car, what was so urgent to get me over here this morning?'

'Jack wanted you to watch him on his horse. Here he comes now.'

'Grannie.' Jack ran into my open arms. 'Thank you. Thank you. Dad wasn't sure whether you'd be too busy but I knew you'd come. I really wanted you to see me ride Whisky for the first time on my own.'

'Well, Jack, I am honoured.' I bent down and kissed my grandson.

'I'm only allowed to walk him today, though. Dan, he's our new groom, reckons it won't be long before I'm trotting across the fields.'

The groom led the pony from the stall and passed Jack his riding cap.

'Let me.' I fastened the helmet under his chin.

'Shall we get the young man up here, then?' Dan patted the horse.

Once Jack was settled on the saddle, he took hold of the reins.

'Now, Jack, you know what to do next?' The groom looked up at my grandson waiting for confirmation.

Jack nodded his head, sat up straight, and gently squeezed his heels. The groom stayed close to his side.

'He's a natural, George.' I smiled with pride. 'It won't be long before he's trotting.'

'I know. And he just loves Whisky. What with Whisky and Ginny I'd say our Jack's a real animal lover.' George chuckled. 'Ha, I hadn't realised before but they've both got alcoholic names.'

'Oh yes. Ginny is gin.' I laughed.

'Did you know he wants a cat now?'

'No, I didn't but I bet my sister had something to say about that.'

'You're not wrong there.' I laughed. 'She said, "George, there's no way another animal is coming into this house. Do I make myself clear? Goodness knows what Mother and Father would have said." So, I answered, "well it's a good job they're not around then." And on that comment, she stormed out of the room.'

'That sounds like my sister. Oh look, here he comes.'

Jack grinned, sat up straight and guided the horse towards us. 'Did you see me, Gran? Did you see me?'

'I saw you, Jack. You and I are going to be riding together in no time at all.' I lifted him off the saddle, letting him hug me.

'You're the best gran in the whole world.'

'And you're the best grandson.'

George ruffled Jack's hair. 'Go and find Mum while I have a quick word with Gran.'

'Okay. See you later, Grannie.'

'I'll see you in a minute.' I blew him a kiss.

'Shall we walk for a while?' George took my arm.

'Sure. This is sounding ominous.'

'Not at all. I've some news to share with you.'

'Can't you tell me now?'

'I could but then it wouldn't be any fun leaving you in suspense for a bit.' He grinned.

I punched him lightly on his arm. 'You always were a tease, George Gilmore.'

'I wonder where I get that from.' He laughed. 'How are things going with you and my best mate Charles?'

'Good. Well better than good actually. I really like him. Is that going to be a problem?'

George squeezed my hand. 'Not at all. It's the best news, well almost the best news I've heard for a while. Let's sit on that bench.' He brushed his blond curls away from his forehead. I loved the way his curls had stayed, even though he now kept it cut shorter for professionalism at work. I couldn't believe he'd be thirty-four in June. Where had that time gone?

We sat down on the wooden seat by the crocus bed with its blue, yellow and purple blooms.

George rested his hand on the back of mine. 'I love spring. A time for new beginnings. Is Charles your new beginning?'

'Maybe. And what's your new beginning?' I looked into his twinkling blue eyes.

He took a deep breath before offering a beaming smile. 'Mandy and I are going to make you a grandmother again.'

My eyes filled. 'George. I knew it' – I hugged my son – 'I just knew it. Oh, George, I am thrilled for you both. I told you it would happen in time, didn't I?'

'You did.'

'When's the baby due?'

'September.'

'Does Jack know?'

'No, not yet. No one knows. We wanted you to be the first.'

'Thank you. Well that's settled then,' I said, 'I definitely can't go swanning off on a cruise.'

'Grace' – George took both my hands – 'You very much can and should. You'll be back before the baby's due. Don't let this stand in your way unless…'

'Unless what?'

'Unless you're using it as an excuse for some other reason?'

'Such as?'

'A certain gentleman?'

'No, I'm not, but Charles is one person to take into consideration and I'm going to have to make up my mind soon. Part of me so desperately wants to go as it was Max's last wish but at the same time there's so much to keep me here.'

'At the end of the day, it must be about you.' He tapped my arm. 'It's getting a bit cold out here. Do you have time for a cuppa?'

'Yes please. I'd like to congratulate my lovely daughter-in-law.'

'Don't forget, Jack doesn't know.'

*

I walked into the studio to find Nancy and Charlotte sitting on the couch drinking tea.

'Hello you two. Sorry I'm late. I got caught up at Granville.' I poured myself a mug of tea and sat down with my friends.

304

'Jack's doing so well on his horse. He's walking it unaided and wanted to show me. He's so proud of himself, bless him. Such a dear little lamb.'

'Did you get a photograph?' Nancy nibbled on a chocolate digestive.

'Unfortunately, no, as I didn't have my camera with me.'

'I'm sure there'll be plenty of other opportunities.' Charlotte turned over a page in the sales book.

'How are the orders going?' I picked up a biscuit and dipped it in my tea. Gosh if Mother and Father had seen me do that. I laughed to myself. It was a habit I'd picked up when married to Jack.

'The ivory V-neck jumper over the cream polo has well exceeded our expectations.'

'Really? How about the slinky trouser suit and pastel florals?' I sipped my tea.

'Not bad, however, the paisley, georgette dress is probably the best seller, but wait for it…' Charlotte flipped over the page.

'Yes?' I wet my lips.

'Vikki's skirt and braces came a close second. I tell you, Grace, that girl is going places. She'll be running *House of Grace* before we know it.'

'I know,' I agreed. 'She reminds me of myself at that age.'

'Indeed.' Nancy got up, strode across to the kitchen area and came back with the milk jug and teapot. 'Refill?' She topped up our mugs. 'Now are we going to talk about the elephant in the room?'

'Elephant.' I laughed. 'I don't see any elephant.'

Nancy sat back down. 'You need to make a decision, Grace, whether you're coming on the cruise or not. We fly out two weeks tomorrow.'

'She's right,' Charlotte said, 'I think you've had enough time to make up your mind. The fashion show was two weeks ago. It's time to make a decision.'

'I just don't know. I want to come, honestly I do but…'

'But what?' Nancy stood up. 'This is what Max wanted.'

'Sit back down, Nancy, and don't pressure her like that.' Charlotte lit up a cigarette.

'You really should give up, you know?' I smiled at my friend.

'Yes. You're quite right. Maybe I'll give up if you come on the cruise.'

'Now who's putting pressure on me.' I crossed my legs.

'Seriously, Grace' – Charlotte puffed out a smoke ring – 'what is it that's holding you back?'

'Lori and Annalise for starters. You seem to forget I have young daughters living at home.'

Nancy slapped my lap. 'That's just an excuse, Grace Gilmore. You know very well they're not the problem. Joan and Ted told you they'd move in here and look after the girls. Annalise and Lori were more than happy with that, and Steph has offered to 'live in' while we're away.'

'I know but I feel bad leaving them.'

Charlotte put her arm around me 'Darling, I won't put pressure on you if you really don't want to come, but I think you're looking for excuses.'

'Well even if I accept that the girls will be fine, what about Alice?'

*

After dinner, Charles poured out a glass of wine as we sat close on the chaise longue in the drawing room. He passed me a goblet. 'To my beautiful woman.'

'To my handsome man'. I clinked glasses with him.

'Seriously, Grace. You know how I feel about you, but…'

'But?' I put my glass down on the occasional table.

'You have this cruise to think of and I don't want to get in the way of that.'

'I know but…'

'Darling' – he squeezed my hand – 'if you want to go, I'll be waiting for you when you get back. If it's something Max wanted… and I know how much you respected his wishes.'

I shrugged my shoulders and sighed. 'I just don't know. There seems to be so much against me going.'

'Darling' – he put his arms around me – 'forget all that. If there was nothing standing in your way, what would you do?'

'I'd probably go. It would be a kind of working holiday. Meeting up with overseas buyers and Max's contacts in the States.'

'Then you should go. And when you get back…' He took a deep breath. 'When you get back, if you'll have me.' He tilted my chin the way Max used to. 'Will you be my wife? I'm sorry but I'm too old and grey to get down on one knee but I love you, Grace, and nothing would give me greater pleasure than you becoming my wife and I'm happy to wait for three months, six months, however long you're away for.'

I stared into his sapphire eyes seeing the love radiate. 'I love you too, Charles, and yes, I will marry you.'

Was Charles right and I should go? It would be one last thing I could do for Max, and if it helped Charlotte through her bereavement, then surely there was no question. Annalise and Lori hadn't seemed bothered, but suppose they changed their minds once I'd gone? And then there was Alice who did indeed look happy. Maybe I'd misread the situation about her and Robert, but what would happen if I hadn't?

What a journey these last thirty-seven years had been since Father had thrown me out of Granville Hall. The chance meeting with Max and him becoming part of my life, like a father, marrying my adorable Jack, losing my beautiful Beth, but since blessed with two wonderful daughters in Annalise and Lori. Then there was Adriéne who had never stolen my heart quite like Jack. I had loved Adriéne but with a more sedate love than the passion Jack and I had experienced. And now there was Charles, and I was to become the new Mrs Charles Redmayne, although I would always be Gilmore for *House of Grace*. Was it time for me to finally bury Jack's ghost and love Charles fully? I looked up.

'Well?' Charles stroked my cheek. 'What's it to be?' He winked, flashing those stunning blue eyes. 'Cruise or no cruise?'

Chapter 20

George

I drove up outside Grace's house. She and Charles were in the garden. It looked like they were going back inside.

Grace said something to Charles out of my earshot. He patted her hand and made his way over to me.

'Nothing wrong is there?' he asked.

'No. It's just a social visit.' I locked up the car.

'It's okay, Grace,' Charles called. 'It's social.'

'I see.' Grace glanced at her watch before making her way inside. Charles and I followed her down the corridor and into the drawing room.

'Ah, here's your mum now?' Nancy moved towards the bar.

Grace looked around the room and spotted Alice. 'Hello, darling, this is a bit of a surprise.'

'A nice one I hope.' Alice crossed her legs, raising her short skirt, showing off her well-shaped thighs.

'Can I get you folks a drink?' Nancy picked up a bottle.

Grace frowned. 'Yes, please. I think I need one.'

'Scotch?' Nancy poured a shot into each glass and added a spray of soda.

Charlotte patted the seat next to her. 'Now, Grace, come and sit down.'

Grace sat down next to Charlotte. 'What's going on? And how come Alice and George are here? I'm beginning to feel like I've been ambushed.'

'I suppose my friend' – Charlotte took Grace's hand – 'in a way you have. We're hoping to help you make a decision.'

Nancy sat down the other side of my mother. 'What is it that's keeping you from coming on the cruise with us?'

'I told you earlier' – Grace took a huge swig from her glass – 'Annalise and Lori for starters.'

'That sounds like an excuse to me.' Nancy poked Grace gently on the thigh. 'We've been through this already. You spoke to the girls and even asked them if they wanted to accompany you if you decided to go ahead with the trip.'

'This is true, but…'

'But nothing. Joan and Ted are here, and Steph has offered to move back in while we're gone.'

'I don't see how you can expect me to leave my girls for that long.'

'We can always make the trip shorter.' Charlotte picked up a packet of Marlboro from the coffee table in front of her and took out a cigarette.

'I'm not sure.'

Charlotte flicked her lighter and puffed on the cigarette. 'The girls think you should go. They don't have a problem.'

'Even so there's still Alice.'

'But, Mum, you don't need to worry about me. Robert and I are perfectly happy. I've told you that.'

'If you're so happy why didn't you model for *House of Grace*? He's controlling you again, isn't he?'

'No.' Alice got up, stood behind Grace and stroked her shoulders. 'I didn't feel up to it, that's all. To be honest I've gained a few pounds and felt uncomfortable at the thought of parading on stage.'

Grace twisted around and took my sister's hand. 'But you look gorgeous. Please, Alice, tell me the truth. Has he been saying you're fat?'

'No. Mum. Honestly, it's the truth. Tell her, George.'

I grinned. 'She'd have told Mandy if he had. And you know I'll look after Alice while you're gone. It's not like you're going forever.'

'All right but then there's...' Grace looked at me and held her gaze.

'You mean the baby? It's okay, I've told them. But the baby's not due until September and Charlotte said you'll be home August at the latest. So, plenty of time.'

Grace got up, walked across to the window and fiddled with the drapes. Charles joined her, wrapping his arms around her. 'And you know you don't have to worry about me. I told you earlier, you should go, so, what's it to be?'

'Yes, what's it to be, Grace?' Charlotte and Nancy said in unison.

Grace looked around the room to each of them in turn. Alice nodded. I smiled. Charles squeezed her hand. Nancy and Charlotte stared straight at her, waiting.

'Well?' Charlotte asked.

'It looks like we're going cruising.' Grace kissed Charles on the lips lightly before moving back to the chaise longue, sank down between her two best friends and put her arms around them both. 'It's what Max wanted so let's do it but I shall phone the girls every day.'

Everyone clapped. Grace got up from the couch again and paced the room. 'We'd better get cracking then as there's lots to do. I want dinner with the whole family before we go. Cases to pack. Set things in order at *House of Grace* for while we're away. Ring up the buyers overseas and book appointments with them.' She held her head. 'So much to do.'

Charles was by her side. 'And you'll get there.'

'Indeed, she will.' I joined them and put my arm around Grace.

'This calls for a celebratory drink.' Charlotte stubbed out her cigarette in the ashtray and made her way to the sideboard. She slid open the cupboard door and took out an ice bucket with a bottle of champagne. 'Good job, I was prepared. Give me a hand will you, Nancy?'

Nancy shot up off the chaise longue and hurried over to the china cabinet. She selected crystal glasses and passed them in turn for Charlotte to fill. Charlotte and Nancy distributed the drinks until we all had one.

'A toast' – I raised my glass – 'to the future.'

'To the future.' Grace turned to Charles and clinked her goblet with his.

Alice sat upright. 'Speech, Mum, Speech.'

'Oh no, surely you don't want me to do a speech.' Grace put her hand to her face.

'I think you should.' I smiled, nodding.

'No, George, as head of Granville Hall, it's you who should make the speech.'

'Quite right, Grace, you tell him.' Charlotte laughed. Nancy and Alice clapped. Charles nodded.

I took to the floor. Coughed. 'Okay, here goes. First of all, I'm glad you've come to the right decision.'

Grace and Charlotte smiled at each other.

'You have nothing to worry about with Annalise and Lori,' I continued, 'you know so long as nothing interferes with their riding, they couldn't care less. Joan, Steph, Alice and I, will all look out for them. And you'll be ringing them every day anyway.'

Grace laughed.

'I promise you I will keep a special eye on our Alice and Robert.' I glanced at my sister.

'There's no need, George,' Alice protested.

'Whatever' – I took a sip from my glass – 'I will anyway.' I looked towards Charles. 'And Charles will be waiting for you on your return.'

'I will.' Charles put his arm around Grace.

'And when you return, we'll look forward to another family wedding. I have to say, nothing makes me happier to have Charles as a stepfather. In fact, it's been my wish since I first introduced you to each other. Two people I love dearly. It's time for a new chapter in your life.' I looked over at Nancy. 'Can you make sure everyone has a top up please?'

'Absolutely.' Nancy rushed around topping up everyone's goblets with champagne.

'Once again raise your glasses to the future and new beginnings.'

'To the future and new beginnings,' echoed throughout the room.

Chapter 21

George

'Boarding now for flight TWA708,' came over the Tannoy.

'That's your flight.' Charles took Grace in his arms and kissed her. As he pulled away, she had tears in her eyes.

I took her hand. 'Don't worry. I'll look after him, just like I'll look after my sisters. Especially Alice.'

'Thank you, George. You're a good boy, your father would be proud of you.'

I held her in a hug and whispered. 'He'd be proud of you too, Mam.'

'You don't know how much it means to me to hear you call me that. I've waited so long.' Grace beamed, wiping her eyes.

'I think I do.'

'Hurry up,' Charlotte called, 'they've just announced our last call.'

I broke our hold. 'Now go.' I lightly pushed her in the direction of Nancy and Charlotte.

Charles and I waved, watching them all disappear through the gate and out of view.

*

After dropping Charles off home, I drove around to the Con Club, pulled up in the car park and waited. Within minutes, as predicted, Robert swaggered out from the entrance. I got out of my car and wandered over.

'You and I need to have a little chat.' I led him round the side of the building.

Robert's face whitened. He licked his lips and said in a shrill voice. 'What's going on? I haven't done anything.'

'I never said you had. I just want a quiet word.'

He wiped beads of sweat from his forehead. 'What... What about? What's going on?'

'I've told you, I just want a little word with my brother-in-law.' I pushed him towards the wall. 'You may think I'm weak but I can be just as ruthless as my grandfather if need be. Do I make myself clear?'

'Yes.' He nodded, blinking his eyes.

'Good. Because if I find out you've mistreated my sister again, I will take you, and your family to pieces. Let me tell you, I have a lot more clout than your father. I am Lord Granville and my grandfather's reputation goes before me. No one crosses me. Do I make myself clear?'

'Yes. Yes. Please...' He straightened his glasses.

'I promised my mother I will make sure nothing happens to Alice and I intend to do that.' I took hold of the neck of his tie and pulled him towards me. 'Now don't make me do my worst or you'll regret it.' I released my hold.

'Can I go now?'

'Yes, go.' I watched him run like a little weasel across the car park to his car. I straightened down my jacket, walked over to my Ferrari and got in.

I hadn't liked doing that to Robert but it was necessary to scare him. I may be a coal miner's son at heart, but I also had enough of my grandfather in me to be ruthless when someone threatened my family.

I closed my eyes while catching my breath, thinking of Grace's face when I called her Mam. I'd wanted to call her that for so long but there had never been the right time. That moment came at the airport when we said goodbye. I forgave her completely, fully realising that she'd always done her best for her children. She had never meant to abandon me. Grace had been made to suffer long enough. I had found my family. My mam and my sisters. I'd never know dear Beth but there was no point blaming Grace any longer. We had to look to the future. The future would bring a new brother or sister for Jack and a new stepfather in Charles, a man I trusted with my life.

I took a deep breath, started up the car, and took the road home to Granville Hall.

Acknowledgements

A special thank you to my friend Maureen Cullen. Not only for her perceptive and thoughtful editing but her continuous support, encouragement and faith in me throughout the *House of Grace* trilogy. And thank you to all my fabulous Beta readers. I'd also like to thank Christine Jackson for coming up with the name Japonica Arms and allowing me to use it.

Thanks also goes to Andy Keylock (Marketing Pace) for the cover image design, and to Colin Ward for formatting my manuscript.

Finally, a big thank you to my husband, children, family and friends for their continued support and faith in me.

The Author

Patricia M Osborne is married with grown-up children and grandchildren. She was born in Liverpool but now lives in West Sussex. In 2019 she graduated with an MA in Creative Writing (University of Brighton).

Patricia writes novels, poetry and short fiction, and has been published in various literary magazines and anthologies. Her first poetry pamphlet *Taxus Baccata* was published by The Hedgehog Poetry Press July 2020.

She has a successful blog at Whitewingsbooks.com where she features other writers and poets. When Patricia isn't working on her own writing, she enjoys sharing her knowledge, acting as a mentor to fellow writers.

The Granville Legacy is the final book in the House of Grace trilogy.

Lightning Source UK Ltd.
Milton Keynes UK
UKHW040945050321
379828UK00001B/66